HAND OF JUSTICE

A Mara Brent Legal Thriller

ROBIN JAMES

If a tornado hit the Blue Pony at 5:27 p.m. that particular Friday night, the Waynetown justice system would cease to exist. It wasn't my scene. Not really. I was more of a wine-in-the-bubble-bath kind of drinker. But my boss, Kenya, had made my attendance at the Pony after work mandatory. "Just try to act surprised," she said. "Oh, and if you try to worm your way out of it, I'll make you cover traffic court for the whole summer."

I laughed until I saw her steely-eyed stare. Kenya Spaulding, Chief Prosecutor of Maumee County, told jokes, but she didn't kid around.

As I walked in, the bar itself was almost empty. A game room with pool tables, vintage eighties arcade games, and pinball machines came in from the right. I bypassed it, heading for the tables. The muscle-bound bartender with the slicked-back hair lifted his chin when he saw me.

"Another lawyer?" he said cheerfully, taking in my crisp dark suit and three-inch Sergio Rossi pumps. "Your group's in the back."

Smiling, I walked around the bar and headed down the

dark hallway into the restaurant. They'd taken up four long tables. In the corner sat Kenya, Howard Jordan (who everyone called Hojo unless they were from out of town), Caro, our office manager, and the entire appellate court team.

The judiciary took up the second table. Judges Saul and Ivey from Common Pleas, along with Judge DeCamp from Muni court. Their spouses. A few of my favorite defense attorneys had a table well in the back, away from the final grouping in the other corner. Detectives Gus Ritter, Sam Cruz, the sex squad, and a few from upper command rounded out the law enforcement group. As I stepped into the dim light of the room, a cheer went up and everyone raised their glasses.

I felt a hot blush creep up my cheeks. Sweat formed beneath my collar. Then Kenya was there.

"First round's on me," she said, handing me a shot glass.

Tequila. I could smell it. The crowd waited. There was no getting out of it.

"Bottoms up!" Hojo called from the end of the table. He had his own shot glass poised for my signal.

"I gotta get home somehow," I said under my breath.

Kenya laughed and pushed the glass closer. I did the shot. She handed me a lemon wedge. I got a round of applause.

"Congratulations," Kenya said, putting her arm around me. She led me to the prosecutors' table. It was then I noticed the banner taped to the wall. Well, not so much a banner as 8 1/2 x 11 copy paper printed with red lettering.

"Congrats, Mara!"

The tequila warmed my belly and loosened my nerves.

"It's okay," Kenya whispered as Hojo held a chair out for me. "Today you get to be happy about it."

She was right. The cause for this little celebration was still folded up in the bottom of my briefcase, the ink barely dry on it. Its timestamp read May 18th, 4:51 p.m. Judgement of the Court. Dissolution of Marriage. Judge Saul had actually been the one to sign it. She must have lit out for the Blue Pony right before me.

I was divorced. Single again. Free. Out of habit, my thumb went to the base of the ring finger on my left hand. I hadn't worn my wedding ring in nearly a year. It sat in a teacup along with my engagement ring on my kitchen ledge next to a succulent my son brought home from school. He'd made the pot in ceramics class.

"I am happy," I admitted. "It's just ..."

"Weird," Kenya answered for me. "I know. I remember." Kenya had what she called a starter marriage years before we met.

"Gets easier," Hojo chimed in. He would know. He'd been married and divorced three times. Kenya just the once, though I'd only recently learned that. The little charge I'd gotten out of the tequila faded a bit. The three of us made up the litigation team for the prosecutors' office. Not one of us could keep our marriage intact. Though, in my case, I wouldn't take all the blame for it. I could have forgiven a lot of things. Jason's cheating wasn't one of them.

"What'll you have?" A waitress appeared. She set a beer down in front of Hojo and a rocks glass in front of Kenya.

"Uh ... I'll do a margarita," I said. "And did anyone order any food?"

"Pizzas are coming," the waitress answered. I thanked her. Settling into my seat, this whole thing felt like a reverse wedding shower. And it kind of was. But Kenya was right. Dang it, if she wasn't always.

It would take time to adjust to my new status. Time to figure out exactly how I'd navigate life as a single mom of a ten-year-old boy with special needs. But today felt good to celebrate.

It got a little crazy after that. I made my way from table to table, thanking everyone for coming. Lord, it felt like a reverse wedding reception. I made it to the "cop table" last. By then, only Gus and Sam remained. The others had bellied up to the bar to catch a basketball game. The Cavs were playing.

"You good?" Gus asked. He too knew his way around divorce court.

"How many for you?" I asked.

Gus held two fingers up. "The first former Mrs. Ritter barely counts, though. That was before I entered the police academy."

"Lucky for you," Sam chimed in. "She'd be throwing pension check parties with the second former Mrs. Detective Ritter."

Gus smiled even wider. "Bought her out. Gave her the house. Had that sucker paid off. Plus, I caught her cheating on me with the neighbor. Got lucky I drew old Judge Mattis. Turns out the first former Mrs. Judge Mattis pulled a similar number on him."

This got a laugh at first from Sam. Then the two of them went silent.

"Uh, sorry, Mara," Sam offered. "Not trying to make light of ..."

"No," I said, putting a hand up. "It's okay. Really. Might as well laugh about all of this sometimes. It's better than the alternative."

"How's Will holding up?" Sam asked. "You know what? Forget I asked. This is a party. And it's none of my business."

I reached across the table and touched his arm. "We're friends," I said. "And I know you're not asking me for gossip's sake, Sam. The answer is, good ... ish."

"Ready for another margarita?" The waitress practically sang it.

I put a hand over the top of my glass. "I'm good." It was then I noticed Sam wasn't drinking at all. He had a glass of ice water in front of him. Gus finished his third beer and waved the girl off from any more.

"He taking you home?" I asked Gus. This garnered a sheepish grin from him and outright laughter from Sam.

"She is," Sam explained. I turned my head to follow his gaze.

"Well, I'll be," I said, whistling. Paula Dudley, the bar's owner, weaved her way through the tables, checking on every patron. She was a pretty woman with striking white hair and black, circular-framed glasses. She'd gotten the bar after *her* divorce from the first former Mr. Dudley whose family opened it in 1962.

"Well done, Gus," I said.

Sam poked him in the arm, still laughing.

"Just make sure you take your heart medication."

"Zip it," Gus said, his voice like sandpaper over gravel. "Both of ya."

At that point, Paula Dudley caught Gus's eye. She was blushing all right. So was Gus. He cleared his throat and scooted out of his chair, leaving Sam and me alone.

"Oh my," I said. "I didn't know Gus had it in him."

"I don't think Paula did either," Sam said.

"I mean ... he's smiling!" I said. "And uh, is that what it sounds like when Gus Ritter laughs?"

Paula sidled up to Gus and threaded her arm through his. She planted a kiss on his cheek and I swear his eyes actually twinkled.

"How long's that been going on?" I asked.

"About a month," Sam answered. "She's got a cousin who

works in the property room. I don't know how she did it, but she fixed them up."

"Well, good," I said. "Gus deserves some fun in his life."

Sam's eyes went a little dark telegraphing his thoughts. I knew what he wanted to say. I deserved some fun too.

"Thanks for being here," I said. "I had no idea Kenya was putting this all together."

A strange expression came into his eyes.

"Wait a minute," I said. "This was your idea?"

Sam cleared his throat. "Not just me. Gus said something to Paula and ..." The rest of his sentence trailed off. There was a dart game going on, and it looked like Kenya had just wiped the floor with Judge Ivey. There was an equal amount of cheers as grumbles as those who'd bet on the game squared up.

"Well thank Gus and Paula for me," I said. "And you. A night out was a great idea."

Sam reached for the pitcher of water. He was about to fill his glass when his cell phone went off. It lit up and vibrated on the table in front of him.

His expression fell when he saw the caller ID. I didn't even ask him about it before I saw Kenya's smile fade to a frown as she pulled out her own ringing phone.

Sam stuck one finger in one ear and held his phone to the other. His eyes caught Kenya's as she listened to whatever bad news her caller delivered.

"How many?" Sam asked. "Are you sure? That can't ... Holy ... Yeah. Okay. You better get B.C.I. down. I'm at the Pony. I can be there in fifteen."

Kenya had hung up with her caller. The partygoers yelled after her as she waved off a rematch.

Sam hung up. He pressed his hand to his forehead. Then he slammed his fist to the table.

"Sam?" Kenya asked.

"It's mine," he answered her. "I'm heading out to the farm now. Can you try to keep this from spreading through the bar, at least for tonight?"

"Of course," she said.

Sam rose to his feet. Gus had his back to him. Sam gave me a pained look, then hustled toward the front door.

Kenya put a hand on my arm. "We need to go," she said. "You sober?"

"Sober enough," I said. "What's going on?"

Kenya pulled us down a dark hallway by the service entrance. We waited as a server hustled past us.

"Multiple homicide," she said. "Out in farm country. Redmond Road. The Sutter family. Sam's going to need us out there. We should go."

The Sutters. They were a big family. Waynetown business owners. It seemed like almost everyone in town could claim some relation to them if you went far back enough.

"How many?" I asked.

Kenya slowly closed her eyes as she found her breath.

"Kenya. How many?" I whispered.

She opened her eyes. "All of them, Mara. All of them."

2

F arm country. This stretch of Redmond Road stretched for miles with nothing but cornfields on either side. The newest structure out here was the new barn Matt Denton built in 1988.

Kenya drove. Her GPS would have taken us straight through a pond past the railroad tracks if we hadn't been able to see B.C.I.'s massive temporary floodlights twinkling in the distance.

"Did you know them?" I asked her.

Kenya gripped the wheel. "I mean, sure. There have been Sutters in Waynetown before there was Waynetown in Waynetown. One of the cousins was in my graduating class. I think he was one of C.J.'s boys?"

She turned toward the lights. The first driveway led us to a two-story brick house with white shutters and well-trimmed hedges. Kenya cut her engine just as Sam walked up to us. He turned back and shouted instructions to a pair of uniformed cops standing on the other side of the driveway.

"They're still here?" Kenya asked, her face dropping. I tracked her gaze. The coroner's van was parked in the adjoining driveway. I realized with icy dread who she meant. The bodies. The victims were all still inside. Of course they were. It had been less than two hours since Sam took over the scene.

"What have you got so far?" I asked Sam.

"Seven victims," he said. "This is Chris and Jenny Sutter's house. Four of them are here."

"Four of them," Kenya repeated. Cameras flashed through the windows as B.C.I. did their meticulous work, photographing every room. Every drop of blood.

"Jenny Sutter, age fifty-six, was found in the kitchen. Shot once in the face. We found Chris, her husband, age sixty-one, in the mudroom off the garage. Garage door was open. My guess is he was coming in after hearing the shot fired into Jenny. He got it in the chest. His daughter, Skylar, is right behind him. She was twenty-two."

Sam held a small tablet. He turned the screen so Kenya and I could see. Jenny Sutter had no face. Just long brown hair soaked in blood. She landed against the refrigerator, her arms and legs sprawled in an X. Chris Sutter had fallen forward, but a massive exit wound blew through the back of his yellow tee-shirt. Beside him, young Skylar Sutter lay slumped against the wall, her eyes still open. The shot took her in the forehead.

I hugged my arms around me.

"Fourth victim from this household is half in and half out the sliding glass door off the kitchen. If I had to guess, he walked in on what happened to Jenny too. It happened fast."

I nodded. "The killer was in the kitchen too?" I asked.

"Kitchen's in the back of the house," he said. "There's a living room in front. He was probably standing in the living room. Mudroom comes off the left."

"Who's this fourth victim?" I asked, looking at the body of

a young man lying on his stomach, shot through the back. He had red hair, cropped short.

"Ben Watson, age twenty-three," Sam said. "Not a member of the family. A friend. Not sure of the relationship yet, but our witness says he was staying here. He was a friend of Skylar's."

"Who's your witness?" Kenya asked.

"Darcy Lydell," Sam answered; his expression turned pained. "Chris and Jenny have another adult kid. Luke. He doesn't live here, but Chris and Jenny watch his son, Charlie. Charlie's just over a year old. We found him in a back bedroom."

"Oh God." Kenya said it for us.

"Alive," Sam quickly said. "Though mad as hell and wearing a heavily soiled diaper. He was still in his playpen. Darcy is his maternal grandma. Luke and his wife Rachel are both nurses. They were working doubles, and Darcy came at five to pick Charlie up and relieve the Sutters. She could hear the baby crying and nobody came to the door when she knocked. So she came around the back and saw Ben's body lying in the slider."

"My God," I said. Later, I knew I would have to listen to what would have to be Darcy Lydell's horrified 911 call.

"What about the other victims?" Kenya asked.

"Kevin Sutter lives in the ranch house over there," Sam answered. He pointed east of us. It was a small house with white vinyl siding and an American flag still up the flagpole in the front yard.

"Kevin Sutter, thirty-two," Sam said. "Chris's cousin. He lives alone. Found him in his kitchen as well. Shot in the chest."

Sam swiped to another photo. Kevin Sutter looked more like a wax figure. Shock frozen on his face as he lay sprawled in the center of a small kitchen, a chair lying on its side next to him. What looked like his entire blood volume had spread beneath him, making grisly lines in the grout of his white tile floor.

"Last two victims are in the house directly behind us," Sam said. "Patty Sutter and Mark O'Brien."

"What's the relationship?" I asked.

"Patty was once married to C.J. Sutter. He died a few years back. She was a second wife. C.J. and Chris were brothers. Kevin's the son of another uncle."

"So Patty's not a blood relation to any of the other victims?" I asked.

"No," Sam said.

"I know Mark O'Brien," Kenya said as she peered over my shoulder to look at the photo of the third crime scene. Patty and Mark were shot in their bedroom. Patty still lay in bed on her stomach, one arm hanging off the side. The bullet took her in the back of the head. Mark was on the floor on his side. His cell phone was near his right hand. He'd been shot in the forehead, like Skylar Sutter. His shattered glasses were still crookedly perched on his nose.

"Mark has a general practice," Kenya said. "Does wills and estates, landlord tenant, transactional stuff."

I nodded. He looked familiar, and I knew I'd seen him around the courthouse a few times.

"They were married?" I asked.

Sam shook his head. "Just living together."

"You have any idea who was killed first?" I asked.

"No," he said. "And we may never be able to tell. Autopsies will tell us more, but it's a pretty safe bet these shootings took place within a few seconds or minutes of each other."

"You think it was one shooter?" I asked.

"I don't know," he said. "With the position of the bodies, I'd say Chris and Skylar got it when they came to see what was going on. Ben and Jenny were probably already dead by then. But I doubt we'll ever know if Kevin was shot first, then the killer came here or what."

"Or the killer offed Patty and Mark then came here?"

"Right," Sam said. "It's going to take days, maybe weeks, to process all of this."

"Are there any other houses back here?" I asked.

"No," Sam said. "This whole plat used to be farmed by the Sutter ancestors a hundred years or so ago. It's about a hundred acres. These three houses are the only ones close together like this."

"Somebody has to tell Grandma George!" a female voice shrieked behind us. I turned. A pretty bleach-blonde woman stepped out of a patrol car. She had a gray blanket wrapped around her shoulders.

"Darcy Lydell," Sam whispered. "Excuse me a second."

"Who's Grandma George?" I asked Kenya.

At that point, Gus Ritter came down the driveway trailed by two patrolmen.

"Hey," I said, not sure it was a good idea for Gus to be here. He wasn't on duty, and I'd watched him down several beers just a few hours ago.

"Relax," Gus said, reading my mind. "Sam's running this."

Sam had said something that seemed to calm Darcy Lydell down. A patrolwoman nodded as Sam gave her instructions. She helped Darcy into another car and left the scene with her.

"Poor Darcy," Gus said.

"Deputy Swain's going to get her over to the hospital. They took the baby there just to give him a once-over. His parents are with him."

"That's Luke and Rachel Sutter," I said, looking back at my notes. "Luke's the son of the victims from this house?"

"And his sister Skylar," Sam confirmed.

"If they'd have killed that baby," Gus said, getting a little choked up.

"They didn't," Sam said, putting a hand on his partner's shoulder.

"What they *did* do is bad enough," I said. "Sam, what about the rest of the Sutter family? Do you think they might be in danger too?"

"Not taking any chances," Sam said. "Officer Swain is going to stick close by. Luke and Rachel live on the other side of town, closer to the hospital. I've sent a crew to the other side of the farm. The Sutters don't farm it themselves anymore. They lease it to a guy named Jeremy White."

"Sam," Gus said. "Somebody's gotta look in on Louie and Georgette. You mind if I take care of that?"

"Grandma George," I said.

Gus nodded. "Yeah. Hell, she used to babysit me, if you can believe that. This is going to kill her. Kevin was her and Lou's only grandson. The others, well, they all call them Grandpa Louie and Grandma George. They live up on the hill through those woods behind these houses."

"Lord," I said. "Has anyone checked? Are they okay?"

"Yeah," Sam said. "She answered her phone. Everything seemed okay. But the media vultures are gonna get a hold of this soon, if they haven't already."

"I'll handle that end of it," Kenya assured him.

"Sam," Gus said. "They can't hear about this from the news."

"I know," Sam agreed. "I'm headed over there now. I have to go tell them half their family is dead. It's going to be a long night."

He was right. It would be for all of us. And right now, there was a mass murderer lurking somewhere in Waynetown. A shiver went through me as I wondered whether he or she was watching us all right now. I wanted nothing more than to go home and wrap my arms around my son.

✣ 3 ✥

By Monday morning, the firestorm began. Kenya and I stood jammed together in the corner of the press room in the City-County Building. Members of the media, citizen journalists, and just about anyone who had any relation or acquaintance with the Sutter family packed the room, spilled into the hall, and went all the way down the steps.

Sheriff Bill Clancy hated these things. He had a head of thin blond hair he still buzzed out of habit from his Marine Corps days. He'd served honorably in the Persian Gulf, then joined the Sheriff's Department two weeks after he came home. He read a brief statement, then opened the mic up to questions. They came in an onslaught. An avalanche.

"Sheriff, can you confirm that killings were carried out execution style?"

"Here we go," Kenya whispered.

"I can confirm each of the victims died from gunshot wounds. As I said in my statement, we don't have official autopsy reports back on any of the victims, so I won't be answering questions about the nature of their injuries beyond that."

"Can you confirm the rumors we've heard that the Sutter family may have run afoul of a drug cartel?"

That one took Chief Clancy by surprise. He was hard to read by anyone who hadn't spent a lot of time with him. Kenya and I had. There was just a slight hardening in his jaw.

"This is an ongoing investigation," he said. "We are pursuing any and all leads. But at this time, no, that's not something I would confirm. I would urge any members of the public who have credible information about the events that took place out at the Sutter farm on Friday morning to call the crime stopper number. It's up on the website. You can also call the Sheriff Department's non-emergency line. But I really want to caution everyone not to jump to conclusions or wild speculations. My department is working round the clock. Multiple law enforcement agencies are involved, including the Ohio Bureau of Criminal Investigations and the F.B.I."

"So you *can* confirm this is being considered an act of domestic terrorism," another reporter shouted.

"No!" Bill shouted back. It wasn't like him. "Like I said, we are in the preliminary stages of our investigation. If and when an arrest is made, I'll make another statement at that time. But out of respect for the families, I hope everyone here can report responsibly. When there's something official to say, you'll hear it out of this office. I'm not going to comment on information that's being passed around on social media. These people are your neighbors, folks. Your friends. For some of you, it's family. I can assure you that my office will pursue all leads as they come in. In the meantime, that's all I have for you today."

"Sheriff." David Reece stepped up to the nearest microphone. He was the crime reporter for Channel 8, the highest-rated local news station. "Is there anything you can say to waylay some concerns we're hearing throughout

Maumee County? There was a similar home invasion in Lucas County just last month. Do you have any indication these crimes were related? Are we dealing with a serial killer?"

"I can't speak to the case in Lucas County," Sheriff Clancy said. "And I hate to sound like a broken record, but when I know more and can divulge it, you'll know more."

"Are you going to step up patrols in the rural areas?" another voice shouted from the back. "How do we know this isn't the beginning of something terrible?"

"You don't," Clancy said. "Because it *was* something terrible. Now you all know I'm not going to comment on field operations at this time. I can assure you, the safety of the people in this county is what I care most about. That and bringing the perpetrators of this hideous crime to justice. Like I said. These were our neighbors. Our friends. I've known Chris and Jenny Sutter since I was a little kid. We've got good people, dedicated men and women working 24/7 to solve this case. And we will. You can be sure of that. There'll be no safe harbor for anyone who comes after people in my town. In your town. Now, I'm going to go back to work. You all should too. And please, please, heed what I said. Think twice about the things you post and read on the internet. This family is suffering. Let's none of us make it any worse. Now that's all I'm gonna say today. Thank you."

When Bill Clancy turned away from the lectern, he had tears in his eyes.

Kenya nudged my shoulder. I followed her down the back hallway. "Come on," she said. "Let's go grab a cup of coffee before we head back to the office."

"Okay," I said, puzzled. Caro made perfectly good coffee for the whole office.

Kenya and I walked out of a side entrance. Her car was

parked one block over on Cleveland Street. We made it halfway there before shouting and screamed obscenities, harsh enough to make my eyes water, made us both freeze.

"This is what happens when you bring that crap into town!" The screaming came from an elderly woman with long white hair. She jabbed her finger into the chest of the younger man standing in front of her.

"That's Dale Conner," I whispered. Dale owned a bowling alley on the east side of town. He was also a county commissioner.

"You gonna deny it?" the woman said.

For his part, Dale kept his hands up and tried to back away. The woman kept advancing. A dozen other people quickly joined her, streaming out of the City-County Building.

"You heard what the sheriff said," Dale tried to reason with her. "They don't know what happened out at that farm yet. I know you're upset ..."

"You're a traitor!" a male voice spoke up.

"Kenya," I said. "This is going to turn ..."

"You and your ilk!" the original old woman spat. "You voted to let those drug dealers into this town. Our town. We've got pot being sold next to the McDonald's. They're coming in. More and more. All to line your pocket. Now we've got people being murdered in their beds over it. I hope you're happy. With your fancy new car. Your big house with your gate."

She lost it then. She reared her head back and spat in Dale Conner's face. Another woman stepped out in front of him and pushed the old lady back.

"Oh no!" Kenya shouted. "Stop. Stop it right now!"

It was too late, though. The two factions squared off on the sidewalk. An even bigger crowd started to form. I pulled out my cell phone. Kenya and I tried to turn and head up the sidewalk the other way.

It was no good. More people from the press conference filed out and hustled toward us to see what was going on.

Kenya got shoved sideways. Her ankle turned. I caught her by the elbow as she tumbled off the curb.

"Kenya!"

"And you don't do enough!" The shouting was aimed at us. Somebody recognized Kenya and me.

"You gonna make sure those murderers get the needle for this? Huh? Or are you going to just look the other way while our kids keep dying?!"

Strong arms came around me. I twisted, trying to shove backwards. Then Sam Cruz's deep voice brushed against my ear.

"Come on!" he commanded. "Let's get you both out of here."

About a dozen deputies ran toward the crowd. I prayed the thing wouldn't escalate. Sheriff Clancy had been right about one very important thing. The people in the street right now were neighbors, friends, family. If they would all just take a breath and remember that.

Sam used his keycard and got Kenya and me in through a service door. He slammed it shut behind us. He had a wild look in his dark eyes as he looked me up and down.

"You okay?"

"Yeah." I nodded. "Kenya, your ankle."

She wasn't putting any weight on it but waved me off. "Rolled it," she said. "I'll live."

"You think it's broken?" Sam asked. "Can you walk on it?"

Kenya gingerly took a few steps. Pain lined her face, but she was mobile.

"It's probably just a sprain," Sam said. "Come on down to

the conference room. We'll get some ice on it." Undeterred by Kenya's protests, Sam got an arm around her and helped her hobble down the hall until we made it to the conference room just off the press room. He made a quick call, and a young deputy appeared with an ice bag from their first aid kit. He pulled up another chair and insisted Kenya elevate her leg. Then he positioned the ice pack.

"Thanks," I said. I went to the window. I could see about four blocks down Cleveland Street from there. The deputies had done their work. The crowd had dispersed.

"What started that?" he asked.

"They went after Commissioner Conner," I said. "I'm guessing he was one of the yay votes when they started granting marijuana dispensary licenses in Waynetown."

"What in God's name does that have to do with the Sutters?" Kenya asked. "They're not growing weed out on that farm, are they?"

Sam's brow shot up. "No," he said. "But you remember they used to own Sutter Bait and General Store?"

Kenya shrugged. "Don't have much cause to fish, Sam."

"It was right off of I-75," I said. "You had to have passed it a thousand times. It had that big sign with the fish and the hook in its mouth?"

"Ah," Kenya said.

"They sold it to Verde a couple of years ago," Sam said. Verde was one of the first recreational marijuana dispensaries that came into town after the licenses were granted.

"How long had the Sutters owned that store?" I asked. "I never went in there myself, but Jason took Will a few times. He grew up fishing the Maumee River. Back when it was more or less okay to eat outta there."

"Longer than I've been alive," Sam said. "Fifty years?

Sixty? I'm not sure. But it's a lead we're pursuing. The Sutters got close to two million bucks for that property."

"Wow," Kenya said. "You can't really blame them for cutting and running. For that kind of money?"

"Sam," I said. "I kind of discounted it. But ... tell me the truth. Do you think these killings were related to, I don't know, drug money?"

His face betrayed nothing. "I think Clancy's got it right. It's pointless to jump to conclusions."

I turned back to the window. A cold chill ran down my spine. The Sutters weren't even in the ground yet, and already tribes were forming out there. I just prayed today's skirmish was an isolated incident. But I felt it in my bones we were in for far worse.

✣ 4 ✣

By late Wednesday afternoon, the autopsy reports on all seven victims were in. My office coordinated with the Sheriff's to form a task force while the investigation continued. We held our first meeting in our conference room. At the moment, too many civilians were milling around the Sheriff's Department offices.

I took my seat on one side of the table. Kenya, Hojo, Clancy, Sam, and Liz Meyer from the computer forensics unit attended our first meeting.

"All right," Clancy said. "Let's get one thing straight. This is Detective Cruz's investigation. Everything goes through him. Nobody talks to the press without him knowing about it. And nobody talks to the press yet. Got it? And that's the last thing I'm going to say on this. Sam, this is your meeting."

"Thanks," Sam said. He moved behind Bill Clancy and stood at the head of the table. "The autopsies were pretty straightforward. All victims died of a single gunshot wound to either the head or chest. We're dealing with a shooter or shooters who knew what they were doing. We've got eleven bullets. Eight went into the various victims. Chris Sutter was the only one shot twice. Two bullet holes in the wall of the Sutter kitchen ... uh ... Chris and Jenny's place. Then, there's a missed shot in the wall above Mark O'Brien's side of the bed."

"Do you have any idea who the first victim or victims were?" I asked.

"Afraid not," Sam said. "Rigor mortis was just setting in. M.E. says time of death was between nine in the morning and two p.m."

"How are you establishing that?" Clancy asked.

"Luke Sutter dropped his son off at six thirty in the morning," Sam answered. "His wife Rachel texted Jenny, her mother-in-law, at eight fifty-three. Jenny texted back at eight fifty-eight. The kid was eating breakfast and Jenny sent Rachel a picture. That's the last contact any of the victims had with anyone outside."

"But you don't know for sure if the victims at Patty or Kevin's house were already dead?" Kenya asked.

"Not for sure," Sam answered. "But Kevin sent a text to a friend at eight forty-five. Patty and Mark O'Brien are the question mark. You wanna say what you have, Liz?"

Detective Meyer referred to her notes. "We can show Mark O'Brien logged into his email at seven thirty that morning. He sent a few replies. Work-related stuff. There's a little social media activity after that, but it looks like he was logged off by nine thirty."

"But they're still in bed?" I asked.

"Spilled coffee on Mark's nightstand," Sam said. "Patty was on her stomach. Doesn't look like she ever knew what hit her. She's shot first. Mark's either asleep or reading beside her but tries to get out of bed. He's sprawled halfway from the bed to the door. It happened fast. And I don't know if we're ever going to be able to show who died first."

"So there's no way to tell whether all of these people were intended targets, or it started against just one ..."

"We'll get there," Sam said. "At least, I hope. At Chris's house, based on the positioning of the bodies, I really think Jenny Sutter or Ben Watson was shot first. Chris and the daughter, Skylar, walked in on it. It's the sloppiest of the three crime scenes. The most missed shots. Patty and Mark were far more surgical killings."

"The Sutter Seven," Kenya said. "You've heard that's what the press is calling this already?"

"Catchy," Clancy said, rolling his eyes. "We gotta be perfect on this one, everyone. This county has taken far too much heat. Sam, make sure your people coordinate every warrant through Kenya's office. No matter what happens, we're gonna have the eyes of the A.G.'s office on us. They're already calling. Pretty soon these meetings are going to have to include them."

"I'm not worried about that," Sam said. "Right now, the more help the better."

"Mara's running point from my office," Kenya said. "If it comes to it ... if ... when an arrest is made, this will be her case."

My heart swelled at the confidence Kenya bestowed on me. We both knew if this went to trial, it would be the biggest, most high-profile case Waynetown had ever seen. A terrible way to make it on the map, but we were all of one mind.

"Good," Sam said, echoing Kenya's confidence.

"Do you have any promising leads so far?" I asked.

"About a dozen," Sam answered. "More money, more problems is the biggest one. These people were millionaires. I gotta admit that shocked even me. They didn't live like it. The Sutters are simple. Salt of the earth."

"You never know until you know," Kenya said.

"Yeah," Sam agreed. "I've got an interview first thing in the morning. Patty Sutter's daughter is anxious to talk to me. She's coming up from Nashville where she lives now. Can you clear your schedule and sit in on this one, Mara?"

"Of course," I said.

"That's a standing order," Kenya chimed in. "Mara, I need you on this full time. Anything else on your plate we're off-loading. Hojo, that's why you're here. Get with Mara later today and have her get you up to speed on the rest of her caseload."

Hojo sat a little straighter in his chair. This was news to him. To me, too. But, for the next few months, it seemed I would live, eat, sleep, and breathe the Sutter murders.

So would Sam. Realization hit him the same time it did me.

"That's all I have for now. Sheriff, do you have a plan for how often you want to meet?"

"Wednesday mornings until there's an arrest. More if something breaks. You let me know if anything comes of the daughter. Um, Patty Sutter's daughter. What's her name?"

Sam looked down at his notes. "Devina Francis. She's not a Sutter. Patty was the second wife of C.J. Sutter. Devina, Dev, she calls herself, is from a previous relationship."

Clancy nodded. "More money, more problems," he said. "Let me guess. Old C.J. left more to the second wife than he did the kids or some such."

"We'll find out," Sam said.

"I'll pull whatever probate records there are on C.J. Sutter," I said. "When did he die?"

"Two years ago," Sam said.

"Got it," I said. "I'll let you know what I find out before the daughter gets here."

"Good," he said. "That way I'll know if she's conveniently

leaving anything out or being kept in the dark. She's coming in at ten a.m. Can you be ready by then?"

"Absolutely," I said, knowing it was going to be a long night, followed by a long day in a series of many more.

"Okay," Clancy said. "That's enough for now. Everybody go home and get some rest. We all need fresh eyes in the morning."

We filed out of the room one by one. The rest of my office staff attempted to look busy. Like the rest of the town, they were on pins and needles waiting for something, anything that could make sense of what happened out on Redmond Road. I'd been at this long enough to know that might never come.

$\approx$ 5 $\approx$

C aro had C.J. Sutter's probate court file couriered over to my house. I got home by six and hoped I could keep that schedule over the next few weeks. Will needed it. He needed me.

My ten-year-old son wasn't at the kitchen island when I walked in. My sister-in-law Kat waited for me there. I didn't like her expression.

"Everything okay?" I asked. I'd gotten no calls from Will's school. Since Jason moved out for good, I held my breath a lot, waiting for something to come to a head with our son.

"He has ... questions," Kat said. "I told him you'd answer what you could when you got home."

She had her tablet in front of her. Kat turned the screen toward me. She pulled up a story about the Sutter murders from Monday's press conference.

"I found these in his room," she said. Kat had a stack of paper. Printouts from news stories about the Sutter case.

"Damn," I said. I'd been down this road with Will before. If we weren't careful, Will would let certain events consume his thoughts to the point of obsession. Some were distant enough to be mostly harmless. His go-to was the *Titanic* disaster and the J.F.K. assassination. Two years ago, though, he'd pulled his own hair out enough to make a bald spot on one side when he started reading about an oil spill in the Gulf of Mexico.

I took the papers and walked up to Will's room. He sat cross-legged on the floor with a newly printed stack of papers. More news stories about the Sutters.

"Hey, guy," I said. "Whatcha got there?"

"They were home," he said. "Don't you find it strange that they were all home?"

"Will," I said. I sat down slowly, keeping some distance between us. I wanted to put my arms around him and pull him to me but knew that would be too much stimulation right now.

"Why wouldn't they have an alarm system?" he said. "Everyone will ask that. Only if it was someone they knew, it wouldn't have mattered. Did they have a doorbell camera on any of the houses? Have the police checked that?"

"Will," I said. "I know this is awful. Awful things do happen sometimes."

He finally made eye contact. "Do you think Mrs. Sutter saw them kill her daughter?"

"Oh, Will," I said. I reached for the papers in his hands. He jerked away, keeping them in a vice-like grip.

"Honey," I said. "You're safe. You're here with me right now. Nobody is going to hurt you."

"They can tell a lot from the trajectory of the bullets," he said. "They'll know where the perpetrators were standing. It had to be more than one. Have ballistics come back? Do they know if it was all from the same weapon? It was probably a nine millimeter, like a Luger? I mean, if it was all from one weapon, the killer would have had to reload."

"Will," I said sharply. "Look at me. Right at my eyes."

He clenched his jaw and cocked his head.

"Will," I said, trying to keep my tone more even. "Right here. You and me. Where are you right now?"

Slowly, he brought his eyes up to mine.

"I'm in my room," he said.

"What's under you?" I asked.

"The carpet. I think maybe I want wood floors. Not actual wood. They make synthetic that's easier to clean."

"Okay," I said. "We can talk about that. What does your carpet feel like? Is it hard or soft?"

"It's soft," he said. "We picked out shag. But I was only five. Dad said it would be softer in between my toes."

"He was right." I smiled. Will's shoulders dropped a little.

"What's the moon doing tonight?" I asked.

"It's a quarter moon," he said. "Two more days of that."

"That's your favorite anyway," I said. "You like it better than a full moon."

"It's easier to look at," he said. "And I can see more stars."

"Right," I said.

I reached out and took the papers from Will's hand. This time, he relaxed his grip and let me.

Breathe in. Breathe out.

"Where are you right now, buddy?" I asked.

"I'm here," he said. It was a game we began playing when he was very little. If I could bring Will out of his own head and into the room, he could find his breath again. His center. It didn't always work. I said a silent thank you that tonight, it had.

"Aunt Kat made meatloaf," he said.

"Did you eat yet?" I asked.

"No," he said. "I wanted to eat with you. We thought you might be late."

33

"No," I said. "Not late."

Then, my son reached out and held my hand. I tried not to so much as breathe too hard. Slowly, deliberately, we got up and walked out into the hallway together.

No. I was not late tonight. No matter what happened with the Sutter case, I knew I could not afford to be late coming home to Will, maybe ever again.

❦ 6 ❧

"You okay with being in the observation room?" Sam asked me.

"Of course," I answered. I was about to say something else when a door opened down the hallway.

"That's gotta be her," Sam whispered.

"She" was in her mid-twenties. Pretty, with short brown hair and wide eyes filled with tears. She held her companion's hand in a death grip. He was tall, lumbering, actually. Heavy-set with a boyish face, he was gentle with her, whispering something in her ear as he pulled her close.

"Ms. Francis?" Sam said, stepping away from me. He gave me a quick gesture. I slipped inside of the nearest doorway. The observation room. I took a chair near the large one-way mirror, giving me an unobstructed view of the interview room on the other side.

After a moment or two of muffled voices from the hallway, Sam led Devina Francis and her companion inside. He shut the door, looked my way, then seated the woman and her friend after they both declined any refreshments.

I took a notepad and pen out of my briefcase. "You mind if I record our conversation?" Sam asked.

"No," she said. "Anything you need." She was more composed now.

"Okay," Sam started. "Just for recording purposes then, why don't you tell me your name again."

"Devina Francis," she said, leaning forward, closer to the small black voice recorder Sam had placed in the center of the table. "But it's just Dev. And this is Owen Stevic, my boyfriend."

Owen stayed silent at her side but kept a steadying arm around Dev's shoulders. She leaned against him.

"Dev," Sam continued. "I'm so sorry for your loss. When we're through here, if there's anything you need in town, just let me know. Do you have a place to stay?"

She nodded. "I still have friends here. Thank you."

"Good," Sam said. "Just because we're recording, can you tell me how you're related to the Sutter family?"

"Patty Sutter is my mom," she said, her lips trembling. "She married C.J. Sutter, my stepdad, twelve years ago when I was thirteen."

"Got it," Sam said. "I'm just trying to keep the family tree straight."

"It's a big one," she said. "C.J., my stepdad, was the oldest of three. Um ... Uncle Chris was in the middle, I think."

"You're speaking of Christopher Sutter, one of the other victims?"

"Yes," she said. "They lived in the house closest to the road. C.J.'s house ... the one my mom lives ... lived ... in was to the west, set back a ways. Then the house where Kevin was living was to the east. Grandma George and Uncle Lou still live in the big house on the north side of the property. There's a woods between them and then the cornfields on the east and west borders."

"I understand," Sam said. He'd pulled out a map of the Sutter farm. Dev marked the homes with Xs as she spoke. "Dev, when you called me, you said you thought you had information about a likely motive for these killings. Can you tell me about that?"

She shifted in her chair. Sam kept a box of tissues on the table. Owen reached for one and handed it to Dev just before she burst into tears again. I respected his strong, silent presence and felt grateful she had someone to support her in what had to be one of the worst days of her life.

"My stepdad, C.J., died a little over two years ago. He had lung cancer. Before that, he was helping run the Sutter store with Kevin. Kevin's dad Tom was another cousin. I think C.J.'s dad, Chet, and Kevin's grandpa ... er ... Grandpa Lou were brothers."

"I've noticed all the family members I've spoken to refer to Lou Sutter as Grandpa Lou, is that right?" Sam asked.

"Yes," she said. "Grandpa Lou and Grandma George. They're the last of that generation. The original brothers who opened the store back in the forties. All the other brothers were dead long before my mom married into the family."

"I see," Sam said. "So how was your mother's relationship with C.J.'s family after he passed?"

"Awful," she said. "That's what I need you to know. Like I said, C.J. and Kevin were running the store pretty much. C.J.'s other sister moved away and didn't have much involvement. I never really knew her. Claudia, I think her name was. We all worked there at one time or another. I think every Sutter kid worked behind the counter at the store as a first job."

Sam smiled. "I remember. My dad took me in when I was

a kid a few times. I remember C.J. too. Big guy. Big smile. Big laugh."

This got a laugh out of Dev. "He was all that. Just a big heart, too. Big talker. He got so thin toward the end of his life. It was a hard way to go. He was sick for a really long time. And that's the thing. It was my mom by his side through all of that. They had ... it wasn't always easy between them. They were separated for a while. Right after I graduated from high school my mom left him. C.J. cheated on her a lot. But when he got sick, they worked through it. She was there for him."

"And that didn't sit well with the other family members?" Sam asked.

"They are very close knit," she said. "My mom was always the outsider. C.J. has two grown kids from his first marriage, Gary and Toby. They don't even live in Waynetown anymore. Never wanted anything to do with the store beyond working there when they were kids. They're a fair bit older than me. In their forties. We were never close. But they hated my mom. I mean, *hated* her."

I had C.J. Sutter's probate file in front of me. I'd tabbed a few things and made a note to bring them to Sam's attention.

"Where was your mom in all this when the store was sold to Verde?" Sam asked, making me smile. It was the exact question I would have asked at that exact moment.

"C.J. and Kevin were the legal partners when that sale went through. I told you, they were the only ones who wanted anything to do with the day to day. Maybe ten years ago, C.J. and Kevin bought C.J.'s sister and Chris out of the business. I don't know for how much. But they drew up papers. I remember my mom and C.J. talking about it a lot when it was all happening. He wanted to make sure they got a fair share and all that. He wanted it to be all legal."

She started to cry again. The door to the observation room quietly opened. Sheriff Clancy stepped in.

"How's it going?" he whispered.

I turned my notepad toward him and pointed to the items I'd flagged in C.J. Sutter's probate filings. Clancy's eyebrows went up, and he shook his head.

"There was a big fight after C.J. died," Dev said to Sam. "The money Verde gave them for the store was crazy. It was an offer-they-couldn't-refuse kind of thing. If you ask me, that money was poison. Everybody was fighting with everybody else. C.J.'s sister and Chris thought they should be cut in, even though they really had nothing to do with that store anymore. Not legally. Not practically. When they sold their interest, they sold their interest. They got a bunch of lawyers involved at first."

"How much was the sale?" Sam asked.

I had the figures in front of me and pointed to them again for Clancy's benefit.

"Two million dollars," Dev answered. "C.J. was the one who negotiated it. They offered, I think, close to half of that at first. C.J. threw the two-million-dollar figure out, never thinking Verde would bite. But they did. The thing is, these pot businesses have a limit on the amount of money they can put in the bank. They're loaded with cash. And that property, you know it, of course. It's right at the exit on I-75. And nothing else was available. So, they gave C.J. and Kevin what they asked for."

"So C.J.'s cut was a million dollars," Sam said.

"Yes," she said. "And he was kicking himself, thinking he should have asked for more. But by then, he was getting sicker. That was the other thing besides not being healthy enough to actually run the business. C.J. saw it as a way to make sure my mom was taken care of after he was gone. He knew he was dying. He was kind of keeping it from my mom, or thought he was. But she knew."

"C.J. died, what, three months after the sale went through?" Sam asked.

"That sounds about right. And then things really got ugly after that. C.J. left a hundred thousand bucks to each of his sons, Gary and Toby. He left the rest to my mom. They didn't take that well. There was a huge, awful fight at C.J.'s funeral."

"I never heard anything about that," Sam said.

"They had a private one," Dev said. "Just for family. It got physical. Claudia's husband actually went after my stepbrother Toby and my cousin Kevin. Kevin's mom's boyfriend went after Uncle Chris. Skylar was fighting with Kevin's sister, Nikki. It was a mess. I thought Grandma George was going to have a heart attack. It broke her heart seeing all the nephews and grandkids ripping each other up like that. Thankfully, Grandpa Lou didn't really know what was going on."

"Why is that?" Sam asked.

"He's got dementia," she answered. "It's pretty bad. The last time I saw him, he didn't even recognize me. Those two were the only ones in the family that made me feel welcome, that I was a Sutter too, no matter who my birth father was."

"I see," Sam said.

"Detective Cruz," she said, leaning forward. "I think maybe you need to talk to C.J.'s sons. Maybe even his sister, Claudia. I think they had something to do with what happened out at the farm. They wanted my mom out of the picture. They hated Mark too. He was her lawyer before they started dating."

It made my stomach turn a little. I wrote a few more notes. There would have been huge ethical issues with Mark

O'Brien beginning to date an active client. Especially one who stood to inherit the kind of money Patty Sutter had.

"So your mom got C.J.'s house after he died," Sam said.

"She did," Dev said. "That was another thing that made a lot of them mad. That's Sutter property, they said. Only Sutters should live there. It was Grandma George who shut that crap down. She reminded them that *she* had married into the Sutter name too, and not a one of them would have even thought about trying to push her off if and when Grandpa Lou dies. I really love her for that. She's the only level-headed one in the bunch, as far as I'm concerned."

"Dev," Sam asked. "Do you have any other reason to think C.J.'s own family might be behind this? Did your mother ever express any specific fears?"

"She was afraid of them all, yes," she said. "I told her to sell that house. Tell Chris and the others if they wanted it so bad, they could pay her for it. But she was happy there. She had it fixed up the way she liked. She was convinced it was all gonna die down, eventually. She was wrong."

Dev began to sob. Owen pulled her into his chest.

"I think that's all I need for today," Sam said. "You're staying in town though?"

Dev nodded. "Yeah. We're having Mom's funeral next week. I wanted to take her home. Have her buried near me in Nashville, but she left instructions."

"I understand," Sam said. He rose and gathered his own notes. Leaning over, he clicked off the voice recorder. "Thank you so much for coming in. I know this has to be unbelievably hard. But you've been helpful."

"Are you going to do something?" she asked. "Are you going to bring C.J.'s kids and his sister in?"

"I'll talk to them; you can be sure of that. In the meantime, it's best you don't talk to them. Or anyone about what we discussed, if you don't mind."

"Okay," she said. "I don't want to do anything that will make your job harder."

"I appreciate that."

Sam showed Owen and Dev out then came to join Clancy and me in the adjoining room. Lines furrowed his brow as he sat down opposite me.

"What's your read?" he asked.

"I think you've got a mess on your hands," I said. "I don't like what I'm hearing about Mark O'Brien, the lawyer."

"Yeah," Clancy agreed. "That raises my slime-o-meter too."

"Patty Sutter inherited over a million bucks from C.J.," I said, showing Sam the probate file. "He renewed his will after the sale to Verde, naming Patty as his primary beneficiary, like Dev said. But here's the thing. There was a settlement. Look here."

I handed Sam a document.

"That hundred thousand a piece Dev is talking about, the money she says he left to his sons. It wasn't really an inheritance in the strict sense. He gifted it to them before he died. And he made them sign a release against any claims they might have filed against his estate. Look at the bottom where it says who prepared it."

"Mark O'Brien," Sam read. "Patty's boyfriend. Victim number seven."

"It's ... icky," I said. "Then Mark moves in with Patty within the last year. But I just don't buy that C.J.'s kids would have killed Patty over this. They agreed to take the hundred K. If anything, their beef would be with Dev now. She stands to inherit everything that's left."

"The other problem," Sam said. "Gary and Toby Sutter live out west now. Arizona. I did talk to both of them over the phone. They haven't been back to Waynetown since C.J.'s funeral two years ago. His sister, this Claudia? She's near Fort Worth. I talked to her son. She's got advanced Parkinson's and lives in a nursing home. That pretty much eliminates all three of them as suspects. Though, they did confirm there's a lot of disharmony among the Sutters. They didn't speak too highly of C.J. *or* Chris and Jenny."

"Better send a deputy over to keep an eye out on Dev anyway," Clancy said. "You get an address as to where she's staying?"

"Yeah," Sam answered. "And I agree. Something just doesn't track. This is all fine and good about the bad blood between Patty Sutter, Mark O'Brien, and factions of the Sutter family. If they were the only victims, it would make sense. C.J.'s brother Chris was on the same side as his kids in this dispute. He's dead. His wife's dead. His daughter. And Kevin Sutter."

"You've got more digging to do," I said. "In light of your other interviews, Dev didn't give you anything solid as far as a credible threat against Mark or Patty."

"Yeah," he said. "I've got enough for some tough interviews with the rest of the family here in Waynetown. Then we'll see who lies and how badly."

"I think you *do* have enough to get a search warrant on some of Mark O'Brien's files," I said. "I'd like to know more about what he was doing for Patty Sutter in a legal sense."

"Good thinking," Sam said. "I'll write one up and run it by you."

"I'll be waiting for it," I said. "I'll get it fast-tracked for you."

"I like this," Clancy said as he stood up. "You two keep at

it. Joined at the hip if you have to be. I don't want a single thing missed. Everything's gotta be airtight."

"We're all on the same page," I said. "The last thing my office needs is anything less than perfect." We'd just been burned by a scathing report from the Attorney General's Office that revealed longstanding corruption with my former boss, Kenya's predecessor, Phil Halsey. Though no one had come out and said it directly, a win on the Sutter case would go a long way to restoring faith in the Maumee County criminal justice system. Both Bill Clancy and the mayor had made it clear they were putting the weight of that on Sam's and my shoulders. If either one of us botched this case, I had a feeling we'd both be out of jobs.

I felt like my thoughts were written on Sam's face as well as Clancy slapped him on the back and left us alone.

"He trusts you, Sam," I said. "So do I. You're going to get to the bottom of this case. You tag him, I'll bag him." I gathered my things and started toward the door.

Sam let out a chuckle behind me. "I'll bag 'em you'll tag 'em. You know you can't pull a phrase like that off."

Shrugging, I adjusted my briefcase strap. "No? Not even a little? I thought I kinda had there for a second."

"You thought wrong, Brent."

He was still shaking his head, laughing, as he turned and headed down the other hallway toward his office.

🦋 7 🦋

I found a smile and froze it in place as I walked into the kitchen on Friday afternoon, two weeks later. Will's two packed suitcases sat in the hallway. I heard laughter coming from the living room and it turned my smile into something genuine even as my heart ached at what was to come.

"Hey, guys," I said. Will was sitting on the couch, his knees drawn up. His eyes stayed glued to an object on the table in front of him. As I drew closer, I saw it was a plastic replica of one of the Space Shuttles. Jason, my newly ex-husband, knelt on the floor and snapped a last piece of the model in place, then handed it to Will.

"Hey, Mara," Jason said. The smile he had for Will faded a bit as a new discomfort grew between us. We hadn't been face to face since the divorce decree became official.

"You all packed?" I asked Will.

"Yep," he said as he turned the shuttle end over end in his hands.

"Great," I said. "You mind if I just do a quick once-over in your room in case you missed anything important?"

The shuttle had already mesmerized Will. I'd seen that

45

look a hundred times before. He'd watched a documentary on the Challenger disaster a few months ago. He must have told his dad.

I gave Jason a look. He could still read my expressions. After patting Will on the head, he made an excuse then followed me upstairs. I went into Will's room and did a quick check of his nightstand drawer, under his bed, and his "lucky drawer" in his tall dresser. My son had told the truth. He had packed all his essentials.

"Everything okay?" Jason asked.

"Mom!" Will shouted from downstairs. "Aunt Kat will be here in seven minutes!"

"Okay," I shouted down.

"What's that about?" Jason asked.

"That's what we're up here for," I answered. I brought Jason into my upstairs home office. I kept it locked so Will could never get in. It was my war room. I had timelines written on the white board on one wall. On another, I'd compiled a Sutter family tree.

As soon as Jason stepped in, I shut the door behind him.

"Ever since the Sutter murders," I said, "Will's showing signs of obsession. He's read every article posted online about the crime. He's worried. He won't come out and say it, but he's scared the killer is going to strike again. He asked me if he could install a family GPS app on his phone. I didn't see the harm in it. He's going to ask you to join his circle so he can track you too."

"Good grief, Mara," Jason said. "This can't be good for him. It sounds like I got here just in time."

I bit back the stinging retort I had in mind. Jason's past infidelities were the major reason we divorced.

"I agree it's going to be good for him to get away from Waynetown for a few weeks." Jason had granted me primary physical custody in the divorce decree. Will would spend six weeks in the summer with his dad and alternating Christmas vacations.

"Has he seen any of this?" Jason motioned to my white boards.

"Of course not," I answered. "You know he doesn't have access to this room. I just wanted you to be aware. Enforce our screen time rules and the parental locks on your television and internet. Promise me."

Jason grimaced. I had the sense he was trying to keep from saying the snarky comment he wanted to as well.

"Kat knows the drill," I said. I was so thankful Jason's sister had agreed to travel with Will when he went to D.C. to stay with Jason. I didn't know how many times she could uproot her life, but for the first year of our new arrangement, she was here for him.

"Mara," Jason said. "I'm sorry, but if this starts to be a pattern with Will, maybe you seriously need to rethink what's best for him in terms of your career."

"Really?" I said. "You want to have a go at me about that today of all days?"

I heard the front door open. Kat was here. Her bright greeting to my son warmed my heart. I knew he'd do at least twenty minutes with her explaining his new toy.

"I'm just saying," Jason said, softening his tone. "You know there are a million offers you could take when you want to leave the prosecutor's office. The U.S. Attorney's office is still interested. You'd be closer to D.C. Closer to your mother."

"Stop," I said. "I will not keep having this fight with you. It's a non-starter. This is my life. Waynetown. You're the one who reneged on that deal, not me."

He put his hands up in surrender. Though I knew we'd

have this fight again, Jason was waving the white flag for now. I'd take what I could get.

"So how's it going?" he asked. "And what are you doing with all of this stuff now?"

Jason stepped around my desk and inspected my white boards.

"Because if and when this case goes to court, I'll be the one trying it."

"Any arrests yet?" he asked.

"No," I said.

Jason shook his head. His expression grew more somber as he looked at pictures of each of the victims.

We'd numbered them. Not because we knew the order of the killings, but to help keep things straight. In the house at the center. Ben Watson was Victim #1. Jenny Sutter was Victim #2, her husband Chris Sutter was Victim #3, and his daughter Skylar was Victim #4. To the east of them, their cousin, Kevin Sutter, became Victim #5. We'd dubbed Patty Sutter and Mark O'Brien as Victims #6 and #7, respectively. The Sutter Seven.

"Who caught it from the Sheriff's Department?" he asked.

"Sam Cruz," I said. Jason nodded his approval.

"Good choice," he said. "He's thorough."

"Jason," I said. "Since you're here, and I think Will's going to keep Kat occupied for a little while, there was something I wanted to ask you about."

He quickly straightened. "Anything," he said. "I've still got contacts in the A.G.'s office."

"No," I said. "Nothing like that. Not yet anyway. I'm just ... I didn't grow up in Waynetown like you did. I knew of the Sutters, but I didn't really know them. Did you?"

He considered my question. We heard laughter coming

from downstairs. Will's voice. Jason took a seat on the loveseat against the wall. I leaned against my desk.

"Yeah," he said. "I knew the Sutters. Two cousins went to high school with me. Does Cruz have any promising leads?"

"Some," I said. "Turns out there was quite a bit of infighting among the family members when they sold that bait shop to the pot dispensary."

"I'll bet," he said. "As I recall, there were four Sutter brothers, originally. Ray, Henry, Chet, and Louie."

"Louie is Grandpa Lou?" I asked. "He's the only one of the original four still alive."

"You mind?" Jason asked. He took a black dry erase marker and started drawing a family tree.

"By all means," I said.

"When I was campaigning, the Sutters were big donors," he said. "I spent some time over at Lou and George's. They're both talkers. I got the entire family history."

He drew the four names he'd just said. Ray. Henry. Chet. Louie. He drew a big X through Henry's name.

"He was a navy pilot, I wanna say. Or army air corps. One of the two. Didn't make it back from World War Two. Ray and Chet did. They're the ones who started the store after they came back from the war. Louie was their baby brother. He couldn't have been over ten or eleven, I don't think."

"How do you remember all of this?" I asked. Of course, I already knew. Jason had one of the best memories of anyone I'd ever met. It served him extremely well on Capitol Hill. I always used to tell him he'd have made an excellent wartime admiral if he hadn't gone into politics.

"I also used to date one of the Sutter cousins," he said, giving me a guilty smile that used to melt me. There was a time I would have forgiven him anything when he flashed that smile. Until he did the one thing I couldn't.

49

"Anyway," he said. "Chet had, I think, three kids. I dated one of his granddaughters. Claudia's oldest girl, Michelle."

"Right," I said. I took the marker from him and drew in C.J. Sutter's name beneath Chet's. Chet's kids all had "C" names. C.J., Claudia, Chris.

"Ray had no kids," Jason said. "Louie had a couple, I think. I wanna say there was a kid who died as a baby."

"Kevin Sutter," I said, pointing to my victim board. "He was a grandson of Louie's, not Chet's."

"Right," he said. "His dad was Tom, I think. He died a while back. He's got a sister. Nikki. Man, she was something. A little too young for me, but gorgeous. I don't think she lives in Waynetown anymore."

"Kevin has a sister," I said. "I'm sure Sam's talked to her."

"I can't even imagine the toll this is taking on Grandpa Lou," he said. "He's just the nicest guy you'd ever want to meet. I even called him Grandpa Lou when I was dating Michelle. I kind of lost track of her. Huh. I wonder if she ever got married. After we broke up, she started dating Guy Harvey. That did *not* go over well with her family."

"Why not?" I asked.

"I don't know the whole story, but the Harveys and the Sutters didn't get along. The Harveys own the farmland to the east of the Sutter farm. I know there was a boundary dispute a long time ago. When I was dating Michelle, we used to go back in that woods and ... well ... let's just say a lot of Waynetown kids got lucky on Sutter property."

"Lovely," I said.

"I just remember Michelle telling me we'd have to be careful to stay to the west of the creek that runs through the two properties. She said the Harveys put bear traps out there. There were all sorts of crazy stories. She said some of her old cousins insisted a Harvey ancestor haunted those woods just to keep the Sutters in their place."

"I've never heard those stories," I said.

"Well, like you said, you didn't grow up in Waynetown."

A car honked out front. My heart did a little flip. It was getting late. Jason had a flight to catch with Will and Kat.

"Thanks," I said. "That's helpful. I'm sure Sam's pursuing all that. I'm just trying to immerse myself in all things Sutter. I want to be prepared."

"Of course," he said. "If I think of anything else, I'll call you."

We walked into the hallway together. "Just ... Jason ... take care of him. Will's never been away from this house, or away from me, for this long. Six weeks seems like forever."

Jason turned to me. He put a light hand on my arm and for once I didn't recoil. "It's gonna be okay, Mama. I love that kid just as much as you do. He's going to FaceTime you every night, just like we said. I've got a ton of cool things planned. We haven't even really seen everything there is to see in D.C."

"Just be careful," I said, forcing back tears. "He can get overwhelmed and ..."

"I know," Jason whispered. "Mara, I know. I need you to trust me. Trust Will."

"Gotta go, Mom!" Will shouted from the bottom of the stairs. He was smiling. Excited. I found my smile and walked down to him. He let me hug him. I put a kiss on my son's cheek.

"Be good," I said. "I love you."

"I love you too," Will said. Kat gave me a reassuring wink over Will's shoulder. Then she and Jason took my son to the waiting car. I was alone in my own home for the first time since Will was born.

❧ 8 ❧

Three days later, I met the sister of Kevin Sutter, Victim #5, by chance. As I loaded groceries into my trunk, she shouted my name across the parking lot.

"Ms. Brent?" she said. "You're Mara Brent, aren't you?"

I turned. She had long, nearly waist-length brown hair with blonde highlights and make-up that looked more New York than Waynetown. She stood in front of a red Honda Accord parked two spots over. A rental, by the stickers on it.

"Yes," I said, closing my trunk. "Can I help you?"

"I'm Nikki Sutter," she said, blinking a little too quickly. I realized she was fighting back tears.

"Oh, Nikki!" I said, recalling the crude family tree Jason had drawn for me. Nikki and Kevin were the grandchildren of the youngest original Sutter brother, Grandpa Louie. As Nikki stepped closer, I saw she wasn't alone. An older woman sat in the passenger seat. She turned her head and fixed an enormous set of green eyes—deeply set in a round face with hard lines, especially around her mouth—on me.

"Nikki," I said. "I'm so sorry for your loss."

Nikki looked back at the passenger in her car. "This is Grandma George," she said.

Grandma George's expression didn't change. She considered me. Then unlatched her seatbelt and stepped out of the car to join her granddaughter.

"It's nice to meet you," I said to the old woman. She came to stand next to Nikki. Nikki put her arm around her. She was taller. Georgette Sutter couldn't have reached even five feet. She wore a green polyester vested pantsuit with a matching blouse.

"They won't tell us much," Nikki said. "I just want to know what's going on with my brother's case."

"I understand," I said.

"It'll be you," Nikki said. "They said on the news when they arrest someone, you're the one who is going to take him or them to trial."

"That's right," I said. I knew that look. I'd dealt with hundreds of crime victims, loved ones of people who had lost their lives in unspeakable ways. I couldn't imagine what it must be like for these two. To lose so many members of their family all at once. To live with the fear that perhaps they, too, were targets.

"I know it's frustrating," I said. "But Detective Cruz, well, he's the best there is." It felt natural to make them the one promise I knew I couldn't make. Though I believed Sam would find the people responsible for these murders, I could offer them no guarantees.

"He's so young," Grandma George said. "So are you. How old are you, honey?"

She stepped forward and put a hand on my cheek. It was a forward gesture. She had recently manicured nails with pink pearl polish, but fingers gnarled with arthritis. She wore a pendant with two lockets dangling from her neck, flipped so

I could see the tiny picture inside. It was a faded black-and-white photograph of an infant.

"Grandma," Nikki whispered, embarrassed by her grandmother's boldness.

"It's okay," I said. "I'm thirty-five, Mrs. Sutter."

"Not so young then," she said. "I read about you. You don't let them push you around, do you?"

Though I wasn't sure who she meant by "them" I took it as a compliment. "No," I answered. "I don't."

"Good," she said, pointing a finger at me. "You make sure. You keep an eye on them. I don't want any mistakes. I've put too many of my babies in the ground, Ms. Brent. You promise me. Right here. Right now. You make sure Detective Cruz and the rest of them get it right."

"That's my job," I said. "And it's his job, too. He's a good one."

She nodded, then pointed her finger at Nikki. Nikki put on a smile and froze it in place as Georgette Sutter walked around her and went back to the passenger side of the car. She braced herself on the hood, her left leg moving slower than her right.

She climbed in, reached over, and turned the key. The engine sprang to life and Mrs. Sutter fastened her seatbelt again.

"Sorry about that," Nikki said. "She talks in riddles a lot."

"No," I said. "It's okay. I get it. I had a grandparent just like that. I'm glad to see she seems to be holding up. How are you? Is there anything I can do for you? I can put you in touch with ..."

"No," Nikki said a little sharply. "We can take care of ourselves. I've been ... I'm going to stay here in Waynetown for a little while. The funeral was pretty rough on my grandparents. She still isn't over losing our dad in a car accident ten years ago. Losing Kevin, his only son, too … well, we haven't even told my grandpa yet."

"I see," I said.

"He's not all there anymore," she said. "He still recognizes me. But I think if he really understood what all happened, I don't think he'd survive it, Ms. Brent. I just … I'm worried what will happen if you have to call either of my grandparents at the trial. Lord, even them *being* in a courtroom."

"Let's not get ahead of ourselves," I said. "I think you're managing well just the way you are. One thing at a time."

I pulled out a business card and handed it to her. "I'm going to put you in touch with a liaison out of my office. If you have questions, if you need anything. You or your grandparents. Whatever time of day …"

"Thank you," she said, taking the card. "This is hard for us."

"Of course."

"No," she said. "We don't, well, Sutters take care of their own. This whole thing has been so public. It's been very difficult for everyone to be on display like this. I know it's only going to get worse whenever they catch who did this. My brother and me … I loved him. Don't get me wrong. He was my big brother. My only sibling. And losing our dad ten years ago brought us so much closer. But he wasn't perfect. I'm just worried about people getting the wrong idea about him."

"In what way?" I asked.

"Kevin was hard to like sometimes," she said. "But he was trying to be a good dad to Ava, despite what his ex says. I'm just so glad that sweet little girl wasn't with him that day at the house."

Nikki's voice broke. Her face went white.

I tried to pull up a mental image of the file we had on Kevin Sutter. He shared a three-year-old daughter with an ex.

I couldn't recall off the top of my head whether they were married or not.

"Nikki," I said. "Is there something you want to tell me?"

"I don't know," she said. "I don't want to make more trouble where there doesn't need to be."

"If you know something. No matter how minor, it could help," I said. "Did Kevin confide something in you?"

"No," she said. "Not exactly. It's just, he was having a lot of baby mama drama over the last few months. Lea, Ava's mom, was suing for primary custody. She was trying to take away Kevin's visitation. Now, with everything that's happening, my grandparents are really worried they're never going to get to see that little girl at all. She means a lot to them. She brings them joy. And we haven't been able to see her since Kevin died. They wouldn't even bring her to her own father's funeral. Is that allowed? Is there some way, some legal way we can get visitation for my grandparents?"

"It wouldn't be something within my power, no. Things are so raw right now, I'd imagine. For both families. Maybe when the dust settles a little ..."

"It'll never settle," she said. "Lea's been so unfair. She tried to poison Ava against my brother. Now, God knows what she's going to raise that kid to believe about him."

"I'm sorry," I said. "I had no idea."

"No, I'm sorry," she blurted. I sensed she was already regretting telling me that much. "I have to get my grandmother back home. We don't like leaving my grandpa alone for too long."

"Take care of yourself, Nikki," I said. "And I meant what I said. Don't be afraid to reach out."

"Thanks," she said. Then Nikki Sutter slid into the driver's side and backed her car out of her spot. My breath caught as she nearly clipped the bumper of the car parked behind her.

I waved goodbye, then got behind my own wheel. I sat for a moment, considering everything Nikki had to say. Before I could back out myself, my phone rang. I pressed the "accept" button on my dashboard home screen.

"Mara?" Sam's voice filled my car. I turned the volume down.

"Hey, Sam," I said. "I was just about to call you. I had an interesting conversation with Nikki Sutter in the Meijer parking lot just now. Do we know how ugly the custody fight was getting between Kevin Sutter and his ex? I know it's a long shot. It would make a certain amount of sense if Kevin were the only victim, but a massacre like that?"

"Lea Shane," he answered. "That's Kevin's ex. They didn't have anything on the docket in common pleas over the kid, but I interviewed Lea two days after the murders. She seemed pretty broken up. She had an alibi. She was staying with her folks that weekend. The kid was with her."

"Hmm," I said.

"Anyway, Mara, I'm calling because I may have a break in the case. I'm getting ready to write a search warrant. Cell records came back on Mickey Harvey, Skylar Sutter's on-again off-again boyfriend."

"Harvey," I said. "You mean from the neighboring family?"

"That's the one," he said.

"I don't remember a search warrant on any of the Harveys' phones, Sam."

"Mara, listen. I got the full forensics back on Skylar's phone. There are some disturbing texts from Mickey to her in the last few days before the murder. And Mickey's phone hit the tower that serves Skylar's house at ten the morning of the murders. He was there, Mara. The kid was there."

My pulse quickened. "Sam, have you interviewed him?"

"Yeah," he said. "He never once mentioned being at Skylar's place. He told me he saw her the day before, not the morning of."

"He lied," I said.

"Bingo," Sam said.

"What do you need?" I asked.

"I just want to run the warrant by you. I want to search Mickey's house. And I want to bring him in for a formal interview."

"I'll be right there," I said, hoping like hell this would be the break we were looking for.

❧ 9 ❧

Sam hoped to keep things quiet when he brought Mickey
Harvey in for questioning. So did I. But by the time the
patrol car pulled up to deposit Mickey through a non-public
entrance to the Sheriff's Department, word had already
got out.

"Come on," Detective Gus Ritter said. He took my arm
and led me through a separate door. We went to the
observation room next to the largest interrogation room the
Maumee County Sheriff's Department had. We'd need it.
Besides Gus and me, Sheriff Clancy and Kenya crowded in.

"You ever met him?" Ritter said to Clancy. Just then,
Mickey Harvey entered the adjoining room. I took out my
notepad and claimed a chair closest to the one-way glass.

I had a bio sheet on Mickey. He had a bit of a record. The
worst of it was a drunk driving charge from two years ago. A
handful of juvenile offenses. Underage drinking, shoplifting a
pack of cigarettes when he was fifteen. But looking at him
now, I'd have guessed he was trying to put all of that
behind him.

He was clean-shaven with dark-blond hair he wore slicked

back and tucked behind his ears. Just twenty-five, he could have passed for much older judging by the bags under his eyes. He was steady, though. No fidgeting. No scratching at his skin or rapid blinking that would have signaled drug withdrawal. It wasn't definitive, of course. But I was already trying to gauge how Mickey would read to a jury if he ever took the stand.

Sam came in a few minutes later holding a clipboard. Mickey didn't realize, but his interrogation had already begun the moment he took his seat.

"Mickey," Sam said. "I want to make a few things clear. You're not under arrest. You're free to leave this room anytime you want. We clear on that?"

"Yeah," Mickey said. He had a gravelly voice. He sat with his hands folded in front of him.

"Good," Sam said. "I have some follow-up questions. You remember we talked a couple of weeks ago? The day after Skylar Sutter's body was found."

"Of course I remember," Mikey said.

"Do you remember what I asked you?" Sam asked.

"You asked me if I knew who might have done that to Sky," Mickey said. His eyes turned red. "I told you, I don't know. I still don't."

Sam took a piece of paper off his clipboard and handed it to Mickey. "You wanna tell me about that?"

Mickey read the paper. Maybe two seconds later, he slammed it down on the table.

"No," he said. "No way." He slid the paper back at Sam.

"That's a partial transcript of some texts we found on Skylar Sutter's phone. You want to tell me what that was about? Two days before she died, she texted you she wanted some space. It sounds like she called off a date you were supposed to go on the night before she was shot, Mickey."

"So what?" he said. "That had to do with her folks, not me. She was worried about what her folks were going to say when we told them we were planning to get married. We were supposed to get married last year. It just got complicated. Her folks, my dad. Trying to please everybody. So we postponed it and were going to elope. It was like that with Sky and me. She had a temper. And her dad was really hard on her. Like she could never please him. He was not a good guy. Ask around."

"I see," Sam said. "You want to explain why you didn't mention this fight when I talked to you last?"

"It wasn't a fight," Mickey said. "Sky was just stressed out. She was studying for an exam. You know she was trying to be a respiratory therapist. That was her dad and brother's idea. Not Sky's. She and me ... we wanted to move out of Waynetown. It was just a lot of stuff coming to a head."

"Mickey," Sam said. "When was the last time you saw Skylar?"

He sat back, draped his arm over the back of the empty chair beside him. I had a copy of Mickey's preliminary cell phone report in front of me. Gus leaned in and looked at the entry I had my finger on.

"Watch this," Gus whispered.

"I saw her the Thursday morning before she died," Mickey said. "She'd spent the night at my place the night before. Instead of going out like I wanted, she just came over. We talked."

"About what?" Sam asked.

"None of your business," Mickey answered.

"You didn't go over there at all Friday?" Sam asked.

"No," Mickey answered.

"Mickey," Sam said, keeping his voice steady. "I'm trying

to figure out who put a bullet into your girlfriend's head. You really want to get in the way of that?"

Mickey dropped his head. He hid his face in his hands and let out a great, sighing breath. When he looked up, tears had filled his eyes.

"We talked about running away together," he said. "This is killing me. Sky was my whole life, man."

"Why were your parents opposed to the two of you getting married, Mickey?" Sam asked.

Mickey put flat palms against the table.

"Sky's family didn't like you, did they?" Sam said. "They liked to meddle. Get in Skylar's ear. Was that it?"

"Yes!" he hissed. "It was just a bunch of stupid crap. Total BS. Her great-grandpa pissed off my great-grandpa or some crap like that. I don't even know. Frickin' boomers. We laughed about it."

"But what about you, Mickey? Huh? You personally. I heard they told you not to come around anymore. I heard Skylar's dad told you he'd kick your ass if he saw you on their property. Is that true?"

"I told you. Not a good dude. He was overprotective," Mickey said. "He and Sky's mom both. And they were completely dysfunctional, those two. Sky's mom used to threaten to leave all the time. She was messed up. Bipolar or something. Sky tried to be the peacemaker. Her brother Luke got out as quick as he could. Not Sky. She told me once she had to stay there to keep them both happy. She was twenty-two years old! They manipulated her. She was going to move in with me. Then, I don't know. Her mom and dad just ran the same guilt trip on her they always did and she changed her mind."

"That must have made you pretty angry with Sky and her parents," Sam said.

"No. Screw that. I didn't shoot them. And I didn't kill Sky. I would never ..." He broke then. "I loved her. Do you get what I'm saying? I *loved* her! If anything, she'd have been more likely to shoot me."

"When was the last time you went over to Sky's house, Mickey?" Sam asked.

"I told you. She came to my place that Wednesday night. I drove her home the next morning. I guess it was Thursday morning. Then that was it. That was the last time I saw her. I swear."

"You're telling me, you were at Skylar's house just to drop her off on Thursday, May 17th? In the morning?"

"That's what happened," he insisted.

Sam pulled out another piece of paper. "You're lying, Mickey. We ran your cell phone records."

"You can't do that!" he said. "That's illegal."

"It isn't," he said. "We got your number off Skylar's phone. Now you want to tell me the truth?"

"I told you the truth. I didn't see her after Thursday. I gave her what she wanted. I gave her space. I was getting ready to go stay with a buddy of mine down in Lexington. I was going to be gone for a week. I figured that'd give us both a chance to cool off."

"Mickey," Sam said. "You were at Sky's house on Friday morning. You went there at ten in the morning. The proof's right here. You see that entry? That's the cell tower on Redmond Road. You were there. You know the county has cameras set up at the Redmond and Whittaker intersections? There's a Valero at Whittaker."

"So what?" he said.

Sam pulled out a file. He'd blown up 8x10 grainy security footage photos.

"That's your car, isn't it, Mickey?" Sam asked. "That's you

heading west on Redmond at nine fifty-two a.m. Friday morning on the 18th. You went to Sky's house, didn't you?"

Mickey was sweating. He licked his lips.

"You know my old man lives over there. You ever think maybe I was going to my dad's, genius?"

"Were you going to your dad's?" Sam asked.

No answer from Mickey.

"The property abuts," Sam said. "But your father's house is off Whittaker. That's not the direction you were heading, son."

"I just drove by Skylar's," he said. "I didn't go in. I was just looking to see if her car was there."

"He's lying," Gus whispered. "Little punk is lying through his teeth. Cell records have him in one location for over an hour. He just put himself at the crime scene."

"I know," I answered. "What the heck is he thinking? He's got to know he's caught."

Just then, there was a soft knock at the door. Clancy stood up and answered it. He kept a finger to his lips. A junior detective stood there. He leaned in and whispered something to Sheriff Clancy. Clancy scowled. He took a thin file from the other detective and shut the door.

He slapped the file on the table and opened it for the rest of us to read.

"Fruits of the warrant we served at Mickey's house," Clancy said.

I reached for a one-page report. They were lab results. Rapid DNA.

"Get Sam," I said. "Gus, can you break him off for a minute?"

Gus was already out the door. He poked his head into the interrogation room. Mickey sat with his face buried in his hands. Sam rose, shut the door, then came to join us in the adjoining room.

I handed Sam the report. "You were there?" I asked. "When they served the search warrant?"

"Yeah," he said. "This mother ..."

"Sam," I said. "Am I seeing what I think I'm seeing?"

"Yeah," he said. He pulled out his cell phone and showed me a picture. Sam had taken photos of several of the items he'd collected from Mickey Harvey's house. On screen, he showed me a crumpled yellow tee-shirt. It was stained brown in front.

Kenya came to my side. "What am I looking at?" she asked.

"Probable cause," I answered.

Sam handed her the report we'd both read.

"We found it in a trash can in Mickey's garage," Sam said. "DNA came back. The shirt is covered in Skylar Sutter's blood."

❧ 10 ❧

"I s it true Skylar Sutter was bound and gagged?"

"We've heard rumors that there was a word carved into her stomach, can you confirm what that was?"

"We understand Ben Watson was dismembered in a very specific way ..."

"There are still many concerns within the community about connections to a drug cartel. What can you tell us as far as that lead?"

A hundred cameras clicked as I stood in front of the bank of microphones with Kenya on one side of me, Sam on the other, and Sheriff Clancy behind us.

"I'm sorry," I said. "We're going to do this one at a time. My office won't be answering any specific questions about the evidence in this case. You have Sheriff Clancy's statement. Michael "Mickey" Harvey has been charged with several counts of first-degree murder in connection with the killings that took place on the Sutter farm back in May. He's being held in the Maumee County jail awaiting arraignment. We'd ask that you please continue to respect the family's privacy. You can imagine it's been very difficult for them."

Nikki Sutter sat in the front row with her grandmother at her side. Georgette Sutter wore a navy-blue pantsuit and her hair combed back. Her face was pale. Her hands shook until Nikki took one of them for support.

"Has the toxicology come back?" another reporter shouted.

It had, just a few hours ago.

"We won't be making a statement on the specifics of the evidence in this case," I repeated. "I know you all want answers. So do we. Mr. Harvey is scheduled to be arraigned the day after tomorrow. That's all I can share with you at this time."

Sam came to the microphone. "Folks, let's report responsibly on this one. There are a lot of people in town who are friends or family to the Sutters. I understand members of the media have knocked on their doors looking for interviews. I've been asked by the family to let you all know they won't be granting any right now. Please respect that. And once again, if there's anyone out there who thinks they have information material to this case, please call my office or the crime stopper hotline. That's all we have for you right now."

More shouting. More cameras flashing. Georgette crumpled against Nikki. I turned to Sam, but he was already of the same mind. He gestured to a pair of patrol officers to get on either side of Nikki and Grandma George. As we left the podium, they brought the Sutter women through the same private door into the bowels of the City-County Building and away from the hungry reporters.

"Can we get her a glass of water or something?" Nikki shouted with alarm.

I turned. Georgette looked pale and sweaty. Lord, I hoped she wasn't about to have a heart attack on us.

Sam snapped his fingers. One of the patrolmen

disappeared down the hall. He returned a few seconds later with bottled water. We put Nikki and Georgette in chairs right outside of Clancy's office.

"Do you feel like you're going to pass out?" I asked Georgette. "Do you want me to call someone?"

"No," she said. "I'll be all right. How can they say all of those things? Did they cut up that boy?"

"No," Sam answered. "Don't pay any attention to that stuff. They're just trying to drum up readers and clickbait."

Georgette sipped her water. Sam also had a soothing effect on her. She put a hand on his shoulder as he leaned down to talk to her. Nikki left her side and came to me.

"Is she okay?" I whispered. "I don't like her color."

"She will be," Nikki said.

"Does she have someone staying with her?" I asked. I knew previous to the killings, Grandma George was living by herself with her husband. Sam had put a pair of deputies in front of her house.

"I'm staying with her," Nikki said. "She's also got a zillion nieces and nephews on her side, as well as shirttail Sutters. Everyone's been pitching in. But she ... she wants me with her over anybody else. There's a lot to sort out. My brother left his affairs in kind of a mess. He and Lea weren't married, and he made out his will before Ava was born. He named me in it. I don't want it all, I swear. Now with Mickey being arrested, I just don't see how I can go back to Seattle anytime soon."

"I'm so sorry," I said.

"They still won't let my grandma see Kevin's daughter, Ava," Nikki said. "That's her great-grandchild."

"Nikki," I said. "This maybe isn't the right time to talk about this, but do you or your grandmother have your own attorney to help you navigate the civil part of this?"

Nikki answered with a shrug.

"I can give you some names," I said. "I know some good family law and probate attorneys that are outside the county. That might not be a bad idea considering how everyone knows everyone around here."

"Thank you," Nikki said. "That would be really helpful. We all just want the best for Ava."

"Of course," I said. Sam had worked his magic, and Georgette looked much calmer. She got to her feet with his help.

"I'm ready to go home, honey," she said to Nikki. "I've had enough of this circus for one day. I don't like leaving your Grandpa Louie for more than an hour. He gets agitated."

"Of course. But it's okay, Grandma. Cousin Jody's over there. And Luke said he'd stop by today too," Nikki said.

Grandma George waved her off. "A bunch of busybodies. And Luke's got his own trouble to deal with. He lost his whole family out there, Nikki. He'll just upset your grandpa."

"Why don't you let the deputy take you to your car," Sam suggested. "I think all the reporters have left, but just in case."

"Thank you," Nikki said.

"I'm glad they picked you," Georgette said to me. She reached up and put her hands on my cheeks, taking me a little off guard. "You'll get 'em. I know you will."

"I'll do my very best for your family," I said.

"Will you come to the house?" she asked, taking her hands away. "I have some questions about what to expect. I talked to that liaison lady, but you're the one who's running this show now. You think you could clear some time for me in your schedule?"

"Of course," I said. "Mickey Harvey's arraignment is Thursday at eleven. How about I stop by around eight? Is that too early?"

"No, ma'am," she said. "I'll put some coffee on. Nikki, you'll pick up some donuts from Brinkley's? That'll be nice."

"You don't have to go to that kind of trouble," I said.

"Want to," Georgette said. Nikki gave me a look that seemed to show I'd be wasting my time protesting.

"I'll be there," I said.

I couldn't help but chuckle as Georgette smiled up at the two strapping deputies Sam picked to get her safely to her car. As soon as they had her out the door, I turned to Sam.

"She's a tough old bird," I said.

"That's for sure."

"I'm going to have to tell her about the toxicology report," I said. "As his sister, Nikki's Kevin Sutter's next of kin. He wasn't married to Ava's mother, Lea."

"Yeah," Sam said. "Kevin's blood was a pharmacy, Mara."

I was still working my way through it all, but Kevin Sutter had high levels of oxy, antidepressants, and worst of all, heroin in his system when he died.

"You think they knew he was using?" Sam asked.

"I doubt it," I said. "I want to talk to Lea Shane though, his ex. Ava's mother. I have a feeling she knew, and that's why she was fighting so hard to keep Ava away from him. Sam, we need to know who his dealer was. I don't want any surprises if this thing goes to trial."

No sooner had I said it before a surprise started rushing down the hallway.

"You!" A white-haired man pointed an angry finger at Sam, then charged him. A pair of deputies standing near the restroom door saw him coming and got in the middle.

"Sir!" one of them said. "You can't be down here."

"What did she say?" the man said. "What did that old bat say to you? Whatever it was, it's a damn lie. This is a set-up.

My boy had nothing to do with killing that girl. You let me see Mickey. You let me see him right now!"

"Mr. Harvey," Sam said. "Not here. Not now."

"And you." The man pointed his finger at me this time. He looked enough like his son, I would have deduced him to be Mickey's father without Sam's declaration.

"I know what your office does," he said. "I've been around a long time. You're Phil Halsey's puppet. That dirty son of a ..."

"Ed!" Sam shouted. "You need to back away from her or I'm gonna have one of these deputies cuff you. Do you hear me?"

"Mickey didn't kill nobody. You hear me? You set him up. You think the Sutters are the only ones around here with money? You better be ready. I'll get the best damn defense lawyer you've ever seen. I'll have your badge. And I'll have her law license before this whole thing is through. And you better believe that's a threat."

Then Ed Harvey hurled a racial slur at Sam that made my stomach churn. Sam took it in stride. He fixed a stony, menacing stare at Ed that made him blanch and take a step back.

"Come on," I said to Sam, putting a hand on his shoulder. "Why don't you walk me to my car?"

The deputies muscled Ed Harvey down the hall away from us.

"Sam," I said. His nostrils flared with fury. His fists stayed tightly curled.

"Sam," I said again, gentler.

Sam muttered something in Spanish under his breath. I recognized but one word and found it wildly appropriate under the circumstances.

"Come on," I said. "It's five o'clock. I know Ritter's got a beer for you somewhere. See if he can scare one up for me as well."

A twinkle came into Sam's eyes. "Yeah," he said. "Now you're talking."

I was still a little shaken, but Sam brushed it off as we made it out of the building in search of Detective Ritter and a couple of cold beers.

❧ 11 ❧

Lea Shane lived with her parents an hour outside of Waynetown. She didn't want to talk to me. She'd spent the last week and a half doing everything she could to avoid me. But finally, I got a tip she was on her way home after picking her daughter up from preschool. I waited in the driveway.

She was pretty. Hair dyed blue with a nose ring and painted eyebrows with a high arch. She struggled with a large shopping bag as she tried to get a crying Ava Sutter out of her car seat.

"Here," I said. "Let me help you with that."

Lea startled. Then recognition dawned. For a second, I expected her to cuss me out. Instead, she dropped her shoulders in resignation and handed me the shopping bag while she pulled Ava into her chest.

"We can talk in the living room," she said. "For a minute. You can't be here when my dad gets home."

I refrained from asking why. A petite blonde woman opened the screen door as she saw us approach.

"Mom," she said. "This is that lawyer lady. The one dealing with Kevin's case. Can you get Ava's lunch?"

Mrs. Shane looked me up and down. She took her granddaughter from Lea and disappeared further in the house with her without so much as a hello. Oh boy. I didn't have high hopes for a fruitful conversation at this rate.

Lea led me into the living room. Things were tidy inside with floral print furniture and an upright piano against the wall. I took a seat on the nearest couch. Ava sat in a deep leather chair across from me and crossed her legs. She wore skinny jeans and an oversized tee shirt that read "Shane's Auto Parts."

"First off," I said. "I'm sorry for your loss. I know this has all had to come as a shock to you."

There were already tears in Lea's eyes. I'd looked into her background some. She was thirty years old. A high school dropout, she'd gotten her GED and worked as a dental hygienist. She had some minor brushes with the law. A shoplifting charge when she was nineteen. She'd crashed her car into a neighbor's fence and left the scene. But by all accounts, Lea Shane was a smart, hardworking woman.

"I loved him, you know," she said. "Kevin. He was the love of my life. When he was good, he was great. It's just, he wasn't good very often."

"He was using," I said. "His sister is his next of kin as the two of you weren't married, but it's going to come out if this all goes to trial. Kevin had drugs in his system when he died."

"I was suing him for full custody of Ava," she said. "God. He made me so many promises. We'd been off and on again for years. Seven, I think. He was clean when we started dating. I mean, I knew. Even before we got close, I knew Kevin Sutter was a junkie. Everyone did."

Tears fell down her cheeks. She wiped them away.

"You were in the middle of a custody proceeding," I said. "I had a chance to look at some of the court filings. You claimed he was using drugs around Ava?"

"Yes," she said. "One time she left her stuffed giraffe at home when he was taking her for the weekend. I brought it over because she can't sleep without it. When I walked in Kevin's house, he was passed out on the couch, completely wasted. Ava was in the other room watching cartoons. That was the last straw."

"He fought you on it," she said.

"His whole family fought me on it. When he sold that store to Verde and got all that money, I thought maybe we'd have a chance. But he started pissing that away. He burned through most of it the first year. There was very little left. He accused me of being a gold digger."

"Lea," I said. "You know Mickey Harvey's been arrested for the murders. Did you know him?"

"Of course," she said. "He grew up on the property next to Kevin's folks. Where Kevin lives ... lived. He was a creep though, Mickey. Just a loser. He dated a friend of my kid sister's a while ago. You could talk to her, but I think he abused her too, maybe."

I ripped a page off my legal pad and handed it to Lea. "Do you think you could write her name down?"

"Do you not have enough? They can prove Mickey did this, right?"

"We're working on building the strongest case we can if this goes to trial," I said. "Lea, you knew Kevin better than anyone, maybe. Can you think of any reason Mickey would have killed him too? We have a solid case on Skylar Sutter's murder. But I just want to make sure I have the fullest picture I can about what happened out there."

"Look," she said. "I just don't have a lot I can say. And I

won't be a part of this. I can't go through that trial and sit there. It's just ... I can't hear about what happened to Kevin. It's just too much."

"I'm not sure I'd need to call you as a witness," I said. "That doesn't mean Mickey's defense lawyer won't for some reason. I don't have control over that."

"Kevin hated Mickey," she blurted. "But you don't need me to testify to that. It was common knowledge. Their families had this stupid feud. Kevin mentioned there was drama over the fact that his cousin Skylar was dating Mickey. But he didn't have much to do with the rest of his family besides his grandparents after his cousin C.J. died. That's the one he ran the store with. His business partner."

"They were neighbors," I said. "You're saying Kevin didn't spend much time at Skylar's house? I was under the impression he was close in age with Chris and Jenny Sutter's son Luke. He'd be another cousin?"

"Yeah, I don't know about that," she said. "It just seemed like there was always drama and in-fighting. They're a big family. And the money made everyone crazy. Including Kevin."

"I see," I said. "But Mickey, though. Why would he want to kill Kevin?"

She paused. I could see her need to unburden her mind with something. Yet, something was holding her back.

"I don't want to be involved in this. I don't want Ava around any of it. We're leaving. Moving down to Tennessee to be near my mom's family. My dad's been looking to sell his store and retire for years. Kevin was trying to block that. Now, there's no reason to stay."

"Of course," I said. "You need a fresh start."

"They questioned us," she said. "My dad. My mom. Me. We had to give them alibis. Did you know that? They thought we had something to do with what happened out there."

"The police needed to fully investigate all leads," I said. "You're not under any suspicion, Lea. You know that. You can tell me what you know."

"I know drugs got Kevin killed," she said. "I know Mickey Harvey hung around the same people Kevin did as far as that goes."

"You think they were using together?" I asked. "Or that Mickey sold to Kevin?"

"Not for a fact," she said. "I just know that Kevin ..." Her voice broke.

"Lea?"

"I feel like it was my fault, okay? If I hadn't pushed him to help my dad out at the auto parts store. Then he wouldn't have ..."

"Wouldn't have what?"

Her fingers trembled. She picked up a pen and wrote something on the paper I'd given her. She handed it to me. I read it. A single name. Scotty Jarvis.

"Who is this?" I asked.

"Scotty worked for my dad for a while. A couple of weeks ago, my dad caught him dealing out of the back of his truck. In our parking lot at the store. He fired Scotty on the spot. He and Kevin ... I think Scotty might have hooked Kevin up with something. Drugs. I think Scotty's behind Kevin falling off the wagon again. And ... and I've seen Scotty hanging around Mickey Harvey. You might want to talk to him. But that's it. I don't want to be involved in this anymore. I don't have anything else to say. I just want to live my life and keep this crap away from Ava. This town is crazy. I don't want to be here."

"Thank you," I said. "This could help. Really."

From the other room, I could hear Ava crying again. I put the piece of paper she gave me in my briefcase and said my goodbyes.

I called Sam as soon as I got to my car and filled him in on my conversation with Lea Shane.

"Scotty Jarvis?" he asked.

"Yes."

"Christ," he said. "I know him. He's in custody."

"You're kidding. On what charge?"

"Possession with intent to sell," he said. "He's looking at ten years if the case is strong."

"Sit on him," I said. "We need to know what he knows about Mickey Harvey and Kevin Sutter. If he can connect the two ..."

"Then we've got a real ballgame," he said.

"Indeed," I said. "I'll have Kenya get over there. I'm a good hour away. If you can flip him, get him to testify, I can pretty much promise she'll write him a deal."

"Outstanding," he said. "I'll keep in touch."

I hung up the phone. I sat for a moment, staring at Lea Shane's parents' house. I hoped she truly could put all of this behind her. I hoped the specter of the Sutter farm had claimed the last of its victims.

𝕊 1 2 𝕊

The next day, we set up the office war room. I usually had more help for this, but in mid-June, all our law school interns had gone home for the summer. We'd get a new crop at the end of August. I'd need them. For now, it was just Kenya, Hojo, Caro, and me.

I wheeled in three white boards, one for each house at the crime scene. I put 5X7 pictures of each of the victims as we found them.

"Our challenge," I said, "and there will be many, is coming up with a plausible theory as to who Mickey killed first."

"Does it matter all that much?" Hojo asked.

"I think it does," I said. "I think a jury might get easily confused sorting out the charges, not to mention the victims."

"Are we going to go with the theory he went there with the intention of killing Skylar Sutter?" Kenya asked. She leaned against the wall near the doorway. I stood near the center white board. We'd marked it as House #1, Chris and Jenny's place. There, we had four victims. Chris, Jenny, Skylar, and her friend, Ben Watson.

"Let's say he didn't," I said. "Let's give him the benefit of that doubt. Say he went there to talk to her. Or spy on her. Whatever. But maybe he sees Ben Watson and gets jealous. We still don't know exactly why Ben was staying with Skylar, but by all accounts, and their cell phone records, they were close. She's texting with him almost as much as Mickey."

"But it's platonic," Caro said. "Right?"

"They appear to be just close friends," I said. "But maybe Mickey doesn't know that, or he doesn't believe it."

"He shoots Ben," Hojo picked up my line of reasoning. I'd glued an overlay on the board with the house's floor plan. Then, I drew crude figures roughly where each body was found.

"He's in the kitchen," Hojo said. "We know that from the angle of the shots. He's arguing with Jenny?"

"Maybe," I said. "Then Ben walks in and he shoots him. Or things escalate with Jenny and he shoots her, then Ben."

"Either way," Kenya said. "If I'm the defense attorney, at a minimum I'm arguing there's no premeditation. He's caught off guard. Heat of the moment. We're at second degree."

"Two counts of second degree," I said.

"I just don't see how he goes there with the intent to kill Skylar," Hojo said. "Her positioning doesn't make sense for that. She's coming in through the mudroom behind Chris, her dad. He's got to get through him to get to her."

"And there's my argument for premeditation," I said. "It only had to be a split second."

"So then what?" Kenya said. "What's the motive for the killings at the other two houses?"

"Get rid of potential witnesses," Hojo offered. "Kevin Sutter in House #2 is found in his kitchen as well. He was awake. Moving around. He's got a clear view of what's happening over at Uncle Chris's house ... er ... cousin Chris ... hell, I can't keep the relationships straight."

"Cousins," I said. "Though don't make me sort through how many removals or levels. Anyway, yes. I think Kevin's definitely close enough to be a problem. Lea Shane, Kevin's ex, provided us with gold. We've got an informant by the name of Scotty Jarvis. He's going to testify that Mickey was dealing and that Kevin might have been one of his customers."

"Just inked his plea deal," Kenya said.

"Kevin Sutter died with drugs he shouldn't have had in his system," she said. "You think Mickey actually provided them?"

"I think it's a distinct possibility," I said. "In any event, it gives Mickey another motive. Lea said Kevin had blown through most of the money he made in the Verde sale. He might have owed Mickey."

Kenya walked over to the third board. "So that just leaves Patty Sutter and Mark O'Brien in House #3. You think he figures he's in for a penny, in for a pound at this point? He's offed Skylar's entire family. He's offed Kevin Sutter. Why not a three-for-one?"

"There was a light on in Patty's bedroom. That room faces east, toward Chris and Jenny's house. So yeah. If the theory is he killed Kevin Sutter to get rid of a witness, he'd have the same risk at Patty's place. Plus, there's one other thing."

I smiled. Caro had brought me a gift just this morning. I hadn't had a chance to tell the others about it.

I took a seat at the table and gestured to Kenya to take one too. She gave me a puzzled look but sat.

I pulled out a Tyvek envelope I'd gotten from Caro. I opened it and pulled out a stapled stack of papers. Court filings.

"Check this out," I said. I turned the papers around so Kenya and Hojo could read the caption.

"Maumee Bank and Trust versus ... oh crap. Edwin Harvey, Jr."

"A foreclosure?" Hojo asked. "I don't get the connection."

"Is this for the property adjacent to the Sutters'?" Kenya asked.

"It's for the commercial land Ed Harvey owned in town," I said.

"His repair shop," Hojo said. "Yeah, he shuttered that a couple of years ago, I thought. Sold the inventory to pay off his ex-wife in a divorce."

"Sounds about right," I said. "But look at who represents the bank."

Both Kenya and Hojo leaned in to get a better look.

"I'll be damned," Kenya said. "Mark O'Brien."

"Well, that's some salt in the wounds then," Hojo said. "O'Brien's shacked up with a Sutter. Mickey's dad's neighbor. And he was part of sticking it to old Ed in court when he couldn't pay the mortgage on his commercial property. I'd say that's an extra motive to get rid of him if he's doing some killing, anyway."

"Do you think there's a theory we should run on Mark maybe being the primary target that day?" Kenya asked.

"They were definitely caught off guard," Hojo said. He pulled the file we had with the crime scene photos. Patty Sutter was in the back of the head while sleeping.

"She was the only one shown any mercy," I said. "M.E. doesn't think she even knew what was going on."

"He hunted Mark O'Brien down," I said. "Shot him while he was trying to run for it."

"So either he watched Patty die or woke up when he

heard the shot. So she's killed the first of those two," Kenya said. "If he was there to kill O'Brien, why kill her first?"

"This was deliberate," Hojo said. "Of all the houses, this one seems the most like a calculated assassination."

"That's where I'm at with it too," I said. "He goes into that house with the intention to get rid of Patty and Mark. Even if we can't get to premeditation on the other five, we have it here. Two counts of first-degree murder."

I trained my eyes on Kenya. This was my case. She'd run with it however I advised her. But this was Kenya's office.

"We go for it," she said. "Of course we go for it. This is a death penalty case if ever there was one, Mara."

I sat back in my chair, feeling the weight of the decision. Death.

One life for seven.

I took no pleasure in the task. I don't think anyone does. But it was my job, and I would do it to the best of my abilities.

"Do you have everything you need for tomorrow?" Kenya asked. Mickey Harvey's first court appearance was still scheduled for eleven o'clock.

"I do," I said.

"Any appearance filed on Mickey's behalf yet?" Hojo asked.

"Nothing's been served on me," I said.

"You don't think he's going with a public defender," Hojo asked.

"He hasn't asked for one," Kenya said. "And he's not dumb enough to try to go this alone."

"I expect we'll know more when he shows up for court tomorrow," I said. "Do we have everything coordinated with the Sheriff's? We're going to draw a crowd."

"We're set," Kenya answered.

"Okay," I said. "I'm going over to George and Lou Sutter's

house first thing in the morning. I promised I'd run them through what to expect."

"You want them in the courtroom?" Kenya asked.

"No," I said. "Not yet. It's going to be a circus. Ed Harvey has already shown he can't behave himself. There's no need to upset those people anymore. We have plenty of trial ahead of us if it gets that far."

"You know it's going to get that far," Kenya said. "Ed Harvey probably has the means or connections to fund Mickey's defense."

"So why did he let his commercial property fall into foreclosure?" Hojo asked.

"I don't know yet," I said. "But trust me, I'm going to find out. I don't want any surprises in this case. It's complicated enough. Everyone in this town already has an opinion on what happened."

"I want it here," Kenya said. "Expect a motion for change of venue. We're not agreeing to that. This town needs to see justice served right here."

"We're on the same page," I said, closing the crime scene photo folder.

"Good," she said. "In the meantime, we need some help with the grunt work. I'll work the budget to get you some summer interns."

"I appreciate it," I said. "Make sure they're good ones. Talk to Rhoda Cochran at U.T. She'll give you a straight answer about who's worth our time."

"Done," Kenya said. "Now go home. Eat something. Talk to your kid."

I smiled. Kenya was both a good boss and a good friend. Since Will left with Jason, she'd made sure to get me out of here in time for our nightly phone calls.

I thanked her, gathered the files I wanted to look over at

home, then shut the lights behind us as we all filed out of the war room.

❧

WILL CALLED AT 7:03 P.M. SAME AS EVERY NIGHT.

"Hey, buddy," I said. I put my feet up and sipped a glass of white wine. "What did you do today?"

"Air and Space Museum," he said. "I looked at moon rocks."

"Sounds interesting," I said. "What did you have for dinner?"

"Aunt Kat made spaghetti," he answered. His favorite. He had her make it at least once a week.

"My blanket isn't right," he said, changing subjects without warning. He did that often. I'd learned to speak Will-ease over the years. It wasn't always linear, but I could track his thoughts.

"Your weighted blanket," I said, kicking myself for forgetting about that one. "Honey, I can send one to you. As soon as we hang up."

"Ten pounds," he said.

"Right," I said. "Not twelve. I'll take care of it. The kind with the cover you can take off. Aunt Kat can wash it for you. You'll have it on your bed tomorrow night or the night after at the latest. Will that work for you?"

"I like the subway. We get off at Ballston if I ever get separated."

That had been my own superstition. The subways moved so fast in D.C. I worried if Will got jostled away from Kat or Jason ... if he got distracted ... I wanted him to know his stops.

"Good," I said. "You're doing great. I miss you."

"They arrested Michael Edwin Harvey," Will said. "Age twenty-five."

"Yes, honey," I said. I sensed the relief in his voice. Will never expressed it, but I knew the beginnings of his obsession over the Sutter massacre stemmed from fear that the killer might come to our house. In that, my son wasn't alone.

"Good job, Mom," he said.

I smiled. "My job's just starting, baby."

"Will they give him bail?" he asked. I knew it might mean a greater conversation with Jason about where Will should spend the rest of the summer. One crisis at a time, I told myself.

"I don't think so," I said. "I think Michael Edwin Harvey is going to stay in jail. It's okay. I'm okay. And so are you."

Will got quiet. I could see him in my mind's eye, counting silently to ten. I counted along with him, moving my lips.

"I love you, Mom," he said.

Opening my eyes, I smiled. "I love you big, buddy. Good night."

"Good night," he said, then hung up the phone.

❧ 13 ❧

Everyone called it the Sutter farm, but that wasn't entirely accurate. I had Hojo blow up a satellite map and hang it on the wall in the war room.

The Sutter family owned one hundred and eighty acres. The largest tract of land in Maumee County, most of it heavily wooded and split on the south-western border by the Maumee River. A local farmer rented just thirty acres of it for corn and soybeans.

The three houses in the southeast became my crime scene. Lou and Georgette Sutter lived in the original house on the northernmost plot of land up on the hill.

I drove up that hill, marveling at the beauty of it. You couldn't see the house from the road or even their winding driveway. I knew from the satellite pictures they had a twenty-acre private lake in the back of the property.

My dad would have loved it here, I thought. My mother would hate it.

I saw a line of cars next to the house, two pick-ups, and an older model Town Car. I parked beside that and cut my engine. Nikki Sutter came out the front door just as I pulled up. I'd seen a trail camera on my way. She'd seen me coming. She waved.

I left my briefcase behind in favor of a single legal pad just in case I needed to write anything down for the family. To my right, the whir of a chainsaw drew my attention. A young kind, maybe twenty, sliced through a pile of wood on the side of the house.

"I'm so glad you came," Nikki shouted above the noise. She wore jeans, no make-up, and a ponytail. It made her look only eighteen, though I knew she was at least thirty.

"Grandma and Grandpa have been antsy," she said. "Come on inside where it's quieter. They have a lot of questions. I think I've got them convinced to stay away from court today."

"That's probably for the best," I said. "Today is just a formality. Just one step in what could be a very long road." The kid with the chainsaw saw us and stopped long enough to wave.

"Come on," Nikki said. "They're sitting on the porch out back. Grandpa takes his morning coffee there. There's a pair of mallards he likes to yell at."

I smiled and followed Nikki through the house. It smelled good. Like freshly baked cookies. Georgette had charming, rustic farmhouse decor, including an antique washboard nailed to one wall.

On another wall, she had two large portraits. One was a young girl, maybe three years old. It was an old photograph. Black and white. The child sat on a mini-rocking chair holding a red ball. She smiled at the camera with dimpled cheeks.

"That's my Aunt Tina," Nikki offered. "Grandma and Grandpa's only daughter. She got sick not long after that picture was taken. I think she was four when she died.

Leukemia. Back then they didn't have treatments as good as they do now. Grandma always wonders whether she'd have lived if they did."

"That's so sad," I said.

"And that's my dad," Nikki said, pointing to the other portrait. He was a handsome young man. He wore a brown suit with his blond hair slicked back. Clearly a senior picture, it had that old-fashioned fuzzy retouch, and an unnatural pose with his fist beneath his chin.

"Thomas," Nikki explained. "He and Aunt Tina were twins. Dad passed away eleven years ago now. We just had the anniversary."

"How awful," I said. I looked out the screen door where I could see Grandma George sitting in a wicker chair next to Grandpa Lou. He threw bread at the ducks.

"They outlived both of their children," I said. I kept the next thought to myself. They'd also outlived one of their grandchildren. Kevin.

Nikki opened the screen door and motioned for me to follow her.

Lou Sutter had thin silver hair and wore a polyester blue golf shirt, khaki pants, and white dress shoes with tassels.

"Get on outta there," he yelled to the ducks as he tossed the bread.

"He doesn't like them on the lawn," Georgette said. "They poop everywhere. I keep telling him the bread doesn't help."

Lou waved her off.

"You're supposed to feed them lettuce or kale or something," Georgette said. "They don't eat bread in the wild, Lou."

He threw a piece of bread at Georgette, but there was no malice in it. His shot was wide. So was his smile.

ROBIN JAMES

"Hello, there!" Lou said, catching my eye. He had a twinkle in his that made me instantly like him.

Everybody's grandpa. Someone had said that. Jason told me Lou was the real draw at the Sutter Bait Shop. Maybe even more than the worms. He said he had a story for every occasion and never forgot a face.

"That's how they first got suspicious he was getting sick," Jason had told me. "He started having trouble remembering names."

"Hello," I said, offering my hand to him. "I'm Mara Brent."

"She's the prosecutor," Georgette said, leaning in close to Lou's ear. His smile faltered. "She's on our side, Lou."

I watched as Lou Sutter escaped to some better place in his mind. He muttered under his breath and retrained his focus back on the ducks.

Georgette sighed. She kissed her husband's cheek, then left his side. She gestured to a small bistro table nearby. I took a seat.

"So," Georgette said. "Nikki said you want to tell us what's going to happen today."

"I do," I said. "Mickey Harvey will be arraigned today. He'll likely enter a plea. Then the judge will decide whether to set bail."

"You think there's any chance he will?" Nikki said. "Could Mickey be out and about after today?"

"I really doubt it," I said. "The nature of this crime ... and to be honest, I think the judge is going to think Mickey's safer in county lock-up than anywhere else."

"He's right," Nikki said. "Ms. Brent, it's getting nuts out there. Everybody thinks they know something. There are so many rumors."

"I'll call you as soon as the hearing is over," I said.

"Mickey's lawyer will be there. I haven't met them yet. But after that, there may not be a lot of activity for a few months. I'll continue to interview witnesses, build the case. It's likely a trial date will be set for sometime this fall. It's important that you not discuss the case around town. I may have to call some of you as witnesses."

Nikki's face fell.

"Probably just you, Nikki," I said. "To establish some background. But there will also be a lot of questions about how the Harveys and the Sutters are connected."

"We're not!" This from Lou. He turned his chair and faced me.

"Lou," Georgette cautioned.

"He's a crook," Lou said. "Ed Harvey's been trying to steal from my brothers and me since my dad was still around."

"It's complicated," Georgette said. "A lot of the land we own now, Lou's grandfather bought from Ed Harvey's grandfather. But that was, oh, ninety years ago. Maybe more."

"He called my brother a cheat!" Lou said, his face lined with fury.

"I'd heard something about an old boundary dispute," I said.

"A long time ago," Nikki explained. "He's talking about Uncle Ray, right, Grandma?"

She nodded. "Lou's oldest brother, Ray, is the one who built the store. My Louie was just a kid then. They had another brother, Henry, who died in the war. Lou always said that's what killed *their* father. Henry was the favorite. Anyway, Ray was the oldest. He and his wife Rosemary more or less raised Lou after that. He grew up in that store."

She got a wistful look in her eyes.

"It's been hard," Nikki said, lowering her voice. "Grandpa

couldn't run the day to day anymore. Then when my dad died
..."

"I can imagine," I said.

"Ray cheated nobody," Lou said. "He paid fair and square
for the west tract. If Ray hadn't come along and offered on it,
Ed Senior would have been sent to the poorhouse. He'd have
been begging on the streets."

"I know, Lou," Georgette said, patting her husband's
hand. "I know. Now you're getting all upset. It won't do you
any good. Come on. Come help me in the kitchen. I can't get
those pickles down from the top shelf."

Lou's face softened as his wife put her arm around him.
He got up and followed her in the house.

"He doesn't really know what's going on," Nikki said. "He
fades in and out. I didn't even think it was a good idea to tell
him what happened to Kevin and the others. Grandma said
he has a right to know. I suppose she's right. But he
remembers what doesn't hurt, I think."

"Nikki," I said. "What about Kevin?"

I'd gone over the toxicology reports with her a few days
ago. I'd left it up to her to decide what to tell her grandmother.

"She doesn't know," Nikki said, looking over her shoulder
to make sure Grandma George and Grandpa Lou were out of
earshot. "I didn't have the heart to tell her Kevin was using
again. What difference does it make now?"

"And you didn't know?" I asked.

She shook her head. "Not really. It's just ... do you have
any addicts in your family?"

I paused.

"Never mind," she said. "I know it's none of my
business. It's just ... I know he was sick. I know it's a disease
process. But Kevin's addiction is part of why I left
Waynetown. Our mother, too. There were other reasons ..."

Her voice trailed off. Then, "But none of that really matters anymore."

"I'm so sorry for what you're going through," I said.

"I tried to get him to come with me. I thought maybe a change of scenery would do Kevin good. Get him out of his old patterns and bad associations. We had an intervention for him a few years ago. My mom and I stuck to our bottom line. We moved to Seattle."

"That must have been incredibly hard," I said. "But also brave."

"It worked," she said. "Kevin turned his life around. Selling the bait store was part of that. He was making changes. I swear, I didn't know he was using. But I'll blame myself forever for not really trying to find out."

"You set your boundaries," I said. "There's nothing wrong with that."

A tear fell from her eye. "Except now it's too late."

"Nikki," I said. "Kevin's full autopsy report is going to come out. I won't be able to keep it out if this goes to trial. Obviously, it's your call how you want to break things to your grandparents. But it will be public knowledge."

She nodded. "I know. It's just ... there's been so much. I've tried to kind of tell them things in stages. She's trying to hold it together for Grandpa. Gosh. She's always done that. We've offered her live-in help. Kevin especially. After he sold the store, he could more than afford it. She's stubborn, though. Now, I'm afraid of what that will mean for me."

"What do you mean?" I asked.

"She wants me to stay," she said. "She hasn't come out and said it. But she keeps saying I'm all she's got left. My dad is dead. Kevin's gone. Now there's a good chance she won't get to see Ava much. We talked to that lawyer you suggested. Great-grandparents don't really have any rights."

"What about your mom?" I said. "Can't she intervene and try to get some visitation?"

Nikki looked down. "She won't. She's trying to process things too. Kevin and I still had a relationship. He burned a lot of bridges with my mom. He didn't treat her very well. He could be mean. But I know that was the drugs talking. They would have both come around. It's just ... they ran out of time, you know?"

"I know," I said. "And I'm so sorry for the pain this is causing you."

"I can't stay here," Nikki started to cry. "Not forever. I know I have to be here for Kevin. For this trial. But I can't move backward. My life is in Seattle."

"What about the rest of her family?" I asked. "You're not the only Sutter left in town, Nikki."

"She has other help," Nikki said. "Just nobody as close as me. Grandma George has a sister. Or half sister ... something. They live a little north of here. Her grandnephew Jody comes out. Runs errands. That's who's out there now chopping wood. She's got him doing her landscaping and lawn care, keeping her cars running. Things like that. There are still a ton of aunts and uncles and cousins. They all check in. Some of my cousin Claudia's family was here yesterday. A few of them will be in the courtroom today. Grandma kicked them out. She thinks they're just buzzing around looking for handouts. Jody's the only one besides me she lets in anymore. She says it's because he's not a Sutter, so he knows he isn't entitled to any of their money. But since I came back, I'm who she wants. I'm the one who hears her crying herself to sleep, and I can't make it better. How in the world can anyone make this better?"

"I'm so sorry," I said.

Nikki wiped her eyes. "No. I'm sorry. I don't mean to lay

this all on you. It's not all dire. Like I said. She still has tons of family around if she wants it."

"But you need to process your grief too," I said. "You can't let yourself get dragged under the weight of this, Nikki. You know what they say about putting the oxygen mask on your own face before someone else."

"Yeah," she said. "Thanks. I mean that. Really. It helps to know you're out there to handle this. I know you're the best. So does Grandma."

"Thank you," I said. "And I'll call you later today after the hearing. Promise."

Nikki wiped her eyes again and rose with me. "Come on," she said. "Let's walk around the side of the house. She gets a hold of you again, you'll be late for court."

Her smile lightened my heart a little. But as we walked around the house, I could feel the gravity of her grief, of all of their grief, and knew this might never be a cheerful place again.

14

"Ho-lee crap," Kenya said. She came up behind me as I sat at the prosecution table in Judge Denholm's courtroom. The judge and his staff were out for an early lunch. His bailiff let me into the courtroom early so I could gather my notes and have a moment of peace before Mickey Harvey's first court appearance started. Ironically, things were quietest inside the courtroom now. Half the town and every media outlet in Ohio waited outside to see Mickey.

"Holy crap." She said it again. I turned in my seat. Hojo walked in behind her.

"You tell her yet?" he asked.

"Tell me what?" I asked.

Kenya handed me a single piece of paper. A court appearance, still warm from the printer. I looked at the caption and back at Kenya.

"Are you serious?"

"I thought she was retired," Kenya said. "Hell, I thought she was dead."

I looked back at the table. In the People of the State of

Ohio versus Michael Edwin Harvey, his defense lawyer had finally entered an appearance.

"Elise Friggin' Weaver," Kenya said. "Weaver the Cleaver."

"You want to enlighten me?" Hojo asked. "I'm sorry I don't have the fancy pedigrees you two do. I just went to good old U.T. Law."

Kenya rolled her eyes at him. "You also don't have the same debt. I'm still paying mine off. You?"

"Elise Weaver," I said. "She taught criminal procedure and trial practice at U. of M. Law School."

"We both had her," Kenya explained. "Though I was a few years ahead of Mara. She sliced students up. Weaver the Cleaver."

"Why do I know that name?" he asked.

"She defended the Greendale killer in the early eighties," I explained. "And Roger McLanathan? The guy falsely accused of being the Carey bomber?"

"Oh yeah," he said. "He got more infamous than the real bomber. See, I don't even remember *that* guy's name."

"Exactly," Kenya said. "Well, son of a gun."

"What in the world is she doing in ..."

"All rise!"

I didn't have a chance to finish my question. Judge Denholm moved quickly when he was ready. The back courtroom door opened and none other than Professor Elise Weaver the Cleaver stormed right in.

She looked exactly the same as I remembered from law school twelve years ago. Four-inch black heels. Impeccably pressed designer suit. Also black, but a pink silk blouse beneath it with a wide floppy bow. Only her hair had changed. Not the style. She still wore that in a neat, short cut, sprayed so it didn't move. Only now, her hair was steel gray instead of black. She had a wide jaw and strong chin that kept her from aging.

"Elise Weaver on behalf of the defendant, You Honor," she said. "I filed my appearance with the clerk twenty minutes ago."

"Cutting it a little close, counselor," Judge Denholm said. Behind me, I heard Hojo mutter a cleaver joke as Kenya shushed him.

Mickey Harvey came in next. Wearing prison orange and shackles, he shuffled to the table sandwiched by two large deputies.

Judge Denholm wasted no time and rattled off the charges against Mickey. Seven counts of first-degree murder.

"Your Honor," Elise said. "We're requesting bail be set at a reasonable amount. My client has strong ties to the community. He doesn't pose a flight risk ..."

"Got it," Judge Denholm. "Ms. Brent, I take it you oppose?"

"Absolutely," I said. "Due to the brutality of this crime and the substantial resources ..."

"Save it," Judge Denholm said. "I'm inclined to agree. Bail is denied. The defendant will be remanded back to Maumee County jail pending trial in this case. That's all for now. I'll see you both back here in two weeks for our first scheduling conference."

He banged the gavel and dismissed the hearing.

"Your Honor!" Mickey shouted. "I didn't get to talk. I didn't get to say I'm not guilty."

Elise grabbed Mickey by the arm and whispered something harsh in his ear. If I knew Elise Weaver, it was something along the lines of shut the heck up before I shut you up myself.

Whatever it was, it caused Mickey's color to drain. He

held his jaw open, then clamped it shut. One of the deputies grinned but tried to cover. Elise gave him a nod, then allowed them to take her client back to his cell.

"Ms. Montleroy," she shouted to me, sending an old fear shooting down my spine. I expected her to make me recite the dissent's analysis in Mapp versus Ohio.

"It's actually Ms. Brent now." I smiled, squaring my shoulders.

"Of course," she said. "Is there somewhere we can talk?"

"Yes," I answered. "My office is just across the street. Give me fifteen minutes to handle a couple of other things while I'm here and I'll meet you there."

I didn't give Elise a chance to answer. I knew her. She'd want to try to put me on neutral turf at a minimum. I wasn't in the mood for that particular game today.

I handed her my card and brushed past her, catching the sly smile on her face from the corner of my eye.

⚜

ELISE WEAVER SHOWED UP THIRTY MINUTES LATER. Caro walked her into my office and I could tell by the look on her face that Weaver had already rubbed her the wrong way.

"Have a seat," I said, gesturing toward one of the two leather chairs in front of my desk. Elise did, but not before taking in the decor.

I kept things simple in here. Just one watercolor painting in a gold frame on the far wall. Sailboats. A local artist. Will picked it out for me at a street fair when he was only five years old. My law degree hung behind my head in a blue and gold frame. On the credenza, I had several of my favorite black-and-white pictures of Will.

"It's good to see you again, Montleroy," she said. "Oh ... right ... Brent?"

"Yes," I said. There was a bit of an edge to Weaver's tone. As if my name was an accusation.

"I've got to tell you," she said. "I was kind of shocked to find you here. When they told me who was prosecuting that boy."

"Mickey Harvey is hardly a boy," I said. "And what are you doing here in Waynetown, Dr. Weaver?"

"Thought I was dead, did you?" she said, laughing at her own joke. "Or wished I was?"

"Or course not. I just didn't think you actively practiced anymore."

"From time to time," she said. "When a case is interesting enough. This one surely is. That poor family. Horrifying."

"It is," I said.

"Sure do have a lot of opinions around town about what really happened," she said, baiting me.

"Are you setting up shop here in Waynetown?" I asked. Her appearance listed an address just six blocks from here. As far as I knew, it was a vacant office building.

"I rented a little place," Elise said. "Just signed the lease yesterday."

"When were you engaged by the defendant?" I asked. The bigger question was why she waited until today to get a hold of me.

Elise looked at my degree hanging over my shoulder.

"You were something," she said. "One of the good ones, Montleroy. You know they were scared of you in class."

"Of me?" I said. "I think they were scared of you."

"You weren't though," she said.

I laughed. "You sure about that?"

"Yes," she said, deadly serious. "You held back sometimes.

I knew you were doing it. Trying to fit in. Trying to pretend you didn't have things figured out before you ever stepped foot in class. I know how that works. You didn't want to be seen as a threat. You wanted to have a social life. Your final essay in criminal procedure, though. Better than some Supreme Court opinions I've read."

"How on earth can you remember an exam I wrote more than a dozen years ago?" I asked. "Besides, I thought you were supposed to grade those blind."

She gave only a guilty smile by way of an answer.

"I remember the good ones," she then said. "All teachers do."

"Coming from you," I said, "I appreciate the compliment."

"You should," she said. "I don't often hand them out. So, how have you been? I have to admit, I caught a little of your story on the news. Jason was also one of the good ones. Look how far he's gone."

"All the way to Washington." I smiled.

"And yet, here you are," she said.

"Here I am," I agreed.

"Interesting. I didn't peg you as cut out for government work."

"What did you peg me as?" I asked, not sure I wanted the answer.

"Oh, I don't know. I figured you'd get snapped up by one of the big corporate firms. Big Park Avenue apartment, maybe. I suppose that's what your mother wanted for you."

"Maybe," I said. "I like it here."

She nodded, then inspected the cuticles on her right hand. "We all make our choices, I guess."

Anger rose in me. It was a veiled reference to the scandal of my third year in law school. I wouldn't take the bait.

"Yes," I said. "We do."

"Well," she said. "It's good to see you, Montleroy. I'm glad you found a way to use your degree. It's noble. Respectable. And I'm looking forward to working with you."

"I'll have your initial discovery couriered over by the end of the day."

She nodded, rose, and showed herself out of my office. Her heels clacked on the tiles as she made her way down the hall.

I waited until I heard the outer door open before leaving my desk. When I did, Kenya met me in the hallway.

"So, what's she think you're offering on Harvey?" Kenya asked.

"You know?" I said. "I'll be damned. She never even asked me about the case."

Kenya reared back, surprised. "So what the heck were you talking about?"

"That old shark was just sizing me up," I said. "I think she's in this for the long haul, Kenya. Which means so are we."

"I don't like her," Caro said, joining us. "Who the heck does she think she is?"

Smiling, I tapped my hand on my door frame. "She thinks she's the person who taught me everything I know."

I left Kenya and Caro staring after me as I went back to my office and shut the door.

15

Three days later, I met Sam at a coffee shop right next to Verde. It was his choice. We sat near the window so I had a view of the pot dispensary that used to be Sutter Bait and General store. There was still a picture of a cartoon walleye painted in the middle of the parking lot, chipped and faded.

"You ready for Tuesday?" Sam asked.

Sipping my coffee, I nodded. "Grand jury convenes at ten. You have everything you need?"

"I have more than everything I need. That's what I wanted to talk to you about."

I set my coffee down. Sam reached beside him and picked up a red file folder he'd brought with him.

"Mickey's lies keep on coming," he said. He opened the file and slid it across the table to me. He'd added an addendum to his main report on the case. Before me were three new interview summaries.

"Jody Doehler, Chad Carmichael, Sarah Bosch?" I asked.

"Sarah was a friend of Skylar Sutter's. Well, all three of

them knew her. Chad's her boyfriend. And this Jody is a shirttail relation of the Sutters somehow."

"You're right," I said. "He was out there the other day doing yardwork when I stopped by to talk to Georgette Sutter and her granddaughter."

"How's she doing?" he asked.

"Nikki?" I said.

"Well, yes. But Grandma George. I need to go out there myself. There's been so much loss in that family. Even before this tragedy."

"I know," I said. "She's got practically a shrine to the children she lost. I can't even imagine it, Sam. If anything like that happened to Will, I don't think I'd survive it. And for it to happen to her twice. Both kids. Now her grandson. She's strong. Puts on a brave face. It's odd to say, maybe, but I almost think Lou Sutter's mental state is helping her?"

"How so?" he asked.

"Well, for one thing, he's not really *in* the grief of this thing. I'm not sure how much of it he's aware of. That's a blessing. But caring for him gives that woman a purpose. Distracts her. Nikki's pretty worried though."

"It's a lot on her shoulders," Sam said. "Nikki, I mean."

"How well do you know her?" I asked.

Sam sat back. "Not all that well. She's what, thirty-one, thirty-two? She was just a kid when I was a teenager. Pigtails. Braces. Always getting in the way at the bait shop. Lou and Tom, her dad, had trouble keeping her occupied. She paints? Something arty?"

"Photographer," I answered. "She's got her own studio in Seattle. She wants to get back to it, but I think she feels obligated to stick around for her grandparents."

Sam clicked his tongue. "Rough break on every level." He looked out the window. His expression turned wistful as he took in Verde. The parking lot was full. In five minutes, we watched at least six people come in and out.

"A gold mine, that," he said. "Sure ruffled a lot of feathers when they sold it, though. But anybody with half a brain couldn't blame them. You know I talked to Kevin not long before they sold it. He said business wasn't anywhere close to what it used to be. I think they were struggling."

"So the offer from Verde came along at a good time," I said.

Sam nodded. "I don't know. It was probably a combination of things. They weren't selling enough worms to keep the doors open, you know? I don't think Kevin's heart was in it after his dad died. Nikki left. C.J. was ... well ... if I'm being honest, he was kind of a jerk. A blowhard. A bully. I never really liked him much. Chris was the one everyone liked."

"And he had zero financial interest in that store," I said. "Only Kevin and C.J. benefited from the sale to Verde. Everyone else had been bought out years before."

"Sure, they're all kicking themselves for that."

When the waitress came by, she topped off our coffees.

"Anyway," he said. "Chad, Jody, and Sarah's statements. I think you're going to want to put one of them on the stand for the grand jury."

Sam gave me a knowing smile. I looked back at the paperwork. My pulse quickened a bit as I skimmed the highlights. All three witnesses described an incident at the Blue Pony, the very restaurant we'd all been at when we got word of the murders.

"Chad's the one who called me," Sam explained. "At Sarah's urging. Then I got a call from Jody last night."

"They'll testify to this?" I said as I scanned the pages. "You're sure?"

"I'm sure," he said. "Chad said he and Sarah were out at the Blue Pony and ran into Mickey and Skylar. They can be specific on the date. Sunday night. April Fool's Day. You know Paula Dudley always has that April Fool's bash. Mickey and Sky got into some kind of argument. Chad and Sarah both say Mickey got rough with her. Grabbed her. Chased her outside. Sarah made Chad go after them. He'd been drinking a bit."

"Chad? Great," I said. "That won't help me if I put him on the stand."

"Except Sarah went too. They both saw Mickey manhandling Skylar in the parking lot. Couldn't hear what they were saying, but it was alarming enough Chad went over to see if she was all right."

I flipped through the statements and read along as Sam spoke.

"She had marks on her arms," I said, finding a line from Sarah's interview.

"Handprints," Sam said. "Chad says he saw Mickey shaking her."

I flipped the page and looked up at him. "Was this an isolated thing? Did you get that sense?"

"No," he said. "That's just it. Sarah said she felt stuck between a rock and a hard place. Skylar was her friend. She didn't want to tick her off by telling her she thought her boyfriend was a creep. But take a look at what Jody Doehler says."

Jody's statement mirrored Sarah's and Chad's. He was at the Blue Pony the same night. He saw Skylar and Mickey arguing. Sam had highlighted a few of the sentences. I read them back.

"I heard him yell at her. You can't do better than me. You even try, I'll make you regret it. I'll bury you. I'll kill you."

"Good Lord," I said, closing the file.

"Same night. Independent witnesses. They all remember because it was the April Fool's bash. Paula does one-dollar pitchers. Decks the place out. You *have* to have gone to at least one in your younger days."

"I've always been a mom since I moved to Waynetown, Sam," I said. "We go to the Pony for the sliders and the kids' menu, not the pitchers. But Sam ..."

"There's more," he said. "I got a tip that Skylar Sutter was meeting with a lawyer. Sarah thinks she at one point had her convinced to get a restraining order against Mickey."

"There was nothing like that in the background check on Mickey," I said.

"She never filed it," he said. "I got the lawyer's name. A Leslie Noble. She did work for Skylar's parents. I'm going to see if she'll talk to me. See if it got to the point of Skylar opening up a file with her. I know attorney-client privilege survives death but ..."

"Let me know if you need any help with that," I cut in. "Attorney-client privilege is one thing, but if this woman had credible information that Skylar was in danger, she would have had certain duties to protect her, regardless of confidentiality."

"I'll let you know. Sarah didn't know for sure. It could be a nothing burger."

"Or it could be the last nail I need to broker a plea deal."

"About that," Sam said. "Elise Weaver?"

I raised a brow. "Apparently so."

Sam let out a low whistle.

"Hey," I said, feigning offense. He smiled and turned a little red.

"Oh, you're more than a match, Mara. It's just ... how the

hell is Ed Harvey footing that particular bill? They were foreclosing on his business."

"I'm getting somewhat of a bigger picture on that. I think Ed Harvey engaged in some creative accounting, shall we say? Hiding assets from his ex-wife."

"Anything you can use?" he asked.

"Probably not. Ed's not the one charged with seven murders. It's enough that Mark O'Brien had a hand in Ed's so-called downfall. I only need a jury to believe Mickey had a score to settle with Mark."

Sam considered my words for a moment. He finished his coffee.

"I've heard Elise Weaver doesn't do plea deals."

"That's her reputation. But she's already playing games." I told him about my visit with her.

"Ah," he said. "That kind. Well, it will be all that much more fun watching you obliterate her at trial."

"Thanks," I said, smiling. "I appreciate the vote of confidence."

He did something then. An innocent gesture, maybe, but it stirred something in me I hadn't expected. Sam reached across the table and put a hand over mine.

The hairs on the back of my neck prickled. I felt a flood of warmth straight down to my toes. My heart tripped and my breath went out of me in the best way. It felt ... good. And that was the problem. I did something I instantly regretted. I jerked my hand away and folded it in my lap.

Sam's eyes flickered, but he deftly recovered, saving what might have been an awkward moment. Something I never wanted with him. Ever.

"Mara," he said. "Don't let Elise Weaver get in your head. What's she got on you?"

"Nothing," I said. "I've known her a very long time. She

was one of my most influential law professors. She. Well. I think she probably likes to think she molded me into what I am today."

He laughed. "Bullcrap. Even I know they don't teach you how to be a lawyer in law school. Just like they don't teach you how to be a cop in the academy. You earn that in the trenches."

"True," I admitted. "But Elise Weaver can skewer people with a glance. And she judges me for the choices I made. Reminds me of my mother, if you want to know the truth."

"What could she possibly judge you for?" he asked.

I don't know what made me do it. Maybe Weaver the Cleaver's words cut me more than I realized the other day. But I told him.

"You know I met Jason in law school. He was a third year. I was a first year. He graduated first in his class. Got the job with the A.G.'s office right away. It was a big deal. Everyone knew Jason was destined for big things. Anyway, I booked my courses with Weaver."

"Booked?" he asked.

"When you get the highest grade in a class," I said, "it brings a certain amount of attention. Expectations. Weaver lined up an interview for me with a big firm in New York. My mother was over the moon about it. I would have probably made my first million in my own right by the time I was twenty-eight."

"But?" he asked.

"But," I said, "I got pregnant with Will. Found out a few weeks before I graduated. It changed everything for me. I made a decision. Jason and I got married. I put my career on hold for a little while. Not forever. But New York just didn't seem as important to me anymore. Elise Weaver wrote me off after that."

"What business is that of hers? Or anyone's?" he asked.

"Well, I was her protege. She felt I was throwing my life away for some guy. I took a year off. Then I went to work for the Ohio Civil Rights Commission part time. I liked it there. But then the opportunity came for us to move here to Jason's hometown. He was already being groomed for the congressional seat he now holds in this district. And Will ... well ... I realized Waynetown would be more his speed than overpriced daycare and nannies in New York."

"Do you regret it?" he asked.

I met his gaze. "Not for a single second. I'm here because I want to be. Not because I have to be. And I like what I'm doing. A lot."

Sam's grin widened. "Good. So do me a favor. Wipe the floor with Elise Weaver."

I picked the red file back up again. "This will help. And now I get the pleasure of seeing her face when I drop it off."

"Now you're talking," Sam said. Over my protest, he paid the bill. Then he walked me out to my car.

eath hung over Lou and Georgette's house on the top of a winding hill. Yet somehow when I visited them a few weeks ago, I could still sense the joy there. As if perhaps, someday, on some not-too-distant holiday or birthday celebration, there would be laughter again.

By contrast, when I walked up the steps to Luke Sutter's home just five miles to the east of the crime scene, I sensed only the weight of the tragedy he suffered. In House #1, Luke had lost both his parents, Chris and Jenny Sutter. He'd lost his sister, Skylar. Now, he faced the knowledge that their deaths and those of the rest of the family had their nexus at his mother's kitchen table.

Luke greeted me, swinging open the screen door to his modest two-story house. There were toys in the yard. A Big Wheel. A baby pool leaned up against the garage. I stepped over crude drawings in sidewalk chalk.

"Hi," Luke said. He greeted me in bare feet, wearing track pants and a faded M.S.U. tee shirt.

There were toys all over the floor in the house too. Mail

stacked up on a table in the hall. Dishes in the sink. But most alarming was the lack of light. Everything was switched off, and the shades were drawn.

"We have to keep it this way," he said. "Rachel's migraines ... We can sit out back. I probably should have you pull around, anyway."

Luke turned on a hallway light so I could at least see my way through the gauntlet of Legos. We made it through the kitchen and out the back sliding door. Not before I saw Rachel Sutter sleeping on the couch in the living room, a cloth over her eyes.

I would have liked to tell him I could come back another time. Or perhaps invite him to my office. But he and Rachel had avoided my calls for days and the grand jury convened tomorrow.

"This is fine," I said as we stepped out on the deck. I took a seat on one of two green plastic Adirondack chairs. Luke took the other. I could see why they picked this spot to build their home. It abutted the woods. I spotted a deer blind just a few yards in.

"How are you holding up?" I asked, instantly regretting it. The "how" was pretty clear.

"Rachel and I both took a leave of absence," he said. "I go back next week, though. We have some savings. We were planning a remodel later this year. Now we're living off that. It's just been really hard to ... Rachel has nightmares. She can't sleep without Charlie beside her. He used to do great in his own room. But he's not even two."

"Is he here now?" I asked.

Luke shook his head. "No. He's at Darcy's today. Rachel's mom. I go pick him up at three."

"How is your mother-in-law faring?" I asked. "I can't imagine how difficult it's been for her.'"

"She's functioning," he said. "Better than we are. I know what this all looks like. She's um ... she's making plans to move in with us. She keeps seeing that house. What she saw that day. I don't know how we're going to do this, Ms. Brent. We relied on my mom and dad for so much. Rachel's mom is trying to figure out how to retire so she can stay with Charlie full time while we work. There's all just so much up in the air. When the trial starts, I want to be there. I *have* to be there. For my family, you know?"

"Luke, you're all doing the best you can. Don't beat yourself up about it. If you've earned anything, it's some grace. I know there are a lot of people in town who are worried about you. Who are waiting for you to reach out and ask for help."

"I can't," he said. "I can't even go out. We tried a couple of weeks ago. Just to the grocery store. Someone left a note on my windshield."

He went into the house and came back with a crumpled-up piece of paper. He handed it to me. It was a flyer for Verde. On the back, someone had written "You Reap What You Sew."

"Didn't even have the decency to spell check," Luke said, trying to crack a smile.

"I'm sorry," I said. "You don't deserve this."

"This is the Harveys," he said. "People are taking sides. Sides, can you believe that? My family is dead. How can there be two sides to that?"

"Luke," I said. "Tomorrow should pretty much be just a formality. I fully expect the grand jury will indict Mickey Harvey. There's no need for you or your family to be there. I can call you or stop by when it's all over and fill you in."

"I appreciate that," he said. "I don't think I can handle the courthouse right now."

"I did want to talk to you about some new facts that have come to light about Mickey and your sister. Do you feel up to me asking you some questions?"

"Of course," he said. "He can't get away with this, Ms. Brent. You don't think he can get away with this, do you?"

"How much did you know about Skylar's relationship with Mickey?" I asked. "Did she confide in you? Ask you for advice?"

"I loved my sister," he said. "But we weren't as close as my mom would have liked."

"There was an age difference," I offered.

"Yeah," he said. "I was eight years older. Mostly Sky was just my annoying kid sister, you know? Always underfoot. Always trying to follow me around. Loud. God. She was loud as a little kid."

The memory brought a smile to his face. I found myself praying Luke would get to a point where his memories of Skylar would bring him more joy than pain. It would take time. Years, perhaps.

"How well do you know Mickey Harvey?" I asked.

"She started bringing him around maybe two years ago. The thing with Sky, she was always pushing boundaries with my folks. She dyed her hair black when she was twelve. Pierced her nose. All that typical stuff. It was almost a cliche. She tried to get a rise out of my parents. Never got it. My mom and dad were the most easy-going people you'd ever meet."

"I've heard that," I said. And I had. So far, the only negative impressions I'd had of Chris and Jenny came from Mickey himself. He'd described Chris as "not a good guy."

"Didn't have a judgmental bone in their bodies," he said. "Until Sky started bringing Mickey around."

"Because he was a Harvey?" I asked. "I understand your family and the Harveys have some longstanding conflict."

"They didn't hate Mickey because he was a Harvey," Luke said, his eyes going wide and red. "They hated Mickey because he was a little punk. Disrespectful. Couldn't hold a job. He made Skylar pay for everything. My dad told me they thought Mickey stole money out of my mom's purse. Stuff started going missing in the house."

"Do you know if he was violent with Skylar?" I asked. "Before she was killed."

Luke shook his head. "I don't know. My folks never said. Skylar never said."

"Did you notice any bruises on her? Any change in her behavior recently?"

"No," Luke said, staring off into the woods. "But I'm not the best person to have been clued into that. Like I said, we weren't as close as I'd like. And I was mad at her. It's hard for me to admit that, but I was. I didn't like how she was constantly pushing boundaries with my parents. There was just always chaos around Skylar. She attracted it."

"It's going to come out if this goes to trial," I said. "But Skylar's last texts to Mickey were disturbing, Luke. She was trying to break up with him. We think ... well, it's likely that's what set him off. From the way they were found, we think maybe Mickey saw Ben Watson as a threat. He might have been killed first."

Luke let out a bitter laugh. "A threat? Well, that's going to blow up in Mickey's face."

"How so?" I asked.

"Ben was a friend of Skylar's, that's all. Have you talked to his parents?"

"No," I said. "The police have, obviously."

Luke bit his lip. I had the sense he was holding something back.

"Luke, I need to know everything. The absolute worst thing that could happen at this point are surprises. It doesn't matter if whatever you know puts one of the victims in a bad light. Or you in a bad light. I need to know about it."

"It's not a bad light," he said. "But Skylar and Ben weren't dating. Ms. Brent, Ben was staying at my folks' house I think because his parents kicked him out of theirs. He came out to them. I'm assuming they didn't take it well."

I jotted a few notes down. "Do you know that for sure? As far as Ben's reasons for being there?"

"It's just the impression I got from Sky," he said. "She said Ben needed a break from his folks."

"Thank you for sharing that with me," I said.

"Will it help?" he asked.

"It might. At least, it might if Mickey's defense lawyer tries to argue Skylar was cheating on him. If she tries to sell that Mickey was a jilted jealous lover acting in the heat of the moment as opposed to the cold, calculating killer I believe he was."

Luke rubbed his eyes. He looked about ready to crash right where he sat.

"Luke," I said. "How much do you know about the dynamics of the other people who lost their lives that day? How close was Patty to Chris? To Kevin? Did the families interact a lot other than being neighbors? I understand there might have been some bad blood around the sale of the bait shop. Were you involved with that?"

"I don't know," Luke said. "Most of it was drama with my Uncle C.J.'s wife, Patty. I hardly ever had anything to do with her. I don't think my mom and dad did much either. My dad and his brother C.J. were kind of on the outs when C.J. died.

The whole money thing. God, I got so sick of hearing about it. I didn't want any part of it. I hardly ever saw my cousin Kevin. We were close once, but he got into a bad scene. Drugs."

"Yes," I said. "I'm aware he struggled with addiction."

"Nikki, his sister, have you met her?"

"I have," I said. "She's been staying with Lou and George since the murders."

"That's good, I guess," he said. "I should pay them a visit. I haven't seen them since the funerals. That was all just kind of a blur. Anyway, Nikki and Skylar pretty much hated each other."

"Do you know why?" I asked.

"Girl drama," he said. "I didn't talk to Sky much about it. They got into some argument or another last Christmas when Nikki came home. God. There was just always drama circling Sky. I should have paid more attention. I just hate that kind of stuff. Maybe if I'd been around ... I know what people must think. I was her big brother. It was my job to protect her from somebody like Mickey."

"I think you can't beat yourself up too much, Luke. You have a family of your own to look out for now."

"Yeah," he said. "Did he ... Ms. Brent. Do you know if Mickey *was* hurting my sister before all this?" His tears spilled as he spoke. "Christ. What difference does that make now? He put a bullet in her. Of course he hurt her. It's just, I can't believe I didn't see it. If I'd have paid closer attention, maybe ..."

"Don't," I said. "Nothing about what happened is your fault."

"I just need to know," he said. "Do you have proof Mickey was violent with my sister before that day?"

I pursed my lips. I hated being the messenger of any more

awful news to Luke Sutter. But he deserved the truth. And it would come out at trial if we got to that point.

"There's some evidence, yes," I said. "We have statements from three witnesses who saw Mickey and Skylar getting into an argument in the parking lot of the Blue Pony. He had his hands on her. It bothered them enough they tried to step in."

"Who?" he asked.

"Sarah Bosch, Chad Carmichael, and Jody Doehler."

"Jody saw it?" Luke said, wiping his cheek.

"Jody says he heard Mickey threatening to kill Skylar if he ever caught her with someone else," I said.

"He never told me. We spent four hours together last month fixing Grandma George's fence."

"Hindsight is twenty-twenty for everyone," I said. "I'm sure Jody and Sarah and Chad are all dealing with their own regret."

"It's never going to stop," he said. "This just gets worse and worse. Mickey Harvey killed my family. But he's not done destroying people. Ben's family. Jody. My mother-in-law. My wife? Ms. Brent, we can't go through this."

"What do you mean?" I asked.

"If there's any way you can spare us from having to go through trial ... I don't know. Tell him you'll take the death penalty off the table. As long as he never gets out of a cage. Just ... I know other members of my family might not share my opinion. But I know them. I know what this is going to do. So if you can, if you can make it so none of us have to relive this. Have it splashed all over the internet. Will you do that? Will you seriously consider it?"

It was at that moment I realized Luke Sutter had likely emerged as the new patriarch of the Sutter family, whether he wanted it or not. It broke my heart even more, but I respected him for it.

"I'll do what I can," I said. "And I promise. You'll be my first call after tomorrow's hearing."

Luke thanked me. We said our goodbyes. Then he walked me around the side of the house, keeping me from walking back through the darkness inside.

𝕬 17 𝕭

Thursday, July 26th, I called four witnesses before the grand jury. Sam, the medical examiner, Luke's mother-in-law, Darcy Lydell, and Jody Doehler. If we got there, I planned to call Chad Carmichael and Sarah Bosch too. But Jody had made one statement I felt made his story the strongest of the three.

"Mr. Doehler," I asked him. "How well did you know the defendant?"

Jody was just a skinny, twenty-year-old kid with thick brown hair and out-of-control acne. He wore a plain white tee shirt and blue jeans. I'd clean him up more for trial.

"Everybody knows Mickey," he said. "The Harveys too."

"But were you acquainted with him? More than just knowing him from around town?"

"Oh sure," Mickey said. "He's a few years older'n me. My sister Ashley graduated with him. They were sort of friends. Mickey's family lives next to my aunt, Grandma George's."

"You're related to the Sutters?" I asked.

"Just Aunt George," he said.

"I'd like to state for the record this witness is referring to Georgette Sutter."

"Right," Jody affirmed. "My grandma is Aunt George's sister. Half sister, I think. Different dads. Anyway, I spend a lot of time at Grandma George and Uncle Lou's. She needs help around the house. I drive her sometimes. Or I drive Grandpa Lou. He can't anymore."

"Okay," I said. "So you knew Skylar Sutter?"

"I did," Jody said. "She was always real nice to me. Patient."

"Did you know she was dating Mickey Harvey?"

"Yeah," Jody said, uttering the word in a bitter laugh.

"Why do you say it like that?"

"Cuz, he's a Harvey. She was a Sutter. Harveys and Sutters have been at each other's throats for like a hundred years or something."

"Okay," I said. "Jody, I want to turn your attention to a night this last April. Do you recall seeing Mickey and Skylar out?"

"Oh yeah," he said. "We were all hanging out at the Blue Pony. Not together. I was just there. Lots of people were. Mrs. Dudley sells dollar pitchers on April Fool's night. That's why I remember. And you get free appetizers if you wear your shirt backward and stuff like that. Anyway, Mickey was drunk. He was loud. He and Sky got into some kind of fight. They were sitting at the bar and she tried to get up to leave."

"Where were you when this was going on?" I asked.

"I was in line for the restroom. It's right by the bar. The hallway to the men's room. They were right directly in front of me so I could see 'em the whole time. Sky was pretty pissed. He grabbed her arm. Sky kind of jerked it away, and Mickey didn't like that. He grabbed it again and pulled her real close to him."

"Did you hear what he said?" I asked.

"Yeah," he said. "He said, who do you think you are? You're mine. You don't walk out of here unless I want you to."

"Do you know why they were fighting? What set them off?" I asked.

"Sky was really pretty. A knockout. Guys were always looking at her. Mickey didn't like that. Anyway, he pulled her real close to him. That's when I heard it."

"Heard what?" I asked.

"Mickey told Sky she better never think of getting with another guy."

"Those were his exact words?" I asked.

"Um ... yeah. He said, I catch you so much as looking at any other guy I'll kill you. He said, you're mine and I'll put you in the ground before I let you sleep with any other guy. But he didn't say sleep. He said the eff word. Can I say the eff word?"

"I think you've made your point," I said. "What happened next?"

"See, you don't tell Sky what to do. She's liable to do the opposite. I couldn't figure that part out. I think if Mickey had just, you know, ignored her, Sky would have done whatever he said. Grandma George always said Sky would rebel against anything."

"Jody," I said, trying to steer him back. "What happened after Mickey threatened Sky?"

"Oh. Yeah. She jerked away from him again and stormed out of the bar. Mickey went after her. The bathroom opened up and so I took my turn. But I seen Chad and Sarah leaving right after. That's why I didn't follow. Sarah was Sky's friend and Chad's a pretty big dude. I figured he could take care of Mickey if he needed taking care of."

"Thank you," I said. "I have nothing further."

I took my seat at the table.

"Can I go now?" Jody asked.

"Not yet," I said. "The jury might have a few questions for you."

Jody looked confused. I'd gone over the process with him last week. This wasn't like a trial with a judge. The jury members could and would question him.

"Mr. Doehler," the foreperson started. He was a middle-aged steel worker. "Just so I'm clear. How did you interpret what Mickey Harvey said to Skylar Sutter?"

"Interpret it?" he asked. "There was only one way. He told her if she screwed anybody else, he'd kill her."

"Was she?" another juror asked. "Do you think Mickey thought she was dating someone else?"

"I don't know," Jody said. "I just know Ben Watson moved into her house a few weeks later. Mickey wouldn't have liked that at all. Ben and Skylar were best friends. Always laughing and joking with each other. You know, come to think of it, I remember this one other time. I was doing some work at Skylar's place. For her dad. He was clearing some bushes before I helped him haul it away with my truck. Anyway, Ben was over and Mickey showed up."

I grabbed a notepad and started scribbling. Jody had mentioned none of this during his interview with Sam or me. The kid could be trouble if I couldn't keep him focused. Elise Weaver would tear him up.

"What happened?" the juror asked.

"Mickey was just a jerk, like always. Treated me like hired help. Which yeah. Chris was paying me to help him. But Mickey strutted around like he was better than me."

I could hear Elise's cross play out in my mind. It wouldn't take much for her to establish that Jody held a grudge against Mickey. If it weren't for Chad and Sarah's corroborating testimony, I might even have to rethink calling him.

"Anyway," he continued. "Ben and Sky were in the house. He was helping her study for an exam. Ben was real smart. He was going to be a doctor, I think. Mickey went in there and broke it up. He told Ben he needed to get going because he was there to pick up Skylar. I could tell Skylar didn't like it, but she was trying to keep them from getting into a fight. So Ben left."

I exhaled. It was a rough landing, but Jody bolstered my case. Still, a contested trial would be far more of a challenge with this one.

The jurors asked a few follow-up questions, confirming dates and times. Then Jody finally finished. He looked at me, his eyes big as the moon. Lord. He wanted my approval. He might as well have just blurted, "Did I do good? Did I say what you wanted me to?"

I gave him a noncommittal smile, then gathered my notes and faced the jurors.

"The defendant, Michael Harvey, stands charged with seven counts of first-degree murder. We allege that Mr. Harvey committed the unlawful, premeditated killing of Christopher Sutter, Jennifer Sutter, their daughter Skylar Sutter, her friend Benjamin Watson, Kevin Sutter, Patricia Sutter, and Mark O'Brien. Based on Detective Cruz's testimony, that of the medical examiner, and the eyewitness accounts, I ask that you find probable cause and return a true bill on all seven counts. Thank you."

The jurors had no more questions for me. I left them to their work.

Jody Doehler was nowhere as I exited the courtroom. I wanted to remind him not to gossip about what happened here today. Instead, Sam found me.

"You worried?" he said, smiling.

"Not in the slightest," I said. "But Jody needs work before trial."

"He'll be all right," Sam said. "He's a good kid. Wants to do the right thing."

"Well, he all but admitted hating Mickey. Weaver will use that to discredit him."

"She can try," Sam said. "We've got him dead to rights on the phone forensics. The threats to Skylar that two other witnesses heard. The physical evidence ..."

I put my hands up in surrender. "You win!"

Just then, my phone buzzed with Will's ringtone. Even Sam knew that one by now. He put a light hand on my arm by way of a goodbye, then left me to take the call.

"Hey, guy!" I said. I plugged the other ear with my finger and tried to find a quieter space down the hall.

"Did they get him yet?" Will asked. "Did they indict him? I saw on the news ..."

"Will," I said. "Remember, you're supposed to let me worry about this case. You're on vacation. How was Mount Vernon?"

"It made me uncomfortable," he said. "George Washington's body was right there."

"Well, he's buried, Will," I said. Though I breathed a sigh of relief. I'd diverted him from the grisly ins and outs of the Sutter Seven. Now, my son spent twenty minutes explaining his theory on the last days of George Washington's life and how his medical care had likely killed him.

It was good to hear his voice, though. The familiar rhythms and cadences. His mind worked faster than most. Sometimes too fast. I walked the two blocks back to my office as Will explained the brief history of bloodletting. I waved hello to Caro as I passed her desk, phone still to my ear. She laughed quietly, knowing who was on the other end.

I kicked my shoes off and curled my legs under me, sinking into my leather chair as Will segued to the Battle of Yorktown.

"Dad said he'll take me," he said.

"To the battlefield?" I asked.

"To a ton of them. There's a program, a junior archeologist's thing. It starts in two weeks. Dad thinks he can get me enrolled."

I sat up in my chair. Will was due to come home in two weeks. I realized then a large part of this conversation was Will's way of asking me a question that made him uncomfortable.

"You'd have to stay in D.C. until August," I said.

"August 27th," he said.

"Is that what you want, buddy?" I asked.

"I miss you," he said.

"I know," I said. "I miss you too. But if you're having fun ..."

"Aunt Kat said she'd call you. I said I wanted to talk to you myself."

"I appreciate that," I said. "Honey, we're all still figuring this out as we go. I'm so proud of you."

"I think it'll be okay," he said. "I don't have an appointment with Dr. Paul until September. I have enough medication refills until then. Registration for next school year is on the 28th. Open house is the 31st."

"Sounds like you've done some planning," I said. I knew it was more than that. Will could probably tell me the school holidays and half days all the way through high school. He was just about to enter the fifth grade.

"I have summer reading," he said. "But there's a library near Dad's office."

"It's okay, Will," I said.

"You have to pay the summer tax bill," he said. "When you paid the mortgage, they won't keep that in escrow anymore."

"I know," I said. "It's due September 14th. I marked it on the calendar."

"Take it to the township," he said. "If you pay it online, they charge you a fee."

"Good to know," I said, my heart full to bursting. "I'll be fine, buddy. I'm going to miss you like crazy. But if you're having fun. If you have a plan ..."

"Dad wants to talk to you," he said.

"I'm sure he does. I'll call him later tonight."

Then Will moved to moon rocks. Jason had taken him to the Air and Space Museum six times already.

The phone call lasted for more than an hour. I shut my office door and finished some motions after that. At almost five o'clock on the dot, Kenya knocked and let herself in.

"They're back already," she said, holding a piece of paper in her hand. "The court clerk called, but we didn't want to interrupt. Caro said Will called."

"Thanks," I said. "He's going to stay in D.C. a few weeks longer."

Kenya's face fell. "You okay with that?"

"Oh, I hate it. I miss him like crazy. But he's doing great and I love him."

"Me too." She winked, stepping further into my office. "Grand jury indicted. Seven counts. First degree. We've got a ballgame, Mara."

She put the indictment on my desk.

"Trial in early November," she said. "It's gonna come up fast."

I read the victims' names again off the indictment. Christopher Sutter. Jennifer Sutter. Skylar Sutter. Ben Watson. Kevin Sutter. Patty Sutter. Mark O'Brien.

"The full slate, Mara," Kenya said. "Death penalty."

I nodded. "Have Caro get Elise Weaver on the phone. No plea deals."

Kenya slapped her palm against the door frame. "Take that, Weaver the Cleaver. We're going to have to start calling you Brent the ... uh ... Torment?"

"Needs work," I said, not looking up from the note I was writing.

"Gimme time," Kenya said, laughing as she shut the door behind her.

❧ 18 ❧

Summer without Will felt strange. I'd never noticed how big my house was. It echoed. I missed his footsteps over my head in the spare room he used to build his Lego sets. I missed hearing constant chatter and random observations. Will-isms, Kat called them. Like his out-of-the blue comment when some political cartoonist drew a map, making it look like Michigan's Upper Peninsula belonged to Canada or Wisconsin. His teachers told me he rarely talked in school. Jason and I always felt he made up for it at home. It could be exhausting and delightful all at once.

Our nightly FaceTime helped a bit, but Will was usually distracted. He was better when he could talk to me while doing a dozen other things. When forced to sit there one on one, he got uncomfortable.

The Sutter trial prep kept me busy, of course. I had virtually no communication with Elise Weaver since the grand jury indictment. She'd left an associate in town and left, promising to move back to Waynetown the month before trial.

In late August, two days before Will was set to return, I finally got Ben Watson's family to meet with me. They put

their house up for sale a few days after Ben's funeral. I'd heard
they were staying with a family in North Carolina. When
they came back to close on their house, I got a tip from the
realtor. They weren't happy about it, but the threat of a
subpoena can work magic with some. We met at my office.

Gina Watson had eighties hair, parted down the middle
and feathered. Ben Sr. was thickly bearded, wearing a flannel
shirt and work boots. Today was a working day for them.
They told me several times about the moving truck they had
to meet at the Stow-N-Go they rented off I-75.

"You're not putting either of us on the stand, are you?"
Gina said, panic in her eyes.

"I haven't decided that yet," I said. "There were just a few
things I wanted to clear up with you. Also answer any
questions you have about the trial process. It can be daunting.
My office will of course arrange for you to have a liaison
available. If it comes to it, you'll be allowed to present victim
impact statements to the judge."

"I can't do that," Gina blurted. "I can't get up in front of
all those people and tell them things that are personal. Ben
was my son. He was murdered. How do they *think* it's
impacted me?"

"We can cross that bridge when we get to it," I said. "And
you will not be asked to speak if you're uncomfortable. It's
completely understandable if you don't want to."

"He did this?" Ben asked. "This Mickey Harvey? You're
sure?"

"Yes," I answered. "But what I wanted to prepare you for
is one of the reasons why. At least, our theory."

"Are they gonna blame Benny?" Gina said. "He wouldn't
hurt anyone."

"Mr. Harvey's defense lawyer is going to be very
aggressive," I said. "She may call one of you to testify."

"For him?" Ben said. "For the guy that killed Benny? What could she probably ask us?"

"Well, I can go over that with you a little today. It's kind of why I wanted to meet. So you'd know what to expect."

"Please," Ben said. "I'm dying to hear this."

"Well, were Ben and Skylar Sutter close friends?"

"Sure," Gina said. "They met at school. College. Not high school. Benny went to private school."

"Sure," I said. "Would you say they were best friends?"

"He talked to her all the time," Ben Sr. said. "She came to the house. They studied."

"What I think ... that is, what we assume Mickey's lawyer is going to say, is that Mickey had the wrong idea about Skylar's relationship with your son."

"What kind of idea?" Gina asked.

"She means were they dating," Ben said. "Did Skylar's piece-of-crap boyfriend kill her and Benny because he thought they were sleeping together?"

"Well," I said. "In a nutshell, yes."

"What difference could that possibly make!" Gina cried.

"I'm trying to put Mickey away for first-degree murder," I said. "If the jury can be convinced Mickey acted out of the heat of passion, as they say, they might go for a lesser charge. Second-degree murder. That's why I'm certain his lawyer is going to go down that route. It's pretty much a textbook defense tactic. So, I need you to know it's coming."

"I appreciate that," Gina said.

Ben Sr. kept a harder look in his eyes. "And you have to prove she's wrong," he said.

"I do, yes," I said.

"Good!" Gina said.

"Gina," Ben said, exasperated. "What this lady is telling us is that she's going to have to air Ben's business in court.

She's gonna ask one of us to tell the jury that Benny was ... that he didn't go for girls. So they understand Benny and Sky Sutter weren't dating."

"You're going to make us look bad." Gina nearly screamed it.

"What? No," I said.

"Gina, calm down," her husband cautioned.

"You think we kicked him out?" Gina said.

"I think no such thing," I said. "I know family is complicated."

"Gina," Ben said. "I think I can handle this. Why don't you go wait in the car?"

She got up. She didn't utter a word of protest. Gina Watson merely turned on her heel and marched out of my office, leaving me alone with Ben Sr.

His nostrils flared as he let out a breath.

"She's not handling things well," he said.

"I understand, Mr. Watson. I cannot begin to imagine ..."

"Our son's sexuality wasn't an issue for us at all," he said. "So if someone's telling you otherwise, they're wrong. Sure, we struggled at first. Mostly out of worry. People are brutal in this world. We wanted to know that he could take care of himself. That he'd be okay ..."

His voice broke on the last word. Then Ben Watson buried his face in his hands and began to cry. I realized then it's why he sent his wife away. And why she went. They could barely handle their own emotions. They weren't able to comfort each other. Not yet.

I reached for the box of tissues I kept on my desk and moved it closer to him.

"Take your time," I said. "Can I get you anything? If you need a minute ..."

Ben put a hand up. He took a tissue, wiped his eyes and righted himself.

"I'm okay," he said. "It just hits you sometimes. A wallop. It takes your breath from you."

"Yes," I said.

"Mickey Harvey knew Ben was gay. But not everyone did. So if he or his lawyer are trying to say Mickey was jealous my Benny and Skylar Sutter were dating, he's lying. Mickey was a bigot, just like his old man."

I nodded. "Yes," I said. "I've witnessed a little of that firsthand with Ed Harvey."

"A bigot and a cheat," Ben went on. "I'm not ashamed of my son. But he wasn't out to everybody. He was still on that journey. So it's not that I care who knows about it. It's that I knew Benny wasn't ready to tell everybody. I know he's gone. It's just hard not to feel like I've still got to protect him."

"Yes," I said. "My son is still young. Only ten. But I imagine I'll feel the need to take care of him as long as I live. I think that doesn't go away."

"I've heard that line. You know the one. Where there's a word if you lose your spouse. You're a widow. There's a word if you lose your parents. You're an orphan. But there isn't a word for when you lose your kids. I think that's because it's unspeakable."

I could offer him no other comfort besides a nod. The depth of Ben Watson's grief clawed at him. And at me.

"I need to ask you. Elise Weaver might, if she calls you to the stand ..."

"You want to know why Ben was living with Sky at the end," he said.

"Yes."

"He was twenty-three years old, Ms. Brent. I didn't kick my son out of my house. Is that what somebody else said?"

I felt protective of Luke Sutter too. I didn't need either of them confronting each other over what might have been a misunderstanding. It would likely all come out.

"It is," I said.

"One of the Sutters, I take it," he said. "Chris and Jenny were sooo big-hearted. Taking my kid in when his redneck family couldn't deal. Is that the line of crap they're peddling?"

This was bad. At the same time, I could almost understand it. No matter the why, this man's son was dead simply because he was in the orbit of Skylar Sutter and her family.

"It's a bunch of petty BS is what it is," he said. "The Sutters brought this on themselves. I told you, Ed Harvey and that kid ... they're worthless oxygen thieves. But this is about money. Some old Sutter grandpa ticked off some old Harvey grandpa and now they can't get along even to this day. They had to make a big damn deal about Skylar dating that boy. I wouldn't have been happy either, but any fool could see the more they pushed, the more she wanted to be with him. Then when he started beating on her, they did nothing. They didn't help her."

"Mr. Watson, did Ben ever tell you if he witnessed violence between Skylar and Mickey? Was he afraid for her?"

"I don't know," he said. "But she was no better than her parents. Always flaunting what she had that Ben didn't. Fancy car. Fancy clothes. I got laid off last year. I was trying to help put Benny through school, but it got tough. So the Sutters swooped in. He enjoyed being there over being at our place because they had air conditioning. He said it was quieter. That's why he moved out."

"Okay," I said. "And thank you for telling me that. I hate that I have to pry. And I hate that it might at times feel like your son is the one on trial. I'll do what I can to keep that from happening."

"I get it," he said. "And I get you don't want me airing my dirty laundry about the Sutters in front of the jury."

"I only want you to answer the questions you're asked ... if you're asked them ... truthfully."

"Yeah," he said. "The truth. Sure. You make that S.O.B. Mickey Harvey fry for this. I'm counting on you. I'll do my part if I'm asked. So will Gina. But you mark my words, those aren't quality people out there on that farm. The town thinks they're damn martyrs now. It makes me sick. But if I gotta go along with it to make sure my kid's murderer gets the needle, you can be damn sure I will."

As he got up, I had a sense of déjà vu. Ben Watson Sr. seemed to hate the Sutters as much as Dev Francis, Patty Sutter's daughter, did. I just hoped the pair of them could keep their anger in check. If Elise Weaver caught wind of it, she'd use it to skewer them all.

❦ 19 ❧

Three days before the start of the school year, I had my boy home. I made things as normal as I could for him. Big transitions, too much fanfare, and he would retreat into himself. So, to commemorate his homecoming, we simply did the normal thing we always did the weekend before his first day of school. We went to the clothing store near the mall that sold the only pair of pants he liked. Track pants with two stripes down the side. Elastic, not drawstrings. A thin layer of fleece on the inside. I could count on him to go up exactly one size each year so far.

He picked a black pair of pants with a red stripe, a blue pair with a white stripe, and a gray pair with a black stripe. I bought two of each and we were off to the shirts.

"I missed you," I said as he was looking through a stack of v-neck tees. We couldn't have tags. If I left it up to him, he'd get all blue ones, regardless if they matched the pants.

"I missed you too, Mama," he said. I held up two fingers as he picked the blue one he liked the best.

"Then two whites, a couple reds. How do you feel about yellow?"

Will shook his head. "I don't want to look like a bumblebee."

"Fair enough," I said. This was the hard part. During all of our FaceTime calls, Jason had been close by. I knew Will had been doing Zoom calls with his therapist, but I wanted to gauge how he really liked D.C. I didn't want to do or say anything that made my son feel like I was spying on his dad.

Once he had a good eight days' worth of new clothes, we headed to the long checkout line. It seemed everyone in Waynetown waited until the last minute to school shop along with us. I bit my lip and hoped Will wouldn't lose it. Waiting in lines was a struggle point for him.

"What was your favorite part about your summer?" I asked.

He didn't answer. He counted people. He looked at their carts.

"We have time," I said. "We'll hit a drive-thru on the way home. You pick."

"I don't really like the subway," he said. "Not after the first couple of times. So Dad had a man come and pick us up. His office is really big. Everybody's in a hurry."

"I expect they are," I said.

"There's a really good hamburger place two blocks from Dad's townhouse. He said we could go there three times a week. But we only went four times total. He doesn't like routines. The people with the cameras can keep track of you that way."

"What people with the cameras?" I asked.

"Oh, you know. The ones who want to know who Dad goes out with."

I felt a tingle of fear crawling up my spine. I wasn't jealous. Jason could do or date whoever he damn well pleased. He was young. Great-looking. A freshman congressman dubbed an up-and-comer within the party. Newly single. I'd read the D.C. gossip sites, even though I knew I shouldn't. Jason's romantic life made news. I just didn't want Will in the center of that.

"It's taking them two minutes and fourteen seconds on average to get through people," Will said. "There are seven people ahead of us."

"That's not so bad."

Will stomped his foot. "Price check."

"It'll be fine," I said. "Let's talk about something else."

"You're sure Michael E. Harvey acted alone?" Will asked, startling me.

A few of the people in line around us heard him. Most looked away politely.

"Not here, buddy," I whispered to my son. "Not a good idea to talk about that in public."

Will considered my words. I could see his wheels turning. He was having trouble letting go of the thread he'd just pulled at.

The line moved up. Will fidgeted, pulling at his collar.

"Yes," I whispered to him. "He acted alone. Don't worry."

"I thought that was her!" Another customer ahead of us stared at me. Middle aged, with wisps of gray hair flying around her loose bun. She wore a pink sweatshirt and ripped jeans.

My Mama Bear instincts kicked in and I stepped in front of my son. She left her place in line with fury in her eyes.

"That boy's innocent," she shouted. "You hear me? Those people think they can buy anything they want now."

"Ma'am," I said. "I'm with my son today. And I can't comment on an active case. Will you please take your place in line?"

I looked frantically for store security as she advanced on

me. She grabbed my cart and pushed it toward me. The woman seemed out of her damn mind. Behind her, a man, her companion, took his nose out of his phone and saw what she was doing.

"Lou Anne," he said. Lou Anne didn't care about him.

"Please," I said. "This is inappropriate."

"Mara Brent," she shouted. "That's who you are. You're dirty. Your whole office is dirty. Everybody knows it. Now you're in the pocket of drug dealers, aren't you?"

"What?" I said. "I'm gonna need you to step back and get out of my face."

"Mom?" Will said.

A crowd formed. I heard whispers. Name-calling. I wasn't entirely sure if they were meant for me or Lou Anne.

"You'll go to hell," she said. "Know that. You railroad that boy, that's where you're headed."

Will put his hands over his ears. White-hot rage poured through me.

I straightened my back. "Turn around," I said through gritted teeth. "You take another step toward me or my kid, you'll regret it, Lou Anne. I'm gonna do my job. And you're going to get a hold of yourself."

Her eyes went big. I think she saw something in mine that let her know I wasn't kidding. She froze, but didn't get out of my way. Her husband put a hand on her. She still didn't move.

"What the heck is wrong with you?" I asked.

She blinked. Her husband prevailed and got her to turn away.

"Mom," Will said. "They're taking four minutes now."

"Come on," I said. "We can get this stuff online. It'll be here in two days. You've got enough for the first day of school."

Will smiled. He let me take him by the hand. Still shaking with rage, I led my son away from the checkout line lunatic and safely back to the car.

20

Two weeks after my incident at the department store, someone threw a brick through Luke Sutter's house. A few weeks after that, someone called a bomb threat into the Verde store. Sheriff Clancy assigned me a bodyguard. Now, Deputy Molly Remick followed me to and from work every day. She was a quiet presence. With just two years with the department, I hoped she didn't feel like this was a demotion. A glorified babysitting job. I would have declined the protection, but Will caught wind of it and endorsed the idea. Clancy also assigned an extra liaison officer at Will's school for good measure.

"You okay?" Kenya caught me staring at the white boards in the conference room.

"Yeah," I said. "Just want to go over everything one more time, you know?"

Smiling, she stepped in. It was Friday. The third one in November. Three days from now, Mickey Harvey's trial would start.

Kenya stood beside me, staring at the board we'd put up detailing the timeline. We had one of the interns superimpose

Mickey Harvey's cell phone tracking data over it. A perfect match. A wide-open window. He had time to commit these murders three times over before he left Skylar's property that morning.

"Everyone buttoned up?" Kenya asked.

"Yes," I said. "I'm starting with Sam."

"Good call," she said. "It's all there with him. You wanna take bets whether Weaver will put Mickey on the stand?"

"You know," I said. "I've been turning that one over in my mind. On paper, he can only hurt himself. He lied to the cops. Pure and simple. His dad's running around town making it worse for him. Did you hear he gave a quote to the *Columbus Dispatch*? About the bomb threat to Verde?"

"I did indeed," she said. "Basically said the Sutters are the scourge of Waynetown and they got what was coming to them."

"I don't get why Weaver hasn't put a lid on him," I said.

"Maybe she can't," Kenya offered. "I've known Ed long enough to tell you he does what he wants when he wants. Classic narcissist. It's sick, but he likes the attention his son's murder trial is giving him. I wouldn't be surprised if he's angling for a book deal or something when all this is over. No matter how it turns out."

My jaw dropped. "You gotta be kidding."

"I am not," she said. "Ed's always looking for a way to advance his own interests."

"Now you almost make me feel sorry for Mickey. Like he never had a chance growing up with Ed for an old man," I said.

"I got a call from a true crime blogger," she said. "Guy by the name of Stewart Cullen. Ring a bell?"

It did, but I couldn't recall why. Kenya saw my blank expression.

"He hit gold with a podcast he does called *Small-Town Killers*. He's working on season two and thinks the Sutter Seven fits the bill."

"Great," I said. "And he's asking you for an interview?"

"For a statement, yes."

"We're on the eve of trial? What in the heck do these people think they're going to get?"

"Well, Elise Weaver," she said.

I shook my head as if I could clear it and Kenya's words would make more sense.

"Don't tell me she's cooperating with this guy," I said. "Kenya, that's not ethical. She's in the middle of representing Mickey. He's facing the death penalty. How on earth is that ethical?"

"Well, this Cullen kid is an investigative journalist. I'm not worried, believe me. But he's been stirring up people around town. I think his plan is to record his podcast in real time during the trial. I'm only telling you in case he reaches out to you. His tactic is a little in your face."

"Thanks for that," I said. "I just can't believe Professor Weaver is risking an ethical violation by cooperating with this kid right now."

"It's the world we live in," she said. "Just don't let it throw you. And stay off the internet."

"It's not me I'm worried about," I said. "It's Will. He knows too much about this case from what he's seen online. I don't want him stumbling onto this podcast. For a while there, he was really afraid. He keeps asking me if I'm sure Mickey acted alone."

"Poor kid. This one has spooked a lot of people, Mara. And everyone's got an opinion."

"Half the town thinks the Sutters deserved to die," I said. "I just hope things can get back to normal after all of this."

153

"They will," she said. We stood shoulder to shoulder now, staring at the faces of the Sutter Seven. Kevin Sutter. Chris and Jenny Sutter. Skylar. Ben Watson. Patty Sutter. Mark O'Brien.

Justice for them was in my hands now. I felt a hollow pit in my stomach as I feared the very fabric of the town I loved depended on how well I could do my job for them.

❧ 21 ❧

Six men. Six women. Four of them over seventy. Three of them under thirty. Five of them between forty-five and fifty-five. Three alternates.

It took most of the first day of trial to weed through the pool of jurors with family connections to either the Sutter or Harvey families. I had expected Elise to move for a change of venue early on. She never did.

So here, nearly six months to the day after five members of the Sutter family and two of their friends were gunned down in their homes, a jury of Mickey Harvey's peers sat ready to decide his fate.

I kept things simple during my opening statements, focusing on explaining who the victims were. What our community had lost that day. I said their names as a mantra. This was complicated. There were so many. I wanted the jury to have them memorized by the time my fifteen-minute opening was done.

"In the first house farthest south," I said, "Jenny Sutter, wife, mother, and grandmother. Chris Sutter, father, husband, grandfather, youngest son of Chet. Their daughter, Skylar

Sutter, studying to become a respiratory therapist. Ben Watson, her best friend. A medical student. In the second house to the east. Kevin Sutter, Lou and Georgette Sutter's only grandson. He carried on the tradition of running the family bait shop as long as he could. Then, in the third house higher up the hill to the west, Patty Sutter, C.J. Sutter's widow. A loving mother to her only daughter, Dev. Finally, Mark O'Brien, the man she'd started to rebuild her life with, gunned down as the two of them slept."

Then, I focused on the web of lies Mickey Harvey spun from the moment they discovered the bodies.

Elise Weaver was a master of body language. She pulled faces, leaned over for hushed whispers to her client. Waited patiently as I gave the jurors a preview of what they would hear over the next two weeks.

"Is he drugged?" Hojo wrote to me as I took my seat and waited for Elise to deliver her opening statement.

It was a good question. Elise had transformed Mickey Harvey. Gone was the greasy-headed, smarmy-looking kid who'd waltzed into Sam Cruz's interview room all those months ago. In his place sat a well-groomed young man in a freshly pressed gray suit and red tie. He'd shorn his slicked-back hair for a close-cropped style that made him look ready to report to a military recruiter, not a courtroom. He sat straight, quiet, stoic as Elise introduced herself to the jury.

"You may want to convict Mickey Harvey," she said. "Of something, anyway. He's made grave mistakes in his life. He's lied. Cheated. If Skylar Sutter was your daughter, maybe you wouldn't have wanted Mickey to be her boyfriend either. But as you'll hear, none of those things make him a murderer. The prosecution's case is nothing more than a good story. It won't hold up to the rigors of their burden of proof. Reasonable doubt. That's the phrase to remember. Not beyond any doubt.

Not the absence of doubt. You can have that. Reasonable doubt will present itself to you in abundance. That's a promise."

She was neat. Efficient. Comfortable in her role. The cadence of Elise Weaver's voice brought me back to a dozen years ago when I heard it every day in a lecture hall. Only today, she wasn't lecturing. She was starting a conversation. She did it smoothly.

"They like her," Hojo wrote. It was true. Every juror kept their eyes on Elise as she leaned on the lectern, only stepping out from behind it once.

"They've only scratched the surface," she said. "They'll only bring you superficial evidence of Mickey's alleged role in this tragedy. It will crumble before your eyes. That, too, is a promise," she said. She turned at the last sentence and I knew her words were meant as much for me.

Weaver the Cleaver had thrown her gauntlet. Now, she expected me to run.

Judge Terrence Denholm sat unimpressed behind the bench. The joke was he and Morgan Freeman were separated at birth. He had the same peppery hair and deep lines around his mouth as his doppelganger. You expected his voice to have the same rich timbre. Instead, Judge Denholm's voice had a nasally twang that could grate after a while.

I liked him. A judge's judge, he didn't grandstand. He didn't show contempt for the lawyers practicing in front of him as some did.

When Elise walked back to the defense table, Denholm looked at the clock on the wall, then at me. Three fifteen.

"I want to go until four thirty today," the judge said. "You ready to call your first witness, Ms. Brent?"

"I am," I said. "Your Honor, the state calls Detective Sam Cruz to the stand."

Sam had waited in the back of the courtroom. He wore a suit I'd not seen him in before. Black with a faint gray pinstripe. A blue tie he straightened as he walked past the bailiff and raised his hand to be sworn in.

"Detective," I said. "Will you please tell the jury your role in the Sutter murders?"

"I am the lead detective," he said. "It's my case."

I took Sam through the discovery of the bodies. One by one, we entered the crime scene photos into evidence.

Ben Watson was first. Shot in the back, half in and half out of the sliding glass door leading into Chris and Jenny Sutter's living room.

"Mr. Watson was shot at point blank range, no more than fifteen feet from his assailant," Sam said. "One shot. Right below his left shoulder blade. You'll see a twelve-foot blood trail leading from the yard into the house."

"Why is that significant?" I asked.

"Well, we think Mr. Watson may have been running away from the killer, Mr. Harvey."

I clicked my laptop and pulled up the next crime scene photo. It showed the trail of blood Sam spoke of in greater detail. The blood became thicker as Ben reached the house.

"Were you able to determine which of the victims was killed first?" I asked.

"Not definitively, no," Sam said. "But these victims were killed quickly. Likely within seconds of each other in some cases. No more than minutes in others."

"Who was the next victim found?" I asked.

"Moving into the Christopher Sutter house, we found Jenny Sutter. She took a shot in the face. She was found lying against the refrigerator. Unlike Mr. Watson, Mrs. Sutter appears to have died where she was struck. There's no trail of blood that would indicate she moved under her own power after she was shot."

"I wouldn't think so," I said. We let the photograph of Jenny speak for itself. Her cheekbone was gone. It was easy to imagine the shooter walking right up to her and pulling the trigger. Later, in closing, I would have them envision the last thing Jenny Sutter would have seen. "Who else was found in the Christopher Sutter home?"

"Christopher Sutter himself, along with their daughter, Skylar."

I had a second screen up with the layout of the home displayed. Sam took his pointer and shone it on the small hallway off the kitchen leading to the mudroom and garage.

"Christopher was found just inside this small hallway. There's a small blood trail behind him, so we believe he took at least a few steps toward the kitchen before falling. Behind him, Skylar was found half in and half out of the doorway leading to the garage."

"Her father was in front of her?" I asked.

"He was. Since Mr. Watson was shot in the back and all the Sutters in this home were shot from the front, we believe Watson was killed first, then the defendant entered the home and picked off the rest of the Sutters as they came toward him to see what happened."

Sam then moved to describe the crime scenes at Patty Sutter's home. Members of the jury recoiled as I displayed the crime scene photo. You didn't have to be an expert to see exactly what had happened.

"Mr. O'Brien was found on his side. His cell phone was knocked off the nightstand beside him. It was found on the ground near his right hand. Mrs. Patricia Sutter was found face down in her own bed. Gunshot wound through the back of her head. We don't believe she ever woke up."

"She never knew what hit her," I said. Surprisingly, Weaver let me.

"She was likely asleep when the bullet entered her brain, that's correct," Sam said. "But this was a quick, violent death for both of them. No other signs of a struggle anywhere in the home."

"Was anything taken from the home, to your knowledge?" I asked.

"No," he said. "Patty Sutter had a jewelry box on her dresser. Among other things, we found a four-carat diamond engagement ring. Her daughter, Devina Francis, confirmed it belonged to her mother. It matched what she filed with her homeowner's policy. It had an appraised value of ten thousand dollars. It was still in the box. There were computers in the home. There was a small safe in the closet. It had five thousand dollars cash inside. Chris and Jenny Sutter also had valuables in their home. Jenny's engagement ring was still on her finger. Christopher Sutter's wallet was on the kitchen counter with two hundred and sixteen dollars inside. Credit cards. Theft was not a motivation in this killing."

"What about Kevin Sutter's home?" I asked.

"As far as valuables?" Sam asked.

"Let's start there," I said.

"He only had twenty dollars in his wallet," Sam answered. "That was found on him, in his jeans pocket. He had guns in the home. Hunting weapons, for the most part. But he kept a .38 in a bedside drawer. It was still there. It hadn't been moved."

"Can you tell me where Kevin was found?" I asked.

"Also in his kitchen, near his kitchen table. We found a bullet hole in the wall, as if perhaps the killer missed. But then, Kevin was shot right through the chest. He fell beside the table, likely taking the kitchen chair with him."

"Detective," I said. "At what point did your investigation begin to focus on the defendant?"

"We did extensive interviews with the remaining members of the Sutter family. This was not a home invasion. As I stated, nothing was stolen from these people's homes. There were no signs of forced entry at any of the residences. So, that strongly indicated that the perpetrator might have been someone known to the victims. Several of the witnesses indicated concerns they had about Skylar Sutter's relationship with the defendant," he said.

"In what way?" I asked.

"I was informed that Mickey Harvey and Skylar were dating. One of the first things I did was secure Skylar's cell phone. Upon searching it, I found a series of texts from the defendant to Skylar that raised some concerns."

I introduced the cell phone records. One by one, the jury saw the texts between Mickey and Skylar. They began the day before the murder after Mickey claims he last saw Skylar.

Mickey: You catch any grief from your dad? I tried to get out of your driveway before he saw me.

Skylar: I don't want to talk about it.

Mickey: Whatever. I'll pick you up after your last class tomorrow. Pack some shit. You'll stay here.

Skylar: Not this weekend. I just want to lie low. I'll talk to you later.

Mickey: What do you mean you'll lie low? Pack some shit.

Skylar: Just drop it. I've got exams. I'm tired.

Mickey: So am I.

Mickey: What time you want me to get you?

Mickey: ??

Mickey: You're ghosting me? Yeah, I don't think so. I'm the one who's tired of this. You need to quit using your daddy as an excuse, Sky. When are you going to grow up?

That was it. The texts ended.

"What did you do then?" I asked.

"I subpoenaed Mickey Harvey's phone records," he said. "I had his number off Skylar's phone. It took a few more weeks to get the transcripts of his other texts. But within a day, I had the tracking data. Mickey Harvey's phone hit the tower closest to Skylar's home at ten a.m. on May 18th. He was there for approximately an hour that morning."

"Then what did you do?" I asked.

"I brought Mickey in for questioning."

At that point, I was permitted to play the interview tape of Mickey's interrogation. The jury saw him from the camera's vantage point in the top corner of the room. Sam's back was to the camera.

Mickey squirmed, fidgeted, sweat, asked for a cigarette. Then, just a few minutes into the interview, Mickey delivered the first lie that later sealed his fate.

"When was the last time you saw Skylar?" Sam asked him.

"I saw her the Thursday morning before she died," Mickey said. "She'd spent the night at my place the night before. Instead of going out like I wanted, she just came over. We talked."

"About what?" Sam asked.

"None of your business," Mickey answered.

"You didn't go out there at all Friday?" Sam asked, giving Mickey the rope he used to tie around his own neck.

"No," Mickey lied.

"What happened next?" I asked Sam after the recording finished.

"The fruits of my search warrant on Mickey Harvey's apartment came in," he said.

"What did you find?"

Sam went through the catalog of items. Finally, he got to the most damning piece of all. I held up the shirt we now had sealed in a vacuum bag. Though brownish now, the bloodstains stood in stark contrast to the yellow cotton.

"After our DNA analysis," Sam said, "we could confirm that the defendant, Mickey Harvey, had blood-soaked clothing wadded up in a garbage can inside his garage. The blood matched Skylar's. Later analysis showed a transfer pattern."

"Meaning?" I asked.

"Meaning this blood was likely wiped on this shirt. He pressed against her. He wiped his hands on it, something of that nature."

"Objection," Elise said. "Assuming facts not in evidence."

"Sustained!' Denholm shouted. Both Sam and I knew we were out on a limb here. But regardless of the judge's ruling, the jury had already heard what I wanted.

"What did you do next, Detective?" I asked.

"At that point, I believed I had probable cause. I arrested Mickey Harvey for the murder of Skylar Sutter, Ben Watson, Chris and Jenny Sutter, Patty Sutter, Mark O'Brien, and Kevin Sutter."

"Thank you, Detective. Your witness, Ms. Weaver."

Elise paused for a moment, then rose to take her place at the lectern.

❧ 22 ❧

"**D**etective Cruz," Weaver started. "So I'm clear. You have no definitive way to determine which of the victims of this tragedy were killed first, do you?"

"No, ma'am," he said.

"And that's because all those things one would normally use to determine time of death were basically the same in each victim, right? Lividity? Body temperature, etc."

"Objection," I said. "Counsel is assuming facts not in evidence. Detective Cruz isn't the medical examiner."

"Sustained," Judge Denholm said.

"Fine," Weaver said. "But back to my original question. Detective, you can't determine with any degree of certainty which of the victims was shot first, isn't that right?"

"Definitively? No. We can make educated guesses based on the positioning of the bodies," he said. "And as I stated on direct, these victims were likely killed within minutes of each other."

"Based on the positioning of the bodies inside Chris and Jenny's house, right?" she asked.

"Well, yes."

"In other words, Kevin Sutter, one house to the east, might have been the first victim?"

"That's certainly possible," Cruz said.

"Or Mark O'Brien might have been killed first, then Patty Sutter?"

"Correct. Though in that crime scene, we have the clearest evidence that Mark was shot first."

"Right. Since Patty appeared to still be sleeping. We're assuming she would have woken up, tried to run, or fight, like it looked like Mark did, right?"

"That's correct," he said.

"And based on your theories," she said, letting her tone drip with contempt, "in Chris and Jenny's house, you don't think Skylar Sutter was killed first, do you?"

"I do not," he answered.

"More than likely, she was shot last? Isn't that right?"

"That's difficult to say," Sam said. "I can only say for sure that her father, Chris Sutter, was likely shot just before she was. He was in front of her. The killer would have had to shoot through him to get to her. They were shot from the front."

"And yet you believe that Skylar's relationship with Mr. Harvey was the primary motive in this case," she said.

"It's significant, yes."

Weaver paused. She went back to her lectern and reviewed her notes. "You never found a murder weapon?"

"None was recovered, no. But based on the ballistics, we know it was a nine millimeter. And we know these victims were all shot with the same weapon. The primer marks were all consistent across the board. The rifling from the slugs recovered from the victims' bodies was all consistent one hundred percent. There is no question that this was the same murder weapon used on all. It doesn't get any more definitive than that."

"But you don't know for sure whether there was one shooter," she said.

"No," he said.

"With that type of weapon, how many rounds are in one clip?"

"Seven," he answered.

"Seven," she repeated. "And you indicated that you found no less than eleven bullet holes at the scene. Some in the victims, some in the walls."

"That's correct."

"Which means the shooter would have had to have reloaded at least once?"

"That's correct."

"Interesting," Weaver said. "Isn't it true, Detective, you found none of my client's DNA at any of the crime scenes?"

"That's true," he said.

"Across three brutal crime scenes, you found none of my client's blood?"

"Correct."

"And you didn't find so much as a single hair matching my client's head at any of these three houses, isn't that true?"

"That's true."

"You didn't find any footprints you couldn't identify?"

"That's true."

"No footprints belonging to Mickey Harvey in the houses?"

"None," he said.

"None of his footprints in the yards between the homes?"

"No," he said. "It was a pretty dry day. We didn't even find any of Ben Watson's footprints and he was found lying half in the lawn at the end of a trail of his own blood. So we know he took steps, he didn't levitate."

"Your Honor," Weaver said. "Would you please instruct the witness to respond only to questions he's been asked?"

"I believe I just did," Sam answered, getting agitated.

"Detective," Denholm said. "Let's none of us lose our tempers here. Just answer defense counsel's specific questions."

"Detective," Weaver said. "These were bloody crime scenes, were they not?"

"Each of the victims bled quite a bit," he said. "Yes."

"And yet you found no bloody footprints belonging to the defendant in Chris and Jenny's kitchen, for example."

"I didn't find footprints that we were able to match to Mickey Harvey, no," he said.

"You searched for fingerprints," she asked.

"Of course."

"I believe in your report you said you found thirty-two distinct sets of fingerprints among the three homes, is that correct?"

"That sounds right."

"How many of them belonged to Mickey Harvey?" she asked.

"None were a positive ID to Mickey. But it should be noted that four sets of prints were of such poor quality as to be unidentifiable to anyone."

"You searched Mickey's car?" she asked.

"Yes."

"You didn't find any blood or DNA evidence belonging to any of the victims in Mickey's vehicle, did you?"

"We did not," he said. "But that doesn't …"

"Detective," Elise shouted over him. "You've already been instructed to answer only what you've been asked."

"Your Honor." I stepped up. "Defense counsel seems to be forgetting the role of the judge in her cross."

"Ms. Weaver, I'll make the rulings. If there's admonishing to be made, I'll make it. You're not a professor here."

Elise looked rattled for the first time. She pursed her lips and gathered her breath.

"Detective," she said. "You weren't able to find a nine millimeter registered to Mickey Harvey, isn't that true?"

"I wasn't able to find a legal registration of that particular weapon in Mickey Harvey's name, that's true."

"But you found other guns registered to Mickey, didn't you? Isn't that true?"

"That's true," he said. "Mickey purchased a .410 Remington three years ago. There is also an AR-15 registered in his name."

This was a risk. One Elise surprised me by taking. If the jury bought every other argument I threw at them, it would help prove premeditation. Mickey went to Skylar's with a weapon he knew couldn't be traced back to him. I made a quick note and saw Hojo writing the same thing on his legal pad.

"Detective Cruz, in your report, you indicated the crime scene unit looked for tire tread matches, isn't that true?"

"We examined tire tread marks at the crime scenes, yes," he said.

"And yet you found none that matched Mickey Harvey's vehicle, isn't that right?"

"That's correct," he said. I wrote down another note.

"So, other than a single hit from a cell phone tower, you haven't got a shred of evidence that Mickey Harvey was on the Sutter property the morning of the killings, do you?"

"You mean other than his later admission that he was there?" Sam said. "No."

"The Redmond Road cell phone tower, you're not claiming the Sutter homes are the only homes serviced by that tower, are you?" she asked. "There are several homes down on Redmond Road that would register a hit if a cell phone was used in their vicinity, correct?"

"That's correct," he said. "But irrelevant. Mickey admitted to being at the Sutters' home, not any of the other homes down on Redmond. If he wanted a better lie, he could have just stuck with his story that he went to his father's. Only he couldn't because we have security footage from the Valero on Whittaker that shows him heading the wrong way, toward Skylar Sutter's where he *admitted* he went."

I hid a smile behind my hand. It was a helluva point. Adjacent to the Sutters', Ed Harvey's property was served by the same tower too. But none of that mattered now.

Elise quickly realized her massive misstep and moved on.

"So you found no murder weapon, no DNA, no footprints, no tire treads, no fingerprints, no physical evidence to indicate my client was on the premises during the murders," she said. "So let me ask you about what you did find, Detective."

"By all means."

"State's Exhibit 19, the so-called bloody tee shirt."

She pulled up a picture of the tee shirt on the wall screen. In it, the garment lay flat on a property room table with a ruler across the top to show the dimensions.

"You indicated this was a positive match to Skylar Sutter's blood," she said. "But Skylar Sutter bled out, did she not?"

"What do you mean?" Sam asked.

"Skylar Sutter's cause of death was listed as cardiac arrest brought on by massive blood loss, isn't that true?"

"That's true," he said.

"Wasn't Skylar wearing a tee shirt when she was found?"

"She was. Exhibit 19 isn't Skylar's shirt. It's the defendant's. As I indicated in my direct testimony, the blood found on Mickey's shirt was transferred. As in, either his hands were covered in Skylar's blood or some other surface was covered in her blood and he wiped it on the tee shirt."

"Thank you," she said. "That's exactly what I'm after. You're not claiming this blood is consistent with a splatter pattern, then?"

"No."

"It didn't get on this shirt because its wearer was standing close to Skylar when she was shot, right?"

"It doesn't appear so, no."

"In fact, you can't even prove when this blood was deposited on this shirt, can you?"

"No," Sam said.

"It could have happened at Mickey's house days before the killings, right?" she asked.

"Sure," he said.

"They *were* dating. Your witnesses didn't dispute that. We know she spent the night at Mickey's as recently as the night before, right?"

"Objection," I said. "Counsel is testifying."

"Sustained."

"I'll rephrase," Elise said. "Detective, it's equally possible that this bloody shirt ended up at Mickey Harvey's by innocent means as anything else, isn't it?"

"I don't understand the form of the question," he said.

"Isn't it true that, in fact, you don't really know how that blood got on that shirt, do you?"

"That's correct," Sam said.

"Thank you," Elise said. "I'm done with this witness."

"Your Honor," I said. "I have just a few questions on

redirect. I'd like to get them in before we adjourn, if that's okay."

"Proceed," he said.

"Detective," I said. "With the obvious exception of Skylar Sutter's fatal gunshot wound, did you observe any other fresh or healing wounds on her body?"

"Not that I observed," he said. "She was found wearing a tee shirt and shorts. I got a pretty good look at her arms and legs."

I left that there. I could circle back and get a definitive answer from the M.E.

I trusted Sam implicitly. He was as sharp a detective as any I'd ever put on the stand. We'd been through this enough times together. It almost felt like a dance. He knew how to take my lead. And he knew how to poke holes in defense theories.

"Detective," I said. "In your experience, what kinds of things would cause a murderer to leave blood or DNA at a crime scene?"

I detected just the hint of a smile in the corner of Sam's mouth. "The most obvious would be from a struggle."

"Were there signs of a struggle at any of the Sutter homes?"

"There were most decidedly not. These victims were gunned down at point blank range. They didn't have a chance to fight back."

"Objection!" Elise shouted. "The witness is offering wild speculation."

"Speculation, yes," I said. "But not wild. This witness is an expert at crime scene investigation. He's qualified to render his educated opinions."

"Let's refrain from hyperbole," the judge said. "Just answer what you know and can reasonably speculate."

"Detective," I said. "Would you have expected to find tire tread marks at any of the crime scenes?"

"No," he said. "All three homes had paved driveways. It had been dry for several days before the murders. We're not talking about muddy trails at all. And I highly doubt the defendant would have driven to each of the homes to carry out these crimes. They were each less than four acres apart. These homes were on top of each other."

"Thank you," I said. "I have no further questions for this witness."

"You're excused, Detective," Judge Denholm said. "And with that, let's call it a day."

Sam was good. Brilliant. My blood raced with adrenaline. The kind of high I only got when I knew I was winning.

❧ 23 ❧

Grandma George came to court dressed in a sharp royal-blue suit and sensible pumps. Her granddaughter Nikki took her to get her hair done. She had it cut in a becoming bob that framed her round face. She walked slowly, but with a straight back, pausing to grab the sides of the wooden gallery benches for support. One of the bailiffs rushed to her side to offer a hand.

"I'm all right," she said. Still, he kept close as she got to the front of the courtroom. It was that last step into the witness box that did her in, though. She gave the bailiff a resigned smile and finally took his hand, needing a hoist into the box.

Behind me, the Sutters came out in force to support her. Luke sat directly behind my table with his wife Rachel. A contingent of more distant Sutter cousins lined the back wall. Patty Sutter's daughter Devina came but I'd counseled her to stay out of the courtroom as I might need to call her as a witness later. Instead, her boyfriend Owen took her place in the gallery.

"Will you state your name for the court?" I asked her.

She leaned in. Too close. Her first word caused feedback into the mic. She adjusted.

"Georgette Constance Mahoney Sutter."

"Mrs. Sutter," I said. "How are you related to the victims in this case?"

This was the primary reason Georgette was here to testify. I needed her to sort through the complex familial relationships of the people who died that day. She could do it better than anyone, and as their grief hardened and became something they all learned to carry, Georgette had done as she always did. She carried on as the rock of the family.

"My husband is Louis Sutter," she said. "He's the youngest of four brothers. There was Ray. Henry. Chet. My Lou. Henry didn't make it out of World War Two. When they got back, Ray and Chet opened the bait store off I-75. That was the start of it. Lou was just a kid then. Eleven years old. Their mother and father ... in their own way ... didn't survive the war either. Lou's dad died of a heart attack not long after his son Henry's funeral. His mother was never the same after losing her son *and* her husband. You can imagine. Anyway, Ray ... remember, that's the oldest brother ... and his wife, Rosemary, took my Lou in and pretty much raised him after that."

"Thank you," I said, trying to gently steer her back to the matters at hand. "Now, what about Chris Sutter and ..."

"I'm getting to that," she said. I saw a little twinkle in her eye. Georgette had the jury's attention, but she would tell her family's story in her own way. Even Elise would be wise not to lob too many objections for relevance. I think she knew it.

"Ray and Rosemary never had any kids. Henry didn't either before he passed. Oh, Henry was a pilot. He got shot down. Did I say that? You know, for a while the navy held out hope he'd made it. But he didn't, of course. I think all of

Waynetown came out for his funeral. You can look it up in the paper. I remember him. I was just a little girl, but he was something, Henry Sutter. I had sort of a crush. Don't tell Lou. Anyway. You wanted to know about Christopher. He was Chet's boy. Chet was Lou's next oldest brother. Chet had C.J. and Christopher. One daughter, Claudia, too, but we don't ever see her anymore. She moved away a long time ago. A couple of her grandkids still live around here. There are some cousins too. Lou's father had two brothers and they have their kids and grandkids too."

She paused. I tried to gently bring her back to the victims at hand. "So Chris Sutter, he was your nephew, through Chet."

"Christopher, Chris, yes," she began again. "He was one of the ones who was killed last May. So he's our nephew through Chet. You got that right."

The outlines of the three homes, three crime scenes, were still up on an easel near the witness stand.

"Let the record reflect that Mrs. Sutter has pointed to house number one, being the home situated in the center of the three."

"So reflected," Judge Denholm said.

"Chris was married to Jenny," she said. "She died too. They had two kids, Skylar and Luke. Skylar died with them. Luke had moved out of that house long ago to start a family of his own. And I guess Skylar had a friend over. That Ben Watson. I didn't know him."

"What about house number three?" I asked, pointing to Patty's house to the west of Chris's.

"Patty," Georgette sighed. "Well, dear, sweet Patty. She was C.J.'s second wife. I told you C.J. and Chris were Chet's boys. Brothers. C.J. died a few years ago. Cancer. He had a rough go of it. Took a couple of years to go through him.

Anyway, Patty's the one who stuck by him. His kids scattered to the four winds. After he died, he left most of what he had to Patty. So, she was living in his house. And she had a new man. Mark."

"You're referring to Mark O'Brien?" I clarified.

"Yes," she said. "He's the one they told me was killed in the bedroom with her."

Her voice stayed steady. But we were getting to the hard part.

"Okay, Mrs. Sutter, how are you related to the last victim?"

"Objection," Elise said. "To the extent counsel has characterized Kevin Sutter as the last victim. Detective Cruz testified there is no definitive way to determine which of these victims died first or last."

"Sustained, Ms. Brent," Denholm said.

"I'll rephrase," I said. "Mrs. Sutter, how are you related to Kevin Sutter?"

She paused. With a shaking hand, she reached for the water bottle the bailiff placed in front of her. She didn't drink it though. Just held it.

"Kevin is my grandson. Louie and I were blessed with two kids. Thomas and Tina. We lost Tina to leukemia when she was little. Thomas passed a little over ten years ago in a car wreck. Kevin was Thomas's boy."

"I'm so sorry," I said.

"You live long enough, you deal with tragedy," she said. "I just ... well, it's not for me to say what God's will is. He must just think I can handle a lot."

"You have," I said. "Mrs. Sutter, what can you tell me about Kevin?"

She let out a long sigh. "I loved that boy. So different from my Thomas, though. Strong-willed. Smart. I really hoped he'd be the one to take over the bait shop one day. For a while he did. But you have to let men ... and women ... find their own paths."

"What was Kevin's path?" I asked. Over my left shoulder, I glanced at Elise. She had a pleasant smile on her face and scribbled notes on a pad. I expected her to object at any moment. For now, I think she understood interrupting Georgette too aggressively might not win her points.

"Kevin had a disease," Georgette said, lifting her chin when she did it. "He struggled with drugs and alcohol. It was better when Thomas was alive to guide him. Losing his dad just broke part of Kevin. Of all of us. I thought he had it beat. I really did. We tried all the things you're supposed to try. Tough love, they used to call it. Now I think intervention is the term. He was good, though. For a long time. What happened came as a shock. Losing him and how. But also what ... what we found out."

"What did you find out, Mrs. Sutter?"

"Kevin was using drugs again," she said. "When he died, they said he was under the influence."

I let that sit for a moment. Georgette's lip quivered and her eyes were red. She took a drink of water and seemed to settle.

"Mrs. Sutter," I said. "What did you know about your niece Skylar's relationship with the defendant, Mickey Harvey?"

"I knew they were an item," she said.

"Did the family approve of him?" I asked.

Her face went hard. "We did not," she said.

"Why is that?"

"The Harveys have blamed my family for every bad thing that has ever happened to them going back about a hundred years."

"Do you know why?" I asked.

"We're neighbors," she said. "A long time ago, I think when the first Sutters settled in this area, the Harveys had the adjacent farmland. Then in the twenties, in the last century, Louie's father bought up some of the Harveys' land. Way I heard it, old Daniel Harvey lost just about everything in the Crash. The Depression hit his family hard. Well, that was all fine and good but I wanna say it was in the fifties, just a few years before I married Lou. There was a boundary dispute over some of the land the Sutters bought. I know it went to court. The Harveys have been accusing Ray Sutter, Lou's oldest brother, of buying off a local judge for decades."

"Objection," Elise said. "We're moving into wild rumors, innuendo, and hearsay."

"Your Honor," I said. "I'm not offering this for the truth of the matter asserted. It establishes the flavor of the relationship between the Harvey family and the Sutters. I'd argue it doesn't matter whether these rumors are true. It only matters that the families believed they were."

"Overruled, Ms. Weaver," the judge said. "But let's rein this in, Ms. Brent."

"Mrs. Sutter," I said. "Prior to May 18th of this year, how would you describe the relations between the Harvey family and your family?"

"They're nuts, Ms. Brent. Ed Harvey, that's Mickey's dad, he still thinks part of our property belongs to him. We've found bear traps out by the stream on Kevin's property. Hidden. I won't even let Louie go for walks on the trail out there. I can't trust he won't lose a leg. He's shot up a couple of my good barn cats. Ed puts political signs along the property line and over on our side. A year ago, we found graffiti painted on three of our trees."

"What did it say?"

"Liar. Cheat. Thieves. One word on each tree. Such petty stuff. And if we run into each other in town, Ed'll scream at Lou. Lou ... his mind isn't what it was. It's upsetting."

"What about the defendant?" I asked.

"When he was a kid, he was as bad as his old man. I used to have to chase him off our property. Caught him shooting his .22 at two at one of those cats one year. Can't prove it, but I think he's the one who killed them. But since he started dating Skylar, I have to admit, I had some hope. I thought maybe once Ed wasn't around, Mickey and Skylar could turn the page on all that nonsense."

"How did Chris and Jenny, Skylar's parents, feel about that?"

"Not good," she said. "They would argue a lot. Chris didn't want Mickey anywhere near Skylar. I know he threatened to kick her out over it once. But then, I started hearing things that made me uncomfortable."

"Mrs. Sutter," I said. "Why were you uncomfortable?"

"I saw bruises on Skylar's arm when she came up to the house earlier this year. She tried to cover them up. But I saw. And she was always checking her phone. If she was with me for more than twenty minutes, she'd call that boy. Like he didn't trust her. Like he was making her check in."

"Objection," Elise said. "Calls for speculation."

"Sustained," the judge said.

I paused at the lectern to review my notes. Georgette had done everything I needed from her. Smiling, I met her eyes.

"Mrs. Sutter, thank you. I have nothing further."

She took a sip of water as Weaver traded places with me.

"Mrs. Sutter," she said. "Your husband sold his interest in the bait shop to your grandson Kevin and C.J. Sutter, isn't that right?"

"That's right," she said.

"Why just those two? You said the bait shop was started by your husband's brothers and that Chet Sutter had several children. Chris Sutter, one of the victims, for example."

"None of the rest of them were interested in running that store," she said. "To be honest, it was mostly my son Thomas who took it over. He tried so hard to keep Kevin out of trouble. He hoped the store would help with that. It did for a while. But then after Thomas died, well, Kevin started to lose interest. C.J., well, he was a lot like his old man. Wanted to just sit around and socialize while Lou or Thomas did the hard work."

"I see," Elise said. "Again though, if I understand the corporate structure, Chet's children and yours owned the business together at one point. When did that change?"

"Oh, maybe fifteen years ago?" she said. "C.J. bought his brother and sister out. Thomas's interest passed to Kevin and his sister Nikki, my other grandchild. So for the last few years the bait store was open, Kevin and C.J. were the owners and the managers."

"But they sold their interest, didn't they?" Elise asked.

"They did," Georgette answered. "They sold it to Verde. One of those pot dispensaries."

"In fact," Elise said. "They sold it for quite a sum of money. Do you know how much?"

"It was close to two million dollars," Georgette answered. "Split between them."

"How did the rest of the family feel about that?" Elise asked.

"It caused some problems," she said. "I think C.J.'s siblings felt a little cheated."

"You're saying Chris Sutter felt cheated? Because C.J. bought him out years before. Do you know for how much?"

"I think they each got somewhere around five thousand

dollars. At the time, the business wasn't what it once was. The value turns out was in the land. Prime location right on the expressway and all."

"Naturally," Elise said. "Isn't it true the fights amongst your family members got violent?"

Hojo made a noise beside me. I stayed stone still.

"There were fights, yes," Georgette said. "C.J.'s kids weren't the nicest people. I know Chris resented my grandson, Kevin, and his own brother for making that sale."

"In fact, you were present at a particularly violent episode the Christmas before last, weren't you?"

"I was," she said.

"Gary Sutter, C.J.'s oldest son, got into a physical fight with Kevin, your grandson, didn't he?"

"They fought," Georgette said. "Those two were always at each other's throats. Families are messy sometimes, Ms. Weaver."

"Messy," she said. "Isn't it true Gary Sutter threatened to kill Kevin that night?"

"Objection," I said. "Calls for hearsay."

"Ms. Weaver?" the judge said. "She's right. The witness is instructed not to answer as to what might have been said between the victim Kevin Sutter and this Gary Sutter."

"Mrs. Sutter," Elise continued. "Isn't it true that your grandson had to go to the emergency room that night?"

"I took him to urgent care," she said.

"He needed ten stitches above his left eye, isn't that right?" Elise asked.

"I don't remember ten. They stitched him up."

"Thank you," she said. "But that wasn't the only time your grandson Kevin had a physical altercation with members of his own family, was it?"

"I already said. Kevin had his demons. Yes. There were

times he got violent. Most of the time, it was the drugs though."

"Mrs. Sutter," Elise said. "Are you aware of what happened to your nephew C.J.'s share of the Verde property sale money after he passed away?"

"I already said," she answered. "He left most of what he had to Patty."

"Patty Sutter," she said. "One of the victims in this case."

"Yes. C.J.'s wife."

"How did that sit with C.J.'s kids? Gary and Toby, for example."

"They were angry," she said. "Far as I know they weren't on speaking terms with Patty or her daughter, Devina."

"In fact," Elise said. "There was a will contest filed, wasn't there?"

"They went to court. Or they settled something. That was between them."

"Thank you," Elise said. "That's all I have."

"Ms. Brent? Redirect?" Judge Denholm said.

"Mrs. Sutter, do you have personal knowledge of the terms of that settlement agreement between C.J.'s sons and Patty Sutter?"

"They paid C.J.'s kids a hundred grand each. I was there when everyone signed the paperwork. Patty asked me to be. She figured everyone would be on their best behavior if I was in the room."

"You're saying Gary and Toby Sutter, C.J.'s sons, accepted a hundred thousand each to settle their claims against Patty Sutter?"

"That's what I'm saying," she said.

"Nothing more from me, Judge," I said.

"All right. You may step down, Mrs. Sutter. You're still under oath if you should be called again."

Georgette nodded and pulled herself to her feet. As she left, her family rose and closed ranks around her. She took Luke's arm as she walked out of the courtroom.

"You may call your next witness, Ms. Brent."

"Thank you," I said. "The state calls Ed Harvey to the stand."

24

Ed Harvey strutted in wearing shirtsleeves and blue jeans. He made a subtle gesture of support to Mickey as he passed by the defense table. A little fist bump. Elise looked straight ahead. She'd clearly counseled Mickey to do the same.

Behind me, it seemed every Harvey in Waynetown had filled the seats vacated by the Sutter contingent.

"Your Honor," I said. "I plan to employ your ruling in my pretrial motion to treat Mr. Harvey as a hostile witness."

"Of course," Judge Denholm said.

"Mr. Harvey," I said. "Please explain your relationship to the defendant."

"He's my boy," Ed said, puffing out his chest. "And he's being railroaded. Let me get that clear right now."

"Mr. Harvey," Judge Denholm said. "I'm going to warn you, you're to answer the questions you're asked. We clear?"

Ed didn't look at him. He kept his hard stare on me.

"Do you have any other children, Mr. Harvey?" I asked.

"Got a daughter, Ashley," he said, then added, "but

Mickey's my only boy." His tone made it seem he felt that meant Mickey was the only child worth anything to him.

"Where do you live, Mr. Harvey?"

"On Whittaker Road," he said.

"You own the property directly to the east of the Sutter farm, isn't that correct?"

"Yes," he said. "Been in my family for generations."

"I understand," I said. "You haven't had a very cordial relationship with the Sutters over the years, have you?"

"They're all a bunch of trash, parading around like they're town royalty or something. Liars. Thieves. Cheats. Every last one of 'em." I hoped it wasn't lost on the jury that he'd used the same three words Georgette described were graffitied on her trees.

"So you don't have a lot of sympathy for what happened out at the Sutter farm in May of this year, do you?"

"Objection," Elise said. "Relevance."

"Your Honor," I said. "The environment in which the defendant was raised is relevant."

"Sustained, Ms. Brent," the judge said. "This witness's feelings about the murders aren't at issue. Ask your next question."

"Mr. Harvey, I'd like to talk about an incident that occurred at the Holman Hardware store in town last year. You were involved in an altercation with Chris Sutter, weren't you?"

"Might have been," he said.

"The police were called. You were asked to leave the premises. When you refused, two deputy sheriffs had to come out and talk to you, didn't they?"

"Wasn't just me," he said. "Chris started it. Called me white trash."

"What was the fight about?" I asked.

Ed crossed his arms in front of him and wouldn't answer.

"You spray-painted graffiti on trees belonging to the Sutters, didn't you?" I asked. "Tell the jury what you painted."

"Those are *my* trees," he said. "They stole that whole area of land west of the creek from me. It's the best hunting spot on the property."

"So you confronted Chris Sutter about that land, didn't you? After he told you not to go on the property again."

He clammed up.

"Mr. Harvey, there were at least six witnesses to the altercation in the store. What was it you said?"

"I said they were gonna be sorry!" he shouted.

"You were humiliated that day, weren't you?" I asked. "You got served with foreclosure papers right there in the store. Right in front of Chris Sutter, isn't that right?"

"They've been trying to bring me down for thirty years," he said.

"Who has? The Sutters?" I asked.

No answer.

"Were you or were you not served with papers on the foreclosure of your business property in downtown Waynetown at Holman Hardware on September 14th last year?"

"Might have been that day. I didn't mark it in my calendar," he said.

"And it was in front of a full store, people in town who know you. Right?"

"There were people there, yes," he said.

"Chris Sutter was there, and you took your anger, your embarrassment out on him, didn't you?" I asked.

"Wasn't embarrassed," he said.

"You weren't alone that day, were you?" I asked. "Your son Mickey was with you."

"Yeah, Mickey was there," he said.

"Since he was a child, you've taught him the Sutter family is your enemy, haven't you?" I asked.

"I've taught him what's right. I've taught him nobody hands you anything in this world for free. I've taught him family are the only people you can trust."

"Of course," I said. "You've been in conflict with the Sutters over that strip of land by the creek for as long as Mickey's been alive, haven't you?"

"It's my land," he said.

"But your family went to court over it, didn't they?" I asked. "That boundary dispute was settled some fifty years ago, right here in this courtroom, wasn't it?"

"Don't care what a piece of paper says," he said. "There's right and there's wrong."

"Mr. Harvey, ten years ago, isn't it true you were charged with criminal trespass on the Sutters' property?"

"That never went to court," he said.

"It never went to trial," I corrected him. "Because you agreed to remove three bear traps you set on the Sutters' property, isn't that right?"

"I took them out, yes," he said.

"Mr. Harvey, who helped you set those traps?"

I had the answer in front of me in the form of the original police report. Mickey had been questioned by Detective Ritter and admitted to setting the traps on Ed's instructions. He'd been just fifteen years old.

"Mr. Harvey, would you like to look at the police report to refresh your recollection?"

"No," he said. "That's my land. My traps on my land. But

I knew the Sutters were gonna keep at it. They've had this court in their back pocket since my Grandpa's days."

"Objection," Elise shouted. "I'd ask that the witness's last statement be stricken and disregarded. He's making baseless accusations against the integrity of this court."

"Mr. Harvey," Denholm said, his voice booming and for once matching his Morgan Freeman looks. "I've had about enough. You spout off like that again I'll hold you in contempt. The jury is instructed to disregard this witness's last statement."

It was working beautifully. I had one goal in putting Ed Harvey on the stand. Show the jury how Mickey Harvey's mind had been poisoned against the Sutters since the day he came into this world. Pure theatre, I knew. But with any luck, it would stick in the jury's minds for the rest of the trial.

"Mr. Harvey," I said. "Let me repeat my last question to you. It was your son, the defendant, Mickey Harvey, who helped you set those lethal bear traps on the Sutters' property, wasn't it?"

"Yes," Ed hissed.

"You taught him well from a very early age that anyone named Sutter was his enemy, didn't you?"

"I taught him how to be a man," Ed said. "I taught him about family loyalty!"

"Family loyalty," I said. "So you didn't much like it when he started dating the enemy, did you?"

"I don't tell my son where to dip his wick."

I recoiled at the crude reference, even as I knew it painted a vivid picture against Mickey. I heard two women jurors in the front row gasp. I gritted my teeth and kept going.

"Mr. Harvey," I said. "You divorced Mickey's mother, Amy, when he was ten years old, isn't that true?"

"Sounds about right," he said.

"And isn't it true that part of your divorce decree included a restraining order against you? You weren't allowed to get within a hundred feet of Amy, were you?"

"That was a long time ago. And you can go to hell for dragging a dead woman into all this."

"Mr. Harvey!" Denholm shouted.

I pressed on. "You had deputies at your house responding to reports of domestic violence no less than nine times during your marriage to Amy, isn't that right?"

"I was wilder in my younger days," he said. "I don't deny that. You better believe Amy gave as good as she got. I've got the scars to prove it. See this one through my left eyebrow? She hit me with a skillet that time. Thought she'd taken my face clean off."

The man actually delivered the line with a wistful humor. My God. He actually seemed nostalgic over a violent argument with his late wife that, from the records, landed them both in the emergency room.

"Your quarrels with your wife were so bad," I said, "Mickey was taken into protective custody twice, wasn't he?"

"You wanna know who called CPS on me?" Ed shouted. "C.J. Sutter, that's who. That fat piece of ..."

"Mr. Harvey!" Denholm yelled.

"Mr. Harvey," I said, going in for the kill. "Back to that foreclosure notice you were served on your property in town. The bank did in fact foreclose on you, didn't they? You don't own the building where you used to operate that business anymore, do you?"

"I let them have it," he said bitterly.

"Them?"

"The bank," he spat.

"The bank," I said. "Better than letting your second wife get it, right?"

"Objection!" Elise said. I raised a hand, conceding the point.

"I'll move on," I said.

"Why don't you tell the court who represented the bank against you in that foreclosure proceeding," I said.

"Is this fun for you?" he asked.

"Please answer the question," I said. "Who came to court and took your business away from you, Mr. Harvey?"

"Mark O'Brien," he muttered.

"Mark O'Brien," I repeated. "Thank you. I have nothing further."

Elise stood up and straightened her blazer. "Mr. Harvey, you didn't like Skylar Sutter very much, did you?"

"Didn't know her," he answered.

Elise looked through her notes. I knew it was for show. "Where were you on the morning of May 18th this year?" she asked.

Ed snapped his neck upward. The question caught him off guard.

"You put her up to this?" Ed said, directing it at his son. Mickey shrank into his chair. He was afraid of his father. Sweat beaded his brow.

"Mr. Harvey," Elise said. "Where were you on the morning of May 18th?"

"Home," he shouted. "Sleeping!"

"Thank you," she said. "I'm done with this witness for now."

"Redirect, Ms. Brent?"

"Just one question," I said. There hadn't been much Elise Weaver could do with Ed Harvey. I knew she wanted him off the stand and out of the jury's mind as quickly as possible. I also knew a few of them would have asked themselves the question Elise just did. Maybe it was Ed who killed the Sutter family after all.

"Mr. Harvey, you weren't alone on the morning of May 18th, were you? In fact, you were one of the first people the police came to question after the discovery of the tragedy at the Sutters' place. Isn't that right?"

"I wasn't alone, no," he said. "I was with my girlfriend. Steffi. Steffi Clark. And her mom's been staying with us. We take care of her. She's got a broken hip."

"Thank you," I said. "I've got nothing else."

Ed stepped down. He'd lost his strut as he passed Mickey's table.

❦ 25 ❦

I got through my scientific witnesses next. The medical examiner delivered straightforward testimony about the fatal gunshot wounds of each of the victims. I spent the most time on Skylar's injuries. He found several older and healing bruises on her arms consistent with being grabbed. He found no recently healed cuts that might have alternately explained the bloodstained clothing in Mickey Harvey's garbage can.

My bloodstain expert provided damning testimony about that clothing. The most likely explanation? Mickey Sutter came home with bloody hands, wiped them on a shirt and threw it away. Elise scored points showing we couldn't tell precisely how long that shirt had been in the trash. Also, it was only Skylar's blood. None from any of the other victims was detected. I planned to argue in closing that perhaps Mickey touched Skylar one last time before she died.

The M.E. also underscored the illicit substances found in Kevin Sutter's system. They would become critical later when I called Scotty Jarvis, Sam's informant. Kevin Sutter was positive for alcohol, oxy, and traces of heroin. The last of which he'd used the night before. The oxy was found partially digested, which meant he'd taken it within an hour or two of being shot.

Elise's cross was simple. The M.E. could not determine who had died first either. And he could not conclusively establish whether there had been more than one shooter. I could almost write Elise's closing for her.

Questions. She would say. More and more questions with very few definitive answers.

That was her story. I just prayed the jury would be able to see through it.

Next, I called my witnesses to Mickey's physical abuse of Skylar Sutter.

"How long had you known Skylar Sutter?" I asked Chad Carmichael.

"Maybe eight years, seven?" he answered. "Sky was close with my girlfriend, Sarah Bosch. We used to double date with Sky and whatever guy she was dating. Went to senior prom together. She was dating a guy from one of the Toledo Catholic schools back then. I think his name was Ted or something with a T."

"Do you know how long she was dating the defendant?"

"Maybe a year?" he answered. "Not a full year. Sarah would know that better than me."

"All right," I said. "Did you have occasion to observe the defendant and Skylar Sutter together?"

"Yeah," he said. "I'll be honest, I didn't much like Mickey."

"Why is that?"

"Even before he started dating Sky. He just kind of comes off as a jerk. He was a year or two older than me in school and he was just always one of those guys I avoided."

"Can you be more specific?" I asked.

"It seemed like anytime there was a fight at school, Mickey would be in the thick of it. He had a reputation of being a bully. He hung around with a rough crowd."

"I see," I said. "Let's focus on the last year, then. You said you and Sarah often double dated with Skylar and her boyfriends. Did you double date with Sky and Mickey?"

"No," he said. "Sarah wouldn't. She didn't like Skylar with Mickey either. He was mean to her. Always putting her down. When Sky was with us, you know, sometimes she'd come over to my place with Sarah. We'd all hang out. She was on the phone with Mickey constantly. And he would upset her."

"Over what? Do you know?"

"No. I couldn't hear their conversation. But Skylar would get agitated during and after their phone calls. She'd go outside to talk to him in private. When she came back in, a lot of the times I could see she'd been crying. Mickey didn't like her hanging out with us. With anyone but him."

"Was there anything else specific that concerned you about Skylar with Mickey?" I asked.

"Yeah," he said. "There was the night at the Blue Pony."

"Tell me about that," I asked.

"Sarah and I went there for burgers one night. Sky and Mickey showed up a little after us. We didn't plan to meet them. It was a coincidence. Anyway, they were sitting at the bar. Right after their food came, Sky stormed out."

"Stormed out?" I asked.

"Yes. He had his hand on her arm. Sky jerked it away, grabbed her purse and left. Sarah was worried, so she asked me to go after her and make sure she was okay. I did. I saw Sky and Mickey in the parking lot and he had his hands on her arms. He was jerking her, shaking her. She was crying.'"

"Could you hear what they were saying?" I asked.

"No," he said. "But Sky was really upset and Mickey was hurting her."

"Objection," Elise said. "The witness is assuming facts. He just said he couldn't hear Skylar or Mickey."

"Sustained."

"Why did you think Sky was being hurt?" I asked.

"Just the look on her face. And she was squirming, trying to get away from him. Mickey's a decent-sized guy. He was twisting Sky's arm to the point she was kind of contorting herself sideways to get away from him. That's when I tried to step in."

"What did you do?"

"Sarah was right behind me. I ran toward Sky and shouted. I told Mickey to let go of her. Asked her if she needed any help."

"Then what happened?"

"Sky seemed shocked to see me. She covered really quickly. She said she didn't want my help, and she got in her car. I was concerned cuz Sarah was right there. Mickey was angry. He told me to mind my own business if I knew what was good for me. I told Sarah to head back into the bar and wait for me. At that point, a big group of people came out of the bar at once. If they hadn't, I don't know. I was getting ready to throw down with Mickey if it came to that."

"Do you remember when this was?" I asked.

"Yes. April Fool's Day. We went to the Pony for the bash. And it's the last time I saw Skylar, I think."

"Thank you," I said.

Elise confined her cross to a few simple questions. Then Sarah took the stand. She backed up everything Chad said.

"Sarah," I said. "Did you ever voice your concerns to Skylar about her relationship with Mickey?"

"I wished I'd done more of that," she said. "Sky was ...

well … she didn't have the best taste in guys. I think she had a self-esteem problem. Over the years, it just got easier for me to stay out of it and let her make her own choices. I regret that. It'll probably be the thing I feel most sorry for for the rest of my life."

"Ms. Bosch," Elise started on cross. "You said Skylar had a history of bad boyfriends. To your knowledge, were any of her past boyfriends violent with her?"

"Yes," Sarah said. "She dated a guy about two years ago, Ty Bryant. He smacked her around a few times. I know her dad went and had words with the guy."

After Sarah's testimony, Elise waived cross but reserved the right to call Sarah during her case in chief. That threw me, but I had an important witness yet to call.

I called Leslie Noble to the stand. Leslie had been Chris and Jenny Sutter's family attorney.

"Ms. Noble," I said. "Can you tell me the substance of your representation of Skylar Sutter?"

"She asked me to help her get a restraining order," Leslie said.

"Against whom?"

"Against the defendant, Mickey Harvey."

I entered Skylar's unfiled petition into the record. Leslie then read the pertinent parts in Skylar's own words.

"The respondent, Michael Harvey has on multiple occasions threatened me with physical violence. I found a tracking GPS device on my car and believe the respondent put it there."

"A tracking device?" I asked. "When did Ms. Sutter discover this?"

"Skylar first came to see me on March 7th of this year. She'd discovered the tracking device sometime before that."

"What was the nature of the physical violence threatened?" I asked.

"The respondent had grabbed her hard enough to bruise her. Skylar showed me those. I took some pictures for my file. She indicated at one time he'd struck her across the face hard enough to break the glasses she'd been wearing."

I entered two photographs of Skylar Sutter into evidence. She had deep purple bruising on each of her forearms.

"Ms. Noble," I said. "What did you do when you learned of Skylar Sutter's murder?"

Leslie Noble dropped her head. "I was approached by Detective Cruz. He'd gotten word from one of Skylar's friends that she might have come to see me. So I gave him what I could."

"Thank you," I said. "I have nothing further."

"Ms. Noble," Elise said on cross. "Why wasn't this petition ever filed?"

"Ms. Sutter changed her mind," Leslie said.

"Did you speak to her about that?"

"No," she said. "She called my office and left a message with my secretary. She asked that her final bill be sent but that she and the respondent ... the defendant, had worked things out."

"Would you say you've filed a lot of restraining order petitions on behalf of clients?" Elise asked.

"I would say so," she said. "I handle mostly family law cases. Unfortunately, domestic disputes require them."

"How confident were you that this particular petition would have been granted had you filed it?" she asked.

"Objection, calls for speculation," I said.

"Your Honor, Ms. Noble is a family law expert. She's just testified that she handles many petitions such as this. As such, this is expert, not lay person testimony. Her opinion is admissible."

"I'll allow it."

"I had hoped to flesh out the affidavit supporting the petition a bit more," Leslie said.

"Flesh it out how?" Elise asked.

"Well, judges in my experience don't like granting restraining orders, especially ex parte ones ... meaning, orders entered without a hearing first ... without a very detailed factual basis."

"So you didn't think Skylar Sutter had provided enough facts to support her request, did you?" Elise asked.

"I'm saying I would have liked to flesh that petition out a little more."

"As Ms. Sutter's attorney, you would have had a legal obligation to notify the police if you felt she was in imminent danger, wouldn't you?"

"Yes," she said.

"But you never called the police, isn't that right?"

"Not until after Skylar was dead, no," Leslie said, her regret written plainly on her face.

"But you stated that you only spoke with the police after they contacted you," Elise said. "Meaning, you didn't even see fit to contact them of your own volition."

"I provided the information I could when they asked," she said.

"So before May 18th, you weren't concerned that Skylar Sutter was in any imminent danger from Mickey Harvey, were you?" she asked.

"No."

"Thank you," Elise said. "You've been very helpful. I have nothing further."

I knew Skylar's restraining order affidavit was weak in that regard too. But it existed. That mattered. I had one more nail to drive into that particular wall.

"Your Honor," I said. "The state calls Jody Doehler to the stand."

❧ 26 ❧

Jody looked terrified as he passed Mickey on his way to the witness stand. He wore a freshly pressed suit with a shiny blue tie. Once seated, he pulled at his starched collar.

"Mr. Doehler," I said. "Can you tell me how you were related to the victims in this case?"

"Um ... not by blood. My grandma is sisters with Georgette Sutter. I call her Grandma George like everybody else. So, I'm not a Sutter exactly, but me and the Sutters grew up like cousins, anyway."

"Do you also personally know Mickey Harvey?" I asked.

"Oh, sure. The Harveys live down the road from Grandma George. Everybody knows 'em. Mickey's older than me, though. I don't know if he knows who I am. But I know who he is if I see him around town and stuff. Maybe even to say hi. Except I know he doesn't like Sutters much and figure he wouldn't care if I'm from the Mahoney side, not a Sutter. So, I guess I've always kept my distance."

"And you were acquainted with Skylar Sutter?" I asked.

"Yeah. I do odd jobs. I'm trying to get certified as an

electrician. To go to school for it. In the meantime, I've always helped around the Sutter farm. Uncle Chris, uh, that's Chris Sutter, he had me doing stuff for him since his son Luke works really long hours as a nurse now."

"What kind of things did you do for them?" I asked.

"Mow the lawn. Change his oil. Fixing fences. Cleaning gutters. Just anything he needed help with. He paid me cash ... oh shoot ... can I say that? I pay my taxes and stuff."

"It's fine, Jody," I said. "Were you aware that Mickey and Skylar were dating?"

"Oh yeah," he said. "Everybody knew that. Chris and Jenny were none too happy. They didn't like when he came around. This one time Chris ran Mickey off. Mickey came up to get Skylar and Chris told him he could just wait in his car at the end of the driveway. Then of course there was that time at the Blue Pony."

"What happened there?" I asked.

"Well, like I told you before when I did this for that big jury. I was waiting in line for the john, this was on April Fool's Day. I mean that Sunday night. Sky and Mickey were at the bar. He was getting real rough with her. Grabbed her arm. Pulled on her. That kind of thing."

"Did you hear what Mickey said?" I asked.

"Sure. He said she better do what she's told if she knows what's good for her."

"Do you know what it was Mickey told her to do?" I asked.

"Told her she wasn't supposed to look at any guy but him. He said he'd seen her flirting. I didn't. I don't know who or what Mickey was talking about. Alls I seen was Skylar sitting there eating a burger with him. They were talking normal at first. Then Mickey just got all crazy. Started up with the manhandling."

"What else did you hear?" I asked.

"Heard him say, you're mine and nobody else's. Got that? I'll kill you if you so much as look at that guy again."

"Is that verbatim, Jody? Were those his exact words?" I had his grand jury testimony in front of me.

"Clear as I can remember," he said. "Oh, wait. Yeah, he said I'll put you in the ground before I let you get with another guy. I'll bury you. Then, like I told you. Sky pulled herself out of his grip and stormed off. Mickey got up to go after her. I was gonna too. Then I saw Chad go after her and my turn came up in the line. Chad's the kind of guy who can handle Mickey. He was a wrestler. I didn't want it to turn into a big thing. So I did my business. When I got done, I didn't see Mickey or Sky. And that was that."

"Thank you, Jody," I said. "That's all I have."

Elise was right behind me. "Jody," she said. "First off, did you ever talk to Skylar after this alleged incident at the Blue Pony?"

"No, ma'am. Didn't think it was my business. Not until after what happened."

"Did you see Skylar alive after this incident?"

"Well, sure. I told you. I did work for her dad. I see them … damn … I used to see them all the time."

"Of course," she said. "Did you talk to Chad Carmichael or Sarah Bosch about what you saw that night?"

"That night? No, ma'am," he said. "I don't think so. They were all gone by the time I came out of the restroom. I didn't see them again, so I assumed it was all handled."

"Did you ever speak to anyone else about what you overheard that night?"

"No, ma'am," he said. "I sure wish I had now. I know Chad and Sarah think the same. They were pretty broke up about it."

"I see," she said. "You said you're not a Sutter by blood. Does that mean you consider yourself one anyway?"

Jody screwed up his face. "You mean like an honorary Sutter?"

"Something like that," she said.

"Well, I guess maybe that's a good way to put it. Grandma George and Grandpa Lou have always treated me like one of their own. I'd say I spend more time with them than I do my real grandparents these days. Now, they're getting on. Grandpa Lou isn't doing all that great. His mind goes in and out. Grandma George worries about him. So, I do what I can for them. I check in. I drive them to their doctors. Especially now, since none of the rest of them are down there on the property anymore. She needs me. Luke, Nikki, they all have their own lives and live far away. So now I can give back. You know, for all the things Grandma and Grandpa Sutter have done for me over the years. I'm happy to be able to help them now."

"Of course," Elise said. "That's very kind of you."

"It's not kindness," he said. "It's about family. You look out for your family."

"Yes," Elise said. "That makes sense. And so you'd also do anything you could to protect your family from people who'd try to hurt them, right?"

"Well, sure," he said.

"And their enemies are your enemies, right?" she asked.

"In a way, I guess," Jody said.

"You don't like Mickey Harvey, do you?" she asked.

"No," he said. "He's a thug. Harveys are all thugs." Mickey's old man doesn't even apologize for the crap he pulls. You know, Grandpa Lou still likes to walk that creek. If he would have stepped in one of those traps Ed set, he could have lost his leg or maybe died. Ed doesn't care. Mickey doesn't care."

"And they got away with it," Elise said, setting her own trap. My blood ran hot. I'd let her. I was the one who'd introduced all the evidence about the Harvey/Sutter family feud. I couldn't very well object to relevance now. I'd known this might be Elise's plan of attack.

"Yeah!" Jody snapped. "They got away with it. And they'll probably try something just as bad when all this settles down. They're all trash. For what they did? Well, that's all I'm gonna say about that."

"Thank you," Elise said. "You've said plenty, Jody. I have no more questions."

Purple-faced with rage, Jody fumed behind the microphone. I did the only thing I could. I got him the hell out of there and let Judge Denholm adjourn us for the day.

❧ 27 ❧

The next morning, I put Sam's drug informant, Scotty Jarvis, on the stand. He almost didn't show. I had Sam put two deputies on his house. They caught him trying to sneak out a window at four in the morning. He came to court disheveled, glassy-eyed, and scared to death.

"Mr. Jarvis," I began my direct. "How long have you lived in Waynetown?"

"All my life," he said, his eyes darting from the jurors to Mickey Harvey.

"And what do you do for a living?"

"Bunch of different things," he said. "I work at Vining Machine Shop. Most recently."

"What do you do there?" I asked.

"Whatever they need. Lots of custodial stuff is how I started. Now I make sure they get what they need on the line and stuff."

"I see," I said. "Are you acquainted with the defendant, Mickey Harvey?"

Scotty chewed his cheek. "Yeah. I mean ... yes."

"How?" I asked.

"Mickey and me worked together at the Quickie Lube. That's the job I had before I got in at Vining. We did oil changes. Then, I left for Vining. I was working on putting a good word in for Mickey."

"Mr. Jarvis, is that the only business dealing you had with the defendant?" I asked.

"Business dealing?" he repeated. I could see sweat start to bead his brow.

"Yes," I said. "Did you conduct any other kind of business with Mickey Harvey?"

"Yeah," he said. "I guess you'd call it business. Mickey ... um ... he used to sell me dope."

"What kind of dope?" I asked.

"Mickey could get anything," Scotty said. "I, uh, I think I had him hook me up with some oxy first."

"OxyContin?" I asked.

"Yeah. But he could get the hard stuff too. I ... that crap is dangerous nowadays. I don't do it as much. Er ... I don't do that now. But there was a time or two where Mickey hooked me up with a speedball."

"What's in a speedball?" I asked.

"That's the thing, you can't be sure anymore. But it's usually like a mixture of heroin or coke."

"How often would you buy drugs from Mickey Harvey?" I asked.

"Once a week. Yeah. Usually once a week. You know. So I'd have something heading into the weekend."

"When did that start?" I asked.

"You mean when did I start buying dope from Mickey? Um, two years ago. Maybe three."

"When was the last time you purchased drugs from Mickey Harvey?" I asked.

"Well, he's been in jail for most of the year, right? So, I

wanna say it was maybe April of this year. Not long before he killed all those people."

"Objection," Elise said. "The witness is not qualified to offer that kind of opinion or speculation."

"Sustained," Judge Denholm said.

"What did I do?" Scotty said.

"Mr. Jarvis," Judge Denholm said. "You are not to speculate on whether the defendant killed anyone unless you personally observed it or he confessed to you."

"Oh, sorry," Scotty said. "I just kind of assumed."

"Don't." Judge Denholm and I spoke in unison.

"Scotty," I said. "Did you personally know any of the victims in this case? Patty Sutter. Mark O'Brien. Chris, Jenny, or Skylar Sutter. Ben Watson. Kevin Sutter?"

"I knew the Sutters," he said. "Everybody knows the Sutters. I don't think I knew the other folks. But I'd say I knew Kevin Sutter the best."

"How did you know him?" I asked.

"Well, I used to go into the Sutter Bait Shop. Did that since I was a kid. Kevin was a couple of years older than me. But he was in there a lot. Worked the counter. We didn't hang out, but I'd say we were friends. We talked when I'd go in. I was closer with his ex, Lea Shane. I worked for Lea's dad for a couple of years at his auto parts store. Oh. Yeah. I worked there when Kevin did too. He didn't work there full time. He had the bait shop until he sold it. But when he'd come in and help out for Lea's dad. Him and Lea had a kid together. I was only at Shane's for a couple of months anyway until I got in at Vining. I was working at the Quickie Lube and Shane's Auto Parts at the same time until then."

"Okay," I said. "Mr. Jarvis."

"Yeah, just Scotty. Mr. Jarvis sounds like my grandpa."

"All right, Scotty. How well did Mickey and Kevin Sutter know each other? Can you tell me that?"

"They were acquainted," Scotty said.

I gripped the sides of the lectern. It was like getting blood from a stone with this kid. He'd been a complete chatterbox in Sam's interviews and mine. Now that I had him on the stand, he seemed disjointed. A pit formed in my stomach. I'd been down this road plenty. I knew what it felt like when a witness was about to go south. I would *not* let Scotty Jarvis screw me over today.

"How well were they acquainted?" I asked.

Scotty met my eyes. I think he could sense my rising anger. I hoped it meant he remembered the power I had over the rest of his day if he didn't cooperate.

"Mickey was Kevin's hook-up too," he said.

"What do you mean hook-up, Scotty? I need you to be specific."

"Kevin Sutter used to buy drugs off of Mickey too," he said.

"How do you know that?" I asked.

"Well, because Kevin came to me one day and asked me if I could get some oxy for him. He hurt himself at work. Had some boxes fall on him. He told me he had a back injury."

"So you're telling me that you are responsible for connecting Kevin Sutter with Mickey Harvey so that he could also score drugs?"

"Yeah," he said. "I took Kevin over to see Mickey. Kevin was pretty hot when he realized where we were going."

"Pretty hot. How?" I asked.

"Angry."

"Why was he angry?" I asked.

"Cuz Mickey's a Harvey. Kevin was a Sutter. Their dads or grandpas or whatever hated each other."

"What happened?" I asked.

"What happened? Nothing happened. Kevin wasn't angry enough to not buy what he needed from Mickey. I knew he wouldn't be. He was pretty strung out when he came to me. Shaky. Sweaty. In a lot of pain."

"When was this?" I asked.

"Um, the first time I put Mickey and Kevin in touch with each other, Kevin followed me to the car wash on Blaine Street. That's where Mickey usually liked to meet. Kevin got what he needed, and that was that. It was about a year ago. Just before Christmas."

"Is that the only time you ever took Kevin to see Mickey for drugs?" I asked.

"There was one other time after that. Kevin called and said Mickey wouldn't answer his phone. He got a new one. He used to use burners. Kevin wanted to know if I had the new number. I did. So, same thing. We met him over at the car wash."

"Do you know what type of drugs Kevin bought from Mickey?" I asked.

"Couple of speedballs. Some oxy."

"And when was that, if you recall?" I asked.

"That was about two weeks after the first time. So mid-January this year."

"Were there any other times you went with Kevin Sutter to buy drugs from Mickey Harvey?" I asked.

"Just the two," he said. "After that, I figured Kevin and Mickey could work their own selves out. I was trying to get clean. The week after Christmas, my girlfriend told me she was pregnant. We were going to get married. I promised her I'd cut that stuff out. We couldn't afford for me to lose my job at Vining."

"Did you stop?" I asked.

"For a while," he said. "By the time it hit the news what happened to Kevin and all the rest of them, I hadn't seen either of them since late January. So five months. But then Cami, my girlfriend. She lost the baby. She took it hard. We broke up. So I kinda lost my way again over the summer. I'm thirty days sober though."

"Good," I said. "Thank you, Scotty. I have nothing further."

Elise charged to the lectern.

"Mr. Jarvis," she said. "You were arrested on June 8th of this year, weren't you?"

"Yes, ma'am," he said.

"For what charge?"

"Possession with intent to sell," he said. "I had some Special K on me. Um, ketamine."

"And what kind of jail time were you facing if you were convicted on that charge?"

Scotty wiped his hands on the front of his shirt. "I was looking at some years."

"Ten years in jail," she said. "It was ten years. But you didn't go to jail. Those charges were dropped, weren't they?"

"Yeah," he said.

"Why was that?"

"I made a deal," he said. "My lawyer talked to the prosecutor and got me a deal."

"Explain your deal," Elise said, her voice dripping with sarcasm on the last word.

"If I gave them the name of my supplier, I could get my charges dropped," he said.

"Did you?" she asked.

"No. I told them about Kevin and Mickey though," he answered.

"Kevin and Mickey. So you knew Mickey Harvey had

been arrested for the killings out at the Sutter farm, isn't that right?"

"Of course I knew. Everybody knew."

"And you just happened to have this juicy information about Kevin and Mickey for them," she said.

"Is that a question? I didn't just happen to have it. It is what it was. It's what happened."

"But Mickey had been arrested some weeks before you were, isn't that true?"

"I don't have a clue when he was arrested. I was popped in June."

"But it was all over the news, wasn't it?" she asked.

"Sure," he said. "Seven people got shot out there. That doesn't happen every day."

"No," she said. "Of course it doesn't."

"There was a sizeable reward for information pertaining to the killings, wasn't there?"

"I think so," he said.

"You're out of work now, aren't you, Mr. Jarvis? In fact, you were fired from your job at Vining in July of this year, isn't that true?"

"They let me go, yes."

"You were fired for stealing cash out of the drawer, isn't that right? And when you were first confronted, what did you tell them?"

"I said I didn't do it," he said.

"You lied. But you were caught because they had you on the surveillance cameras, isn't that right?"

"Yeah," he said. "I'm not proud of it. And I'm trying to turn my life around."

"There was a ten-thousand-dollar reward offered by crime stoppers relating to the Sutter murders. And yet you didn't see fit to come forward with what you claim you knew about Kevin and Mickey, isn't that right?"

"I told them what I knew," he said.

"You told them your story only after you were in hot water," she said. "You did it to save your own skin, isn't that right?"

"I made a deal to keep myself from going to jail and give me a chance for a fresh start," he said.

"Wouldn't a ten-thousand-dollar reward have given you a fresh start?" she asked.

"I could use money like that, sure," he answered.

"And yet, you didn't come forward then. You only came forward after the prosecutor in *this* case offered you a deal." Elise sighed. "Thank you, I have nothing further."

"Ms. Brent?" the judge said. I shot Elise a hard look as she passed me on the way back to her table. She'd just implied my office had done something shady. I found it beneath her. I chose to take the high road for now.

"Scotty," I asked. "Why didn't you come forward sooner with what you knew about Kevin Sutter and Mickey Harvey?"

"Because I was afraid," he said. "And because in the middle of the summer and around the time Kevin got killed, I was still using pretty heavy. I was just trying to survive. And I was afraid what happened out there had to do with Mickey's dealing. I figured he pissed off somebody bigger than him. I was afraid I'd be next."

"What changed your mind?" I asked.

"Mickey can't hurt me from jail," he said. "And it weighed on me. Don't think it didn't. Those were nice folks out there. Not with Kevin. He had his issues. But the Sutters were good people. I couldn't live with myself if I didn't say. And yeah, I didn't want to go to jail. So I did what my lawyer recommended. And I'm telling the truth. Everything I've said here today is the truth."

"Thank you," I said. "I have nothing further."

Scotty stepped down. Judge Denholm dismissed the jury so we could spend the afternoon on a few remaining evidentiary motions.

I felt spent. Drained. I could not read the jury during Scotty's testimony. Elise got in some hits. I had one more big decision to make.

❧ 28 ❧

I got home after dinner, breaking a deal I made with Will. Kat waited for me in the kitchen. Will had already gone upstairs to take his bath.

"How angry was he?" I asked.

"He's okay," Kat said. "He knows how important this trial is. He wants Mickey Harvey to go to jail forever."

My heart twisted. "He shouldn't have to even think about it. I thought he was getting better."

"So did I," Kat said. By her expression, I knew she was holding something back.

"Out with it," I said.

Kat picked up Will's tablet from the kitchen table. She brought it to me and opened the home screen.

"He left this behind when he went to answer a call from Jason," she said. Kat tapped the screen and pulled up Will's browser. He had several tabs open, all news stories about the Sutter murder trial.

"And this," she said. She opened his podcast app. "He's been listening to the one they're doing on the trial. *Small-Town Killers*. I found a notebook in his room."

"He's taking notes," I said. "I don't know how I missed this all."

"Mara," she said. "You should talk to my brother. Jason was really worried about him this summer. When he came back, he really seemed to have put all this out of his mind."

"Kat," I said, the first seeds of panic rising in me. "I have to do my job. I have to find a way to …"

"No," Kat said, putting a hand on my shoulder. "Don't worry. I'm not saying I think Will should go back to D.C. It's just, he listens to Jason. And this is clearly something that Will's worried about. They should be talking about it too."

"I know," I said. I worried Jason might use it against me. Would he try to say Will's best interests might be served living in D.C.?

"Mom!" Will said. He came down the stairs, hair still wet, wearing his blue flannel PJs and the robe Kat got him last week.

"Hey, bud," I said. "I'm sorry I missed dinner. It won't happen again. This thing will be over in a week with any luck."

"Have you rested yet?" Will asked, sliding onto a kitchen stool.

"Not yet," I said. "Maybe tomorrow."

"Do you think the defense will call Michael Harvey to the stand?"

I exchanged a look with Kat. Though it seemed a harmless question on the outside, I knew Will could easily spiral into an obsession that could disrupt his routine.

"I don't know," I answered.

"You wouldn't," he said. "If you were on the defense side, would you? Too many risks involved."

The question surprised me. I could practically see the wheels turning behind Will's eyes.

"I mean, you're good," he said. "You'd get Harvey to trip up. Expose all his lies."

"Yes," I said. "Generally, that's the strategy."

Then Will's face changed once more. He got a far-off expression as he nodded. The boy was working out some other problem in his head. One he might never even tell me about. Or it would come out some time down the road. Nobody else but me would remember the context. It would seem random. Only I knew that wasn't it. It was just that my son had many puzzles spinning around in his brain. When the solution for one presented itself, he had to express it no matter where he was or what he was doing.

"She won't call him," Will said. It was then I noticed the small book he held under the crook of his arm and half hidden by the folds of his robe. It was a dog-eared, green-and-gold-bound textbook. He put the book on the island.

"Where did you get that?" I asked.

"It was in your study," he said.

"Will, that's not a good place for you," Kat said as she mouthed an "I'm sorry," over his head.

"I didn't touch anything," he said. Blood rushed to my toes, but I breathed a sigh of relief. Just last week I'd removed all the pictures on my cork boards of the crime scene. Lord, I prayed Will hadn't been in there then. He couldn't have. We kept the door locked. Only three people had keys: me, Kat, and my cleaning lady.

Will opened the book to a page with a pink sticky note inside.

"What is that?" Kat asked.

"Modern Trial Practice for New Attorneys," Will answered her. "Written by Professor Elise M. Weaver, J.D. University Press, 1998."

Will ran his finger down the page. "The pitfalls of calling

a criminal defendant in his own defense almost always outweigh any potential benefit."

"Weaver?" Kat asked. She covered her mouth to suppress a laugh. "Are you telling me she wrote the literal book on trial practice?"

"A book, not *the* book," I said, smirking. I took the thing from Will. "I don't think I've cracked this thing open since the night before I took her exam."

Will and Kat shared a glance. Kat shrugged. Will turned to me.

"Well," he said. "How'd you do in her class, Mom?"

"I got an A." I laughed. "The only one she gave out." I turned the book over and opened the front flap.

Professor Weaver made a habit of inscribing her textbook and gifting it to the highest-grade earner in each of her courses. At the time, it was considered quite an honor.

"Wow," Kat said. "She's insufferable."

I couldn't help but laugh. "Yeah. Looking back, I guess that's pretty pretentious. At the time it was fun knowing how jealous everyone else was about it. And in her defense, Professor Weaver wasn't the only one who did that."

"Well, I think it's cheesy," Will said. "But she thinks she's going to win."

"Why do you say?" I asked.

"She only takes cases she can win," he answered. "She's tried four cases in the last fifteen years. This one's the fifth. Every time she says she came out of retirement for it. The last one was the Red Mountain strangler in Southern Indiana."

Behind him, Kat took her coat off the hook. She mouthed good luck as she slid her arms in the sleeves. Will was still rattling off Elise Weaver's win/loss record as if it were fantasy football statistics as Kat slipped quietly out the back door.

"Will," I said, when he finally let me get a word in edgeways. "We have a good case."

"Are you scared?" he asked.

"Of what, honey?"

Will didn't answer at first. He fingered the edges of Elise's book. I knew the better question here was whether he was scared.

"Of losing?" I asked. "Well, I never like to lose. But we wouldn't have brought this case forward if I didn't believe Mickey Harvey was guilty."

"If he's not guilty," he said. "If the jury says he's not guilty, then that's it. Right? You don't get a do-over."

"No," I said. "That's right. If Mickey Harvey's acquitted, then our constitution prevents me from charging him with this crime again."

"Then won't he be mad at you? If they acquit him. Won't he blame you for trying to put him in jail?"

"Will," I said. "I'm not scared of Mickey Harvey."

"There are others though," he said. "You don't always win."

I smiled. "Well, I happen to win most of the time."

"Eighty-two percent of the time," he said. "Dad said that's an incredible average."

"Are you kidding? You counted?"

"It wasn't hard," he said. "You can find it all on the internet."

"Will," I said. "Have you been reading about my other cases?"

He went quiet. It told me everything I needed to know.

"Oh, honey," I said. I ran a hand down the back of his head, smoothing his hair. That he let me made it clear how upset he really was.

"Will, look at me."

He did.

"You don't have to be afraid of Mickey Harvey. He's not going to get away with this."

"You don't know," he said. "Not really. Juries are unpredictable. She says that on page one hundred sixteen."

"Baby, you're safe. We're both safe. Do you hear me?"

Slowly, Will lifted his eyes to meet mine. God. I'd been such a fool. This was my son, feeling so out of control. I thought he'd adjusted to Jason and my separation. Outwardly, he had. But this growing obsession with the Mickey Harvey trial had nothing to do with the Sutters at all.

"Come on," I said. "It's about time to give your dad a call. Why don't we do it on Zoom? We'll all talk together. Would you like that?"

Will's shoulders dropped. "Yeah," he said.

"Okay." I took him by the hand and let him into the living room where I kept my personal laptop. Eight o'clock on the dot and Jason was expecting the call.

For now, it was enough. Will told Jason about his science fair project. He was animated, even smiling a few times. I'd defused this little bomb today, but knew the next one might not be so easy.

❦

TUESDAY, THE SECOND WEEK OF TRIAL, WE WAITED UNTIL after the lunch break. I walked into the courtroom with Hojo at my side.

"Ms. Brent?" Judge Denholm said. "Are you ready to call your next witness?"

I looked at Hojo. Behind us, Sam Cruz sat. He gave me a barely perceptible nod. I'd briefed him early on my strategy for the day.

"Your Honor," I said. "At this time, the prosecution rests."

Denholm looked at the clock on the wall behind the jury. One fifteen.

"All right," he said. "It's early yet. Ms. Weaver, are you prepared to call your first witness?"

The highlighted pages from Elise's textbook swam in front of my eyes. Would she do it? Would she actually put Mickey Harvey on the stand? I'll admit, my pulse raced at the prospect. I wanted it. Could taste it.

"Yes, Your Honor," she said. "The defense is more than ready to call our first witness."

"Let's hear it then," Denholm said.

Elise shot me a look. A smile. Pure theatre, of course. Then she raised her chin and named her witness for the judge.

❧ 29 ❧

"The defense calls Devina Francis to the stand," Elise said. Her entire posture changed. Elise reminded me of a racehorse at the starting gate. Someone had just fired the gun. She strode to the lectern, gripping the sides as Dev Francis worked her way through the gallery and up to the witness box.

"Why's she putting her up?" Hojo whispered beside me.

"To make a mess," I whispered back.

"Ms. Francis," Elise said. "Let me start out by expressing my sincerest condolences. You lost someone very close to you on May 18th, didn't you?"

"I lost my mother," she said. "Patty Sutter was my mom."

"Patty Sutter. If you don't mind, can you explain to the jury how she fit into the Sutter family as a whole?"

"Not well," Dev said. She seemed far different from when I interviewed her months ago. Then she was still in very deep grief. Now, she kept a straight posture with narrowed eyes. She never once looked at Mickey Harvey. That was my first inkling that something big was about to happen. And it was something I wouldn't like.

"What do you mean by that?" Elise asked.

"My mother was C.J. Sutter's second wife. C.J. had two kids. Sons. My older stepbrothers. Gary and Toby. They didn't much care for my mom. And they made it a point of letting her know."

"How?" Elise asked.

"When C.J. died, Gary and Toby tried to keep my mom from inheriting anything from his estate. He died with quite a bit of money on account of the sale of the bait shop to Verde."

"How much?" Elise asked.

"Over a million dollars," she said. "C.J. left most of that to my mom. But he set up a trust for Gary and Toby. They accused my mom of unduly influencing C.J. at the end of his life."

"May I approach?" Elise asked. She held a single document in her hand. She gave it to Dev.

"Do you recognize that document?" Elise asked.

"I do," Dev said. "It's the paper my stepbrothers filed in probate court to try to take my mom's money away from her. Like I said, they claimed my mom tried to brainwash C.J. into cutting them out. That wasn't true."

"Objection, Your Honor," I said. "The state of C.J. Sutter's estate is not at issue in this case. He's not a victim. He died of natural causes almost three years ago now. Additionally, the settlement documents regarding this probate matter have already been introduced."

"She's right, Ms. Weaver. What's the point of all of this?"

"Understood, Your Honor," Elise said. "If you'll allow me another question along this line, I think the relevancy will become apparent."

Denholm waved a dismissive hand. "Ask your question."

"Ms. Francis," Elise said. "In the weeks and months leading up to your mother's murder, did you have occasion to talk to her about her relationship with your stepbrothers?"

"I did," she said. "My mother was in fear of her life."

Blood rushed to my head. I caught myself shaking it to clear it. Had I heard what I thought I just heard? I had briefed Dev Francis after charges were brought against Mickey. I'd done so for all the victims' families. At no time had Dev expressed anything other than relief that we'd caught the man who killed her mother.

"Why was that, Ms. Francis?" Elise asked.

"My mother told me she ..."

"Objection!" I practically shouted the word. Hojo stood up and shouted it with me.

"Your Honor," I said. "Defense counsel is eliciting hearsay testimony from this witness to the extent she's asking what her mother might have told her."

"Approach," Denholm said. I grabbed a notepad and charged to the bench. Denholm leaned down and covered the microphone with his hand.

"Out with it, Ms. Weaver," he said.

"This conversation with Patty Sutter and the witness goes to Patty's state of mind. Ms. Francis just said her mother was in fear. I can't think of a better example of a hearsay exception under the rule if I were writing it for a textbook, Your Honor."

"Ms. Brent?" he said.

"If she's about to say what I think she's about to say, a statement by Patty Sutter is about to be offered for the truth of the matter asserted."

"I disagree," Denholm said before Elise could counter. "The witness herself said the conversation centered on her mother's fears. I'll allow it. Your objection is noted for the record, Ms. Brent. Let's proceed."

I clenched my fists as I went back to the table.

"Ms. Francis," Elise said. "Let me go back to my question. I asked you what you knew about your mother's relationship with her stepsons in the weeks leading up to her death. Do you want me to have the court recorder read back your answer?"

"No, ma'am," Dev said. "I remember what I said. I remember what my mother told me. She was in fear for her life."

"Why?"

"The probate stuff had been settled. My stepbrothers each got about a hundred thousand dollars. They signed off on it. But they were still unhappy. They were still trying to make my mom's life miserable. Calling her names. Not letting her see C.J.'s new grandson when he was born. Harassing her on social media. My mom ran into one of Toby's kids at the grocery store. She told me they told her they were going to appeal the settlement. They were going to drag her back into court. They were going to tie up her funds and throw her out of her own house. They told her she'd never find peace in Waynetown so she'd better just get out or else."

"Or else what?" Elise asked.

"It wasn't clear. But my mom was scared. She was thinking about putting the house up for sale. That's why Mark O'Brien moved in with her. They'd gotten close after he helped her with the court stuff. Actually, I called him right away when my mom broke down and told me all this crap about my stepbrothers. Mark said she didn't have anything to worry about, that you can't appeal a settlement, only a court judgment, or something like that. Anyway, he said he promised me he'd handle my stepbrothers and that I shouldn't worry."

"Handle them how?" Elise asked.

"I don't know," Dev said. "Take them to court or

something. I just wanted my mom to sell that house and come live near me. I'd been begging her to do that. The Sutters ... I mean, other than Grandma George, the rest of them just weren't very nice to her."

"Ms. Francis, how well did you know Chris and Jenny Sutter?"

Dev squirmed in her seat. It seemed an odd reaction. I made a note of it.

"I knew them. He was Uncle Chris. She was Aunt Jenny. I was thirteen when my mom married C.J. We lived in that house. They always lived in the house just down the road from us."

"And you knew Skylar Sutter as well?"

"She was a cousin by marriage, yes. But she and her brother were a little younger than me, so I can't say we really hung out a lot. And they were ... well ... I got the impression that most of them were more loyal to C.J.'s ex-wife, Doreen. That's Gary and Toby's mom. It was tough. See, C.J. had a drinking problem. I know it caused a lot of disharmony between his first wife and his kids. I always had the impression they resented that C.J. got sober and married my mom. Like, we got the best of him and they didn't. They'd call him A.A.C.J. Patty got to marry A.A.C.J. while Doreen got a drunk. It was cruel. But I get that. I understand it. He was a different dad to me than he was to them. A different husband to my mom than he was to Doreen."

"I see," Elise said. "Did you consider yourself close to Chris and Jenny?"

She looked down. "Not ... not close emotionally. But they were always around because of proximity."

"What about Kevin Sutter, the victim in the third house? Were you close with him?"

"No," she said. "Of course I knew Kevin. His dad and C.J.

were first cousins, I think is how it goes. I was closer with his sister, Nikki."

"Ms. Francis," Elise said. "If I can refer back to the will contest your stepbrothers filed, beyond undue influence, what was the other basis for the challenge?"

"They ... um ... they said my mom and C.J. were legally separated at the time he died."

"Is that true?"

"It wasn't. I mean, yes. My mom filed for separation from C.J. something like five years ago. But they worked it out. When C.J. got sick, she moved back in and took care of him."

"Why did your mother separate from C.J. Sutter in the first place?"

"Objection," I said. "Your Honor, we have gone so far afield of relevance. This is not divorce court. This is not probate court. Again, C.J. Sutter was not a victim in these killings. The state of his marriage has no bearing ..."

"Overruled," Denholm said. "I'd like to hear the witness answer."

"Your Honor," I started.

"Overruled," he said again.

I sat back down. Hojo had written a note expressing my sentiments. What in the actual hell was Denholm doing?

"I don't ... it was ... very personal," Dev said. "Do I have to answer that?"

"You do," Elise said sharply.

"They just started growing apart. My mom felt C.J. was sweeping things under the rug and wanted him to stand up for himself within the family."

"Stand up for what?" Elise asked.

"He just ... Grandpa Lou always ran the business how he wanted to. C.J. didn't feel like they were equal partners, even though they were on paper. When Kevin took Grandpa Lou's share, it was the same old same old. My dad felt ignored a lot of the time. My dad, C.J., he was giving a lot of money to his brother, Chris, and his sister who moved away from Waynetown. He bought them out years ago. My mom felt it was too much money because they never lifted a finger to help. Then, when C.J. and Kevin sold that business for all that money, it just brought out the worst in everybody. They wanted more and more. Not just my stepbrothers. Chris, too. Aunt Claudia. It was just ugly. Hateful."

"I see," Elise said.

"Toxic," Dev said. "And it's why I left Waynetown. I didn't want to be around it. I knew it was going to end badly. I knew it."

She cried.

"It's all right, Ms. Francis," Elise said. "I have no further questions."

I looked down at the note I'd written Hojo when this all started. Elise Weaver was looking to make a mess. She'd succeeded.

"Ms. Francis," I started. "You said your mother told you she was afraid of your stepbrothers. They never hurt her physically, did they?"

"Not that I know of," she said, dabbing at her eyes.

"We spoke at length several months ago, do you remember that?"

"I do," she said.

"And you never saw fit to tell me that your mother was in fear of anyone, did you?"

"I don't know if I said that," she said. "But I told you if something bad happened to my mom, I knew it had to do with money."

"You no longer live in Waynetown, correct?" I asked.

"That's correct. I live in Nashville now."

"And on May 18th, you were in Nashville. You didn't actually see your mom that day? Or even the day before?"

"No," she said. "I didn't see her."

"Did you speak to her?"

"No," Dev answered. "The last time I spoke to her was May 16th. We had a long phone conversation. I didn't ... I wished I'd known then that was the last time I'd ever get to talk to her."

"You're not suggesting Gary and Toby Sutter had anything to do with what happened out at that farm, are you?"

"I'm not ... that's for you guys to figure out," she said.

I took a chance. "Ms. Francis, when was the last time you spoke with either of your stepbrothers?"

"It's ... I haven't seen them since my mom's funeral. But they've sent me letters."

"You're in the middle of settling your mother's estate, isn't that right?" I asked.

"Yes," she said.

"Have Gary and Toby Sutter made that difficult for you?"

She looked down. "Toby's lawyer filed some paperwork with my lawyer. Yes."

"So your stepbrothers are still trying to get C.J.'s money, aren't they?"

"It's my money now," she said. "My mother left it to me and he left it to her."

"Have Gary and Toby Sutter filed claims against your mother's estate?" I asked.

"They have, yes," she said.

"Thank you," I said. I hesitated but decided to end Dev's testimony. In my closing, I would have to imply she was using this trial as a way to get back at Gary and Toby Sutter for filing claims against Patty's estate. "I have no other questions."

"Ms. Weaver?" the judge said.

Elise rose but didn't take to the lectern. "Ms. Francis, you in fact told the police if something happened to my mom, I have no doubt Gary and Toby had something to do with it. Isn't that true?"

"That's true," she answered.

"Would it shock you to learn that neither of your stepbrothers was ever even brought in for questioning?"

"What?" she said.

"Objection," I said. "Counsel is testifying now."

"Sustained," the judge said.

"I have nothing further," Elise said.

I was fuming. It was a cheap trick. I would call Sam back for rebuttal when I got the chance. No. He'd never brought the Sutter brothers in for questioning because he spoke to them on the phone. He didn't need them at the station. They had ironclad alibis. They were vacationing with their families in Myrtle Beach during the weekend of the murders.

But now, that little misdirection would get the chance to marinate in the jury's mind for days. And I stupidly walked right into that one.

Never again.

"Call your next witness, Ms. Weaver," the judge said.

"We call Nicole Sutter, Your Honor."

Hojo gave me yet another confused expression. Lord, I thought. Not only was Elise making a mess, she was putting me in the position of having to attack the victims' family members.

She was good. Brilliant. Dirty. And I had to do better. Right now.

30

Something was wrong. Nikki Sutter wouldn't look at me as she took the stand. She fidgeted in the witness box as Elise got her notes together and took a sip of water from the bottle on her table.

"Ms. Sutter," she said, starting her questioning in the pattern she established. "Can you enlighten the jury as to how you're related to the victims in this case?"

"My brother," she said. "Kevin was one of the victims. Chris Sutter was our dad's first cousin. Patty Sutter was married to another of my dad's first cousins."

"So you're familiar with your brother's home?" she asked.

"I am," she said. "I grew up there. Kevin lived in our mom and dad's old house. That whole parcel of property, the Sutter farm. It's been in the family for years. Lou Sutter, that's my grandpa, he has the house at the top of the hill. He gave the house where Kevin was living to my dad, Thomas Sutter, when he married our mom. The other two houses were originally owned by Grandpa's other brothers, Uncle Chet and Uncle Ray. One Sutter or another has always lived in those homes."

"I see," said Elise. "I can't imagine the kind of shock it must have been for you to hear what happened out at the farm."

"It was," she said. "But ... I was always worried something would happen to my brother."

"Why is that?"

She looked down. "It's already out now. Kevin had his struggles. Um ... with drugs."

"That must have been difficult for your family. Do you know when Kevin began using?"

"When we were teenagers," she said. "He ... I can't ..."

"Take your time," Elise said. "Just let me know if you need a break."

"No," she said. "I'm okay. Kevin was, I think, sixteen when he started smoking pot. He hung around with kind of a rough crowd. He was a rebel."

"Did that cause friction within your immediate family?"

"It did," she said.

"Isn't it true that your brother OD'd on multiple occasions?"

"What?" she said. "Is that something I have to talk about?"

"Your Honor," I said. "I fail to see the probative value of this line of questioning."

"The state has opened the door," Elise said. "In her case in chief, Ms. Brent took great lengths to introduce evidence of Kevin Sutter's drug problem and made accusations of my client's alleged role in that. That relationship is very much at issue."

"Agreed," Judge Denholm said. "You may answer, Ms. Sutter."

"Yes," Nikki said. "Kevin OD'd."

"At sixteen, he was taken by ambulance to St. Mary's, was he not?"

"Yes," she said. "He was ... my mom found him in his bed. He was late for school. He wouldn't wake up."

"That's not the last time an ambulance had to come to your home for Kevin, was it?" she asked.

"No," Nikki said. "There was another time about a year later that I found him in the garage."

"What did your brother OD on that time?" Elise asked.

"Heroin," Nikki said. "By then he'd moved on to heroin. That's when we were able to get him into rehab."

"Kevin went to rehab at seventeen?" she asked.

"Yes. My dad found a place in Florida. He stayed there for three months during the summer between his junior and senior year of high school."

"Did he stay clean?" Elise asked.

"For a few years, yes," Nikki said. "When he got back, after he graduated, my dad brought him into the store full time. Kevin took classes at community college and worked at the bait shop."

"But he fell off the wagon again, didn't he? In fact, you had to call an ambulance again for him, didn't you?"

"I did," she said. "That was some years later. I was going to Eastern. I was home on break. I think it was my junior year. So Kevin was twenty-three, twenty-four."

"Did he stay clean after that?"

"No," she said. "Not long after that relapse, my father died in a car accident. Kevin kind of spiraled for a while. He left Waynetown. It was a good two years before we got him back."

"But you didn't stay, did you?" she asked.

"I stayed for a while. It was ... it was tough with Kevin. He blamed my parents for a lot of his trouble."

"Why was that?" she asked.

"Just ... he resented them for a lot. For not ... for not being there in the way he thought they should be. And he felt kind of trapped. Like he was never given another option besides running that store."

"I see," Elise said. "But your father was dead by then. He could have left whenever he wanted. After all, you did?"

"I just couldn't be around them anymore," she said. Nikki was tearing at a tissue.

"Who's them, Nikki? Who couldn't you be around?"

"Just ... all of it. My mom and Kevin weren't in a good place together. I told you, he blamed her for everything. I was stuck in the middle all the time. I loved my brother but ..."

"But it takes something from you," Elise said. "Isn't that right? Dealing with an addict?"

"I loved my brother," she said. "But I wanted a different life than the one I had in Waynetown."

"You got as far away from Waynetown as you could, didn't you?"

"Objection," I said. "We've moved off Kevin Sutter's issues. There is no relevance here."

"Your Honor," Elise said. "If you'll permit me just a bit more latitude. You'll see that Nikki Sutter's decision to leave Waynetown is very relevant to what transpired on May 18th of this year."

My skin tingled. Nikki still hadn't looked my way once during her entire testimony. What on earth was Elise talking about?

"I don't like this," Hojo wrote on the notepad between us.

"Ms. Sutter," Elise said. "The drama with your brother's addiction disease wasn't the only reason you wanted to get out of Waynetown, was it?"

"There were a lot of reasons I left," she said. "I was studying photography. I had a friend in Seattle who had connections there. I thought I'd thrive better away from a small-town mentality. Start fresh."

"Nikki," Elise said, dropping her voice. "I know this is painful. But it's time for the truth to come out. If not now, when?"

She tore the tissue in half.

"Your Honor," I rose.

"Ms. Sutter," Elise said. "Isn't it true you had a falling out with Skylar Sutter before you left for Seattle?"

"I don't see why that matters," Nikki said. Finally, she looked to me for help. Wherever Elise was going with this, it appeared Nikki didn't want it to either. What on earth had she not told me?

"Neither do I?" I said.

"Again, the state has made wild accusations about my client's relationship with both Skylar Sutter and Kevin Sutter. I believe this witness can shed light on the true nature of that relationship."

"Overruled for now," the judge said. "But my patience is wearing thin."

"The truth, Ms. Sutter," Elise said.

I could feel the gallery behind me start to shift as people moved in their seats. My blood ran cold. I felt as if I were about to experience a slow motion train wreck.

"You left Waynetown because you didn't want to be anywhere near Christopher Sutter, isn't that true? Isn't that what you confessed to Skylar Sutter?"

Nikki began to cry. Her lip quivered. She looked straight at Mickey. "She told you that? It doesn't matter. They're all dead now."

"Objection!" I said. "Your Honor ..."

"I've made my ruling," Denholm said.

Elise practically stalked in front of the lectern. "Ms. Sutter, please answer. Why did you really leave Waynetown?"

"Yes," she said. "I didn't want to be around them anymore. It took me a long time to really process what happened to me."

"What happened to you?" Elise asked.

"Why do I have to say?" she implored. "What difference does this make?"

"Your Honor, please instruct the witness to answer."

I felt a trap door open beneath me.

"Please answer the question, Ms. Sutter," the judge said.

Nikki Sutter took one heaving breath. Then she answered. "Uncle Chris was ... he'd been inappropriate with me."

There were gasps behind me. I knew Luke and Rachel Sutter sat in the corner of the gallery. I heard Luke shout something, then the doors to the courtroom slammed shut. Hojo swore under his breath.

"Inappropriate how?" Elise asked.

"Your Honor," I said. "This has no bearing on ..."

"Overruled," Judge Denholm said before I could even finish my objection. He couldn't. He wasn't ...

"He molested me," Nikki said. "Okay? Is that what you want me to say? My Uncle Chris was a pervert."

Mickey Harvey's words during his interrogation flooded into my brain. He'd said Skylar's father wasn't a good guy. There was only one way Mickey could know this secret. Skylar had to have told him. I wanted to be angry with Nikki for keeping it from me. But how could I?

"When did this happen?" Elise asked.

I was still on my feet. "Your Honor," I said. "I implore you. We have gone so far down the road away from the issues at hand in this case."

242

"Overruled, Ms. Brent," the judge said. "You may answer, Ms. Sutter."

Lord. Good lord, no. Nikki Sutter was falling apart. Pain etched deep lines in her face. No matter what else happened today, I knew in my gut she was telling the truth.

"It started when I was about twelve," she said, hiccupping past a sob. "I used to babysit Skylar. I was asleep on the couch after she went to bed. She was little. Like four. I woke up and Uncle Chris was ... he was drunk ... and he had his hands on me. Under my shirt, over my pants, between my legs."

"Was that the only time this happened?" Elise said.

Nikki shook her head. "No," she said. "It went on for a long time. I didn't ... I didn't know what to do. He would corner me. Touch me. There was so much chaos with Kevin, I didn't want to tell my parents. They had so much to deal with. I thought maybe I was imagining it. And he ... Uncle Chris ... he told me if I ever told anyone, he'd hurt me. Or he'd hurt my mom and dad. I believed him. You have to know ... he was ..."

"He was what, Nikki?" Elise asked.

"It took a long time to process this. I've been working on myself in therapy since I left Waynetown. I thought it was my fault. I thought maybe I'd done something to bring it on. But then ..."

"Then what?" Elise asked.

"I found out it wasn't just me," she said, sniffling.

"You're saying your Uncle Chris didn't just molest you?" she asked.

Nikki shook her head. "No," she said. "There were other cousins. My Uncle C.J.'s granddaughters. They don't live in Waynetown anymore either. I think it's because of that."

"Objection," I said. "Counsel is eliciting hearsay testimony about what the witness's cousins may or may not have told her."

"Sustained," the judge said. "Ms. Sutter, you will need to confine your testimony to things you personally observed or experienced, not what you may have been told."

"Ms. Sutter," Elise said. "Did you ever confront Chris Sutter about what he'd done to you?"

"Yes," she said. "Right before I left for Seattle. A few years ago."

"What happened?"

"Nothing happened. He laughed it off."

"Did you ever tell anyone else in the family about what happened to you?" Elise asked.

"My mom knows. It's why she left Waynetown as well. She lives in Seattle with me. She wants nothing to do with the Sutter family anymore. Especially now that Kevin's gone. It's hard. They weren't in a good place before he died. I think given time, they would have repaired their relationship. At least, I'd like to think that. I didn't know Kevin was using again. I thought he was doing so much better."

She quietly cried.

"I'm so sorry," Elise said. "I'd just like to say I think you're very brave, Nikki. I have just a few more questions. Did you know if Jenny Sutter was aware of your accusations against her husband?"

She wiped a hand across her brow. Her fingers trembled.

"I don't know," she said. "Skylar knew."

"How do you know that?" Elise asked.

"Because we got in a fight. The last time I talked to her, she ... she called me a liar. It got ugly."

"When was this, if you recall?" Elise asked.

I chanced a look behind me at the gallery. All of the Sutters had left the courtroom. Of the victims' families, only Ben Sr. and Gina Watson remained. Both had tears streaming down their faces. Ben Sr.'s face reddened with rage.

"Last Christmas. I came to town to spend it with my brother. My mom took a vacation with my stepdad. I didn't want Kevin to be alone. We got into a fight. Skylar had been drinking. She said some things. I said some things. I told her about what her father did to me. My therapist told me she thought it would be good for me. It just came out all wrong. She didn't believe me. She called me a liar and a slut and a bunch of other things. I just regret it all."

"Where did this conversation take place?" Elise asked. "Who else was present?"

"It was just Sky and me. We were at Kevin's. She and Mickey were over at Kevin's because she was fighting with her folks. They didn't approve of Mickey."

"Did you?" Elise asked.

"I don't ... I didn't see them together. Mickey was on his way out. He was at my brother's with Sky, but he left. They'd just gotten into an argument too."

"Do you know why?" Elise asked.

"He said Sky got violent when she drank and he didn't want to be around that energy," Nikki said. It was barely more than a whisper.

"Can you repeat that?" Elise asked.

"I said hello to him in passing as he was leaving Kevin's. Mickey looked upset. He was on his way out. He said he couldn't stay because Sky got violent when she drank."

"Skylar got violent," Elise said. "Thank you, I have no further questions."

I rose. Anger clouded my vision. I stared straight at the judge and asked if I could approach. My nails dug into my palms as I made my way to the sidebar. Elise was right behind me.

"Your Honor," I said through clenched teeth. "At this time, the state would like to move for a mistrial."

Judge Denholm straightened. "Bailiff, will you please excuse the jury for the day?"

Then he turned to us. "You two, in chambers. Now."

31

"Your Honor!" I said. He'd asked us to sit. I was in no mood. Instead, I paced at the back of Judge Denholm's office chambers. Elise sat calmly in the chair in front of him. His court reporter sat with her fingers poised over her keyboard. We were on the record.

"Make your motion, counselor," he said. "It's just the four of us. No one to perform for in here."

I felt my cheeks heat. I needed a ten count, or I was going to blow. I took one attempt at a calming breath, then whirled around.

"This entire line of questioning was improper and prejudicial. As sickening as we may find it all, Chris Sutter's alleged conduct toward his niece more than fifteen years ago is irrelevant. It should never have been allowed."

"I disagree, Ms. Brent," Denholm said. "I ruled on your objections in the courtroom. I haven't changed my mind."

"Then I'd like to renew my motion for a mistrial," I said. "There is absolutely no way the jury can come to an impartial decision. We've veered so far off the map of the true issues in this case. Chris Sutter isn't on trial. He's dead, for God's sakes. Nikki Sutter wasn't even living in Waynetown when these murders took place. She's not a suspect and never was."

"Any response from you, Ms. Weaver?" Denholm said.

"Your Honor, I think it's patently obvious this case was rushed to trial. The police were never interested in exploring any other plausible motive for these killings. It is absolutely within the defendant's rights to explore alternate theories of the case. They've got the wrong guy. I'm allowed to show the jury other potential suspects."

"Who?" I asked. "Who exactly are you trying to say killed those people instead of your client? The one who was overheard threatening to kill Skylar Sutter just days before her death. Who has a history of violence against her. Who supplied another of the victims with elicit narcotics and had a legitimate beef with every single victim on that farm, Dr. Weaver?"

"That's the detective's job," Elise said, wryly. "My burden isn't to solve this case for you, Mara. It's to raise reasonable doubt."

"I take it you formally object to the prosecution's motion for a mistrial?" the judge asked.

"Certainly," Elise said. "The state has failed to show adequate grounds that there has been any procedural error or misconduct that would amount to an unfair trial. Courts aren't permitted to grant mistrials just because the prosecution has come to realize it's losing."

"This has nothing to do with that," I said. "This has to do with this court allowing the defense to use this trial as a vehicle to air things that have nothing whatsoever to do with what happened to that family on May 18th. She's going for headlines and podcast fodder, not what's legally relevant here."

The smarmy look on Elise Weaver's face took me back to my first year of law school. She knew it.

"Your Honor," she said. "Again, it is entirely within the defense's province to explore alternative theories about what happened that night. These are relevant issues. And as you've stated, Ms. Brent had the opportunity to raise her objections in open court. There's no prejudice here."

"With all due respect," I said. "Your Honor has lost control of these proceedings. They've become sensational, tabloid material, nothing more. For heaven's sake. Just look out your own window."

He did. Judge Denholm's office faced Cleveland Street and the front of the courthouse. They parked three live news trucks along the curb. A crowd had formed.

"My God," I said as I stepped closer to the window. "That's your clerk! Elise ... your office is giving a press conference?"

"There's no law or order against that," she said. "And I've authorized no such thing. I can't help it if there is a public interest in this trial."

"No," I said. "You're counting on it."

"Enough," Judge Denholm said. "I'm not granting a mistrial in this case. You haven't raised sufficient grounds. You're free to make your argument to the jury during your closing arguments, Ms. Brent. And you'll have your shot at rebuttal. The case goes forward."

He looked at the clock on the wall. "But not today. It's past three. We'll adjourn until bright and early tomorrow morning."

He left me speechless. It took everything in me not to storm out of there and slam the door in Elise Weaver's face as I left.

"Mara," she said softly as we both entered the hallway.

"This is beneath you," I said. "All you're doing is revictimizing that family. This isn't about justice. This is about you drumming up interest so your agent can get you an on-air gig or a book deal."

Her lip twitched. A small tell, but I knew I'd hit on it.

"No," she said, composing herself. "This is beneath you, Mara. What are you *doing* here?"

"My job," I spat back.

"You don't belong here. Waynetown, Ohio? Really? I understood it when I heard you'd taken this job. It made sense in light of your husband's aspirations. Though I'll admit, it disappointed me. You were always a more talented lawyer than he was. But you got complacent, Mara. You've settled."

"What I do with my personal and professional life is none of your business," I said.

"Isn't it?" she said. "I gave you everything I could. I invested in you. But you should be heading the Justice Department. Solicitor general. Even a governor."

"This is my town," I said. "Do you get that? My town. I'm not going to stand by while you rip it apart to further your own jaded ambitions, Elise."

"You're more like me than you think," she said.

"We're done here," I said. "I'm going home. And I'll sleep easy tonight. Can you honestly say the same?"

Her eyes flickered. I knew I'd scored a hit. But she said nothing. She just pasted on a smile, readjusted the strap of her briefcase and turned on her heel.

She got into the elevator as Hojo was coming out. He came to me.

"What was that?" he asked.

"Disaster," I said.

"Come on," he said. "Let's get out of here. You look like

you could use a drink. I'm buying. We'll have to sneak out the service entrance. The street's crawling with reporters. They're out for blood."

A sobering thought, knowing the blood they meant to draw was mine.

32

The look on Kenya's face told me news of my mistrial motion had already reached her. Hojo had beat me back to the office by a few minutes.

"What the hell is he thinking?" Kenya asked. I met her in her office. For the moment, I didn't want to go back to mine. I didn't want to go to the war room and see the lifeless faces of the Sutter Seven staring up at me from the crime scene photos. Judging me. Pleading at me from the grave.

"He's thinking about his career," I spat. "He's thinking about making himself famous."

"That podcast about the case is charting," Hojo said. "It's the number one true crime show in the U.S. right now."

"Can we shut it down?" I asked. "Is there any way to ..."

"No," Kenya said. "Like it or not, the Cullen kid's got a right to put on his show."

"Well," Hojo said. "Denholm should close the courtroom to spectators then."

"Not happening," I said. I went to Kenya's window. There were picketers lined up in the streets. Some pro-Sutter family, some pro-Harvey family.

"Did we know?" Kenya asked. "All this stuff about Christopher Sutter?"

"No," I said. "I had no idea. I interviewed Nikki Sutter and Dev Francis. So did Sam. They never said a word to me. At the same time, I never asked."

"Why would you?" Hojo said. "Like you said in court, whether he was a monster or not, Chris Sutter is one of the victims in this case. He's not on trial."

Heavy footsteps drew my attention from the hallway. Breathless, face flushed, Sam Cruz got to Kenya's office.

"Good," Kenya said, her tone hard. "You were my next phone call. What the hell, Sam? Why are we just hearing about these allegations against Chris Sutter now?"

"You think I would have kept something like that out of my report?" he said. "Christ, Kenya. You know me better than that."

"She's going to say you rushed to judgment on Mickey Harvey," Kenya said. "That's her whole closing argument."

"She's brilliant," I said. "And I've let her play me from day one."

Rage came over me, boiling my blood. I held my notebook in my hand. Before I could stop myself, I hurled the thing against Kenya's wall.

Kenya pursed her lips but did little more than give me an approving nod. I sat down hard in one of her chairs. Hojo took one against the wall. Kenya leaned against her credenza and gestured for Sam to take the seat beside me.

"Fine," she said. "Get it out of your system. All of you, get it out of your systems. But then we need to figure out how to fix this."

"The case is solid," Sam said. "Mickey's a liar. He was *at* Skylar Sutter's house the morning of the murders in the timeframe those people were killed. He's got the motive."

"You've got witnesses who saw and heard him threaten that girl," Hojo added.

"She can misdirect all she wants," Kenya said. "But Elise Weaver hasn't produced a single witness who can refute what we have. Who can offer a plausible theory as to who else would have killed those people if not Mickey?"

"Because nobody else did," Sam said.

"She's muddied everything," I said. "If this were a civil trial, this thing would be overturned on appeal so fast if I lost. Denholm is just flat out wrong. The jury should have never heard a single word about what Chris Sutter might have done to Nikki or anyone else."

"She's giving the jury a reason to think the creep deserved to die," Hojo said.

"If it were just Chris," I said. "If he were the only person killed out on that farm that day, I could almost go there with her. But he wasn't. He might have been the devil himself, but I know in my gut, everyone in that courtroom believes Chris Sutter died trying to protect his daughter."

"It's noise," Kenya said. "That's all it is. Weaver is trying to amplify the noise. Confuse the jury."

"And that's exactly why Denholm shouldn't have allowed it. It's his job, for crying out loud!" I shouted.

"Well," Kenya said. "He's shown his true colors today. He's not interested in justice for those people. He's interested in making some kind of name for himself. These are the cards we've been dealt. So now what?"

"It's solid," Sam said again. "I'm telling you. That jury isn't stupid. I've been watching them. They'll see through all this BS. Mara, you're a hell of a closer. You'll convince them."

I didn't feel so sure. Something must have registered on my face. Kenya stepped around her desk.

"Mara," she said. "Sam's right. This is your case to win or

lose. Not Elise Weaver's. She's slick. Fine. But you're letting her get into your head."

I looked up at her. I wished I could argue the point.

"Forget all of that out there." She gestured to the window and the chaos beyond it. Even from up here, we could hear the shouts and angry name-calling.

I tried to center myself. Closing my eyes, I let the images of those victims come to me. No. We couldn't prove who was killed first. Not scientifically. But there had been a choreography in the way their bodies lay. I *saw* it. It was right there.

"Shooter hits Ben Watson from behind," I murmured. "Mickey's angry to find him there. Skylar won't return his calls. Won't come see him. Ben is running."

From what?

"He saw Mickey coming at him," I said. "Maybe they argued first. Ben sees the gun. He's trying to get away. Or he's trying to warn the others."

"Mickey shoots him in the back." Sam picked up my narrative. "He enters the house. Jenny Sutter is in the kitchen."

"He shoots her before she can run," I said. "Then Chris and Skylar come in from the garage because they've heard the shots."

"Bam. Bam!" Sam said, visualizing their quick deaths just as I was.

"I just don't believe Chris Sutter was the primary target," I said. "Not him alone. I think ... it's just something ..."

"Like it got out of hand," Sam said. We were of the same mind.

"Except that doesn't explain what happened at Kevin Sutter's or to Patty and Mark O'Brien. That wasn't chaos."

"And if this was some kind of retribution against Chris, their murders don't make sense," Sam said.

"Right," I answered. "That's the thing in all of this. It's where any of Elise Weaver's alternate theories fall apart."

"You've got this, Mara," Kenya said. "You take that jury through that beautiful mind of yours, just like you did now. When they see it, they'll know. This was Mickey. Killing Skylar was the ultimate way to control her. We've seen this pattern so many times. The rest? Who knows?"

"Adrenaline," I said. "He's there. Patty and Mark and Kevin all live close enough to have heard or seen what was happening. And even if they didn't, he's got reasons to want them dead."

"He went hunting," Hojo said. "And Daddy Harvey raised him to hate the Sutters. It's enough, Mara. It's going to be enough."

"And beating Elise Weaver at her own game will just be the cherry on top, my friend," Kenya said. "When this is all over, it's you who'll be famous. And me who'll have to worry about it going to your head."

I smiled. "I'm not after fame, Kenya. My name's been in the news enough. Some quiet anonymity sounds like heaven."

"The podcast vultures will move on as soon as this trial is over," Sam said.

I was about to say it wasn't podcast listeners who worried me. The shouts from the street had died down, but the emotions behind them hadn't. This trial, those murders, had ripped open a fissure in Waynetown that I feared might not close when this trial did, however it turned out.

I didn't get the chance to say it. Sam's phone rang. He answered and his expression darkened.

"I'll be right there," he said, then clicked off.

"Trouble?" I said.

"Yeah," he said. "Couple of knuckleheads got into it out at the hardware store. Ed Harvey's nephew Doyle and one of the Sutter cousins."

If they were calling Sam in, it had to be bad.

"Sam?" I asked. He met my eyes.

"Doyle Harvey's in awful shape," he said. "Graham Sutter ran him over with his car. Doyle's in surgery now. They've got Graham in custody. I'm heading over there now."

"Lord," I said.

"Some other injuries to bystanders," he said. "No way to tell who threw the first punch, but the E.R.'s hopping. I gotta get down to the station."

"Go," I said, my heart sinking.

The weight of it seemed to settle on Sam's shoulders as he rose. I had every belief that no matter the outcome of my trial, things might get far worse in Waynetown before they got better.

33

Sheriff Clancy tripled the security outside the courthouse as we began what should have been our last day of trial. Friday, December 7th.

Deputy Remick escorted me into the building, as she did Elise and her contingent of litigation paralegals. We went on the record and I renewed my call for a mistrial. Judge Denholm renewed his denial. Elise called her next witness.

"The defense recalls Sarah Bosch," Elise said. I braced myself. Nikki Sutter had ghosted me since giving her testimony. Doyle Harvey was in critical condition with a torn artery in his lung. He'd miraculously survived the night. Graham Sutter, the victims' third or fourth cousin, was in custody awaiting charges for attempted murder.

As I stood there, I realized I might be prosecuting Sutters and Harveys well into the New Year.

"Ms. Bosch," Elise said. "Please be reminded you're still under oath. And can *you* remind the jury how you knew the victims in this matter?"

Sarah was already in tears. Denholm granted Elise's motion to treat her as hostile.

"Skylar was my best friend," she said. "Since seventh grade. We were like sisters."

"Like sisters," Elise repeated. "When was the last time you spoke with Skylar?"

"The day before they found her," Sarah said.

"Did you see her in person? Did you talk on the phone? Text? What was the nature of that contact?"

"I saw her on Thursday," Sarah said. "We went and got chicken wings from Derby's. We hung out for a while. Then we texted a few times throughout the day on Friday. Until I went to bed. Then, Saturday morning, I texted her, and she didn't answer. She never answered again."

"I see," Elise said. "I am truly sorry for your loss. Let me make that clear. But I've got to ask you some hard questions. When you had dinner with Skylar on Thursday, did you have any concerns about her well-being?"

"What do you mean?"

"Well, you gave a statement to the police after the fact that you'd witnessed Mickey and Skylar have an altercation, didn't you?"

"Yes," she said. "I already testified to all of this. I saw them get into a fight at the Blue Pony a few weeks before she died. She didn't talk to me for a long time after that. She made it pretty clear that if we were going to stay friends, she didn't want me bringing Mickey up. That dinner at Derby's was the first time I'd seen her in a really long time. I purposely avoided talking about Mickey with her."

"Let's get back to the night at the Blue Pony all those weeks ago. Remind me, you never heard what they were saying, Mickey and Skylar?"

"No," she said. "I just saw Mickey grab Skylar. He was rough. She was angry. I had my boyfriend, Chad, follow them out to the parking lot to make sure she was okay."

"Was she okay?" Elise asked.

"She was mad. But yes."

"And you don't claim you ever heard Mickey Harvey threaten Skylar, do you?"

"I don't ... I didn't hear him threaten to hurt her. No. But I told you. I saw him grab her arms. Really hard. And I didn't like how he treated her overall."

"Other than seeing Mickey grab Skylar by the arm at the Blue Pony, you never saw Mickey get physical with Skylar though, did you?"

"Like hurt her? No. But he was very possessive."

"Ms. Bosch, isn't it true that in fact you witnessed Skylar Sutter physically assault Mickey Harvey?" Elise asked.

"Um, well, I saw her slap him once. Across the face."

"Isn't it true that this slap you're talking about came about after Skylar threatened Mickey?"

"I don't know what you mean?" Sarah asked.

"All right. You were in the room and witnessed Skylar hit Mickey, right?"

"Yes," she said.

"What provoked it, if you know?"

Sarah looked at me. I kept my face a mask of neutrality. She had to tell the truth, no matter what.

"Skylar was drunk," Sarah said. "She ... she'd heard a rumor that Mickey had been out with another girl, Audrey Taylor. Skylar hated Audrey. She'd bullied her, well, both of us in high school. Anyway, Skylar confronted Mickey about it."

"She confronted him. Isn't it true she did more than confront him? Isn't it true Skylar threatened to kill Mickey if she found out there was any truth to this rumor?"

"Objection," I said. "Statements allegedly made by Skylar Sutter would constitute hearsay. The witness can testify to what she observed, her impressions, but not statements made by out-of-court declarants."

"Your Honor," Elise said. "It doesn't matter whether these statements were true. That's not why we'd offer them. It goes to Skylar Sutter's state of mind, nothing more."

"Sustained, Ms. Weaver. Ms. Bosch, you'll refrain from testifying about things Skylar Sutter told you or that you overheard."

"Ms. Bosch, describe what you saw," said Elise.

"Skylar was drinking. I told you. She wasn't acting like herself. She was upset. Mickey was laughing at her. Taunting her. Egging her on. Skylar just kind of lost it for a second. She slapped him."

"She drew blood, didn't she, Ms. Bosch?"

"She did," Sarah said. "With her fingernails across his face."

"Did Mickey react?" Elise asked.

"What do you mean?"

"Well, did he pull her away? Push her away? Grab her?"

"No," Sarah said. "He just ... he stood there."

"Stood there. So you're telling me that when Skylar Sutter physically assaulted Mickey Harvey, he did not respond in kind, isn't that right?"

"He didn't put his hands on her that night," Sarah said. "But I told you. I saw him get rough with her a few weeks after that at the Blue Pony."

"Ms. Bosch, are you aware of allegations made by members of Skylar Sutter's family against Skylar's father, Chris Sutter?"

Once again, Sarah looked at me. Once again, I kept my face blank.

"I know there was trouble," Sarah said. "I know there was something going on at home that had Skylar upset."

"And when was this?" Elise asked.

"Skylar came to spend part of Christmas break with me. She didn't ... she didn't want to be at home. There was drama when her cousin Nikki came home from Seattle. Skylar didn't want to deal with her. So she stayed with me for a few days."

"Do you know the nature of that drama?" Elise asked.

"You said I'm not allowed to say what Skylar told me," she said. "Isn't that right?"

"Did you ever personally witness any drama, as you describe it, between Skylar and, say, her cousin Nikki Sutter?"

"They weren't real close," Sarah said. "Like Skylar would always kind of roll her eyes or grit her teeth whenever anyone brought up Nikki. And she wasn't a huge fan of Kevin, Nikki's brother."

"Do you know why?" Elise asked.

"Well, Kevin could be volatile. I knew he had a drug problem. And it was sad. I'll have to admit. When we were younger, I had a pretty big crush on Kevin. We used to hang out over there when her Uncle Tom, Nikki and Kevin's dad, was alive. After he died, there was some kind of falling out."

"Ms. Bosch, I'm going to have to ask you one more time. Isn't it true that you witnessed a violent altercation between Skylar Sutter and her cousin, Nikki Sutter, in January of this year?"

"Objection," I said. "Once again, we have moved out of the realm of relevance. Nikki Sutter isn't on trial. Chris Sutter isn't on trial. There's no dispute that Nikki lived halfway across the country at the time of these killings."

"Your Honor," Elise said. "Once again, I need to remind the state that we are within our rights to explore other potential motives for this heinous crime. In light of the fact that none of these issues appear to have been explored in the investigation of these crimes ..."

"Save it for closing, Ms. Weaver," Denholm said. "I'm overruling the objection. You may answer the question."

"Yes," Sarah said. "There was an argument at Sky's house. I came over to pick her up. We were going to go return some stuff we got for Christmas. But it wasn't Nikki who was doing the yelling."

"Who was doing the yelling?" Elise asked.

"Nikki's boyfriend, Olliver. He had Sky's dad backed into a corner of the kitchen. They were all yelling. Nikki got in the middle of it and pulled Olliver away from Sky's dad. It was ugly."

"Isn't it true that Olliver Harrold, Nikki Sutter's boyfriend, threatened to kill Chris Sutter?"

"Objection," I yelled. My vision clouded. None of this. Nikki had told us none of this.

"Overruled," the judge shouted back.

"Yes," Sarah answered. "I heard Olliver tell Chris Sutter that he'd end him. Those were his words. I'll end you. We left after that."

"Thank you," Elise said. "I have nothing further. Your witness, Ms. Brent."

I shot up. "Ms. Bosch," I said. Fuming. Blood roared in my ears. "You were questioned by the police for two hours after Skylar Sutter's murder, isn't that true?"

"I don't know how long, but yes," she said.

"And you sat down for interviews with my office, isn't that true?"

"Yes."

"And yet you never once bothered to mention these allegations of threats by Olliver Harold, isn't that true?"

"It's Skylar's family business," she said. "It wasn't my place to ..."

"Not your place?" I said. "You came forward to tell

Detective Cruz about what you witnessed between the defendant and Skylar at the Blue Pony, isn't that right? That's how you initially became involved in this case, correct?"

"Yes," she said, crying.

I was flying blind. Running on emotion. I existed almost outside of myself. The reasonable, calculating part of me wanted to stop this. Get her off the stand. Regroup. But I kept on going.

"And you were aware that your friend Skylar Sutter was pursuing a restraining order against her boyfriend Mickey, isn't that true?"

"Yes," she said. "That's true. I was afraid for her."

"Why were you afraid?" I asked.

"Because Mickey's dangerous," she said. "He was controlling. Possessive. Skylar changed when she was around him. I already told you that. And things were getting worse. It got so she stopped taking my calls or texting me back when he was around. He'd get so jealous."

"Why was it getting worse?" I asked.

"Mickey freaked when Ben Watson moved in with Sky. Even though the two of them were not romantically involved at all. Ben wasn't interested in Sky that way. They were just friends. Mickey didn't care. He wanted Sky all to himself. And he did this. He killed her. There is no doubt in my mind."

"Objection!" Elise said. "Your Honor, the witness is not permitted to speculate in this manner. I ask that her response be stricken, and the jury admonished to disregard her last statement."

But they'd heard it. It was messy. Chaotic. But they'd heard it.

"Sustained," Denholm said. "Members of the jury, you're

to disregard statements made by this witness regarding her belief as to who killed Skylar Sutter."

"Your Honor," I said. "I have no further questions."

"Fine," Denholm said. "Then we'll adjourn for the weekend."

He banged his gavel. Sarah Bosch left the stand in near hysterics. I sank into my seat and tried to remember how to breathe.

I didn't get the chance. As I gathered my things, a text came in from Sam Cruz. Doyle Harvey had just succumbed to his injuries. We had one more murder on our hands.

❦ 34 ❧

I didn't make it home until well after midnight. I had met
Sam at headquarters as they processed Graham Sutter.
They'd picked the kid up blitzed out of his mind, trying to
leave town before the cavalry showed up. The media broke
news of Doyle Harvey's death. They swarmed the Sheriff's
Department. Sam worried it wasn't safe for me to head
straight home in case they followed me. So, he had me
dropped off in an unmarked car. Will was already asleep. I
crawled into bed beside him and neither of us woke until
almost ten the next morning.

Kat was downstairs making pancakes and bacon. I saw no
good reason to object when she offered to move in until the
trial ended. I'd left a trail of broken promises in my wake
about making it home by six.

"It's almost over," she said, flipping a perfectly executed
Mickey Mouse cake on Will's plate. He had one at Disney
when he was five and had been nuts for them ever since.

Will was quiet. As of this morning, the *Small-Town
Killers* podcast had entered the top ten for most downloaded

true crime shows in the country. He knew about Graham Harvey.

I helped Kat clean up the dishes as Will disappeared into the den. He had science homework he insisted he didn't need help on. At noon, he had a video call scheduled with Jason.

"He's been listening," I said to Kat over the running water.

"Yep," she said. "Mara, I don't know how to keep any of it from him. I think it's worse if I try."

"Yeah," I said.

She slid a plate into the drying rack and turned to me. "He's not worried about the Sutters or the Harveys, Mara. He's worried about you. He's afraid no matter what happens in that trial, that one side or the other is going to try to take it out on you."

"I know," I said.

"Mara," Kat said. "I'm worried about you. You're barely eating. You're not sleeping. Have you stepped on a scale lately?"

The question caught me off guard.

"I ... no," I said. "Kat, it's almost over. This time next week the jury will have this case. Then maybe we can get back to normal. I just ... thank you. My life just wouldn't work if you weren't here. I feel like you're the one constant in Will's life. You could have bailed on me. Jason's your brother."

"Stop," Kat said, raising a hand. "We're family, Mara. I love my brother. I'd like to brain him half the time. But I love Will more. Just don't tell either one of them. And I love you too. I'm where I want to be."

"Are you sure? Because I know Jason's offered to move you to D.C. I know he's still offering."

Kat went quiet. She didn't know I knew. Well, in truth, I didn't know for a fact. But I knew it was exactly the kind of thing Jason would have done.

"I'm staying put for now." She smiled. "Besides, you're not the only reason I have to stay in Waynetown."

I caught a blush in her cheeks.

"Oh, really?" I said, drying the last of the dishes. "You wanna tell me about it?"

"Maybe later," she said. "It's new. She's ..."

"Is it the girl from the coffee shop?" I asked.

"No," Kat said. "Ugh, that's so cliche. We met through a friend."

"Does she have a name?" I teased.

"Bree," she said. "And that's all I'll say. Don't dig."

"Oh, I'll dig," I said. "With a big ol' shovel. I have no life outside of Will and work, remember? I need something exciting to talk about."

Kat rolled her eyes and stepped around me.

We had an uneventful day after that. Will lit up, talking to Jason. They made plans for the holiday break. I got Will Christmas Eve, then he and Kat were flying to D.C. after Christmas morning. He'd spend New Year's out there and come back the Saturday before school started.

Later, Will asked for sliders. There was only one place in town to go for them. Kat came along and I begged her to invite this Bree.

"If she can leave work early enough," Kat said.

"So what does she do?" I pried. "That she's working past dinner on a Saturday?"

"You're worse than your mother," Kat said as we pulled into the Blue Pony. We had reservations at six.

"How dare you!" I feigned indignation. Will ran ahead of us. He liked the pinball machines and wanted to play while we waited for our food.

We asked for a table in the center of the restaurant. All the booths were taken. I saw the back of a familiar head at the bar. Sam sat nursing a beer. There was a woman sitting beside him I didn't recognize. She laughed at something he said. He saw me come in and his eyes lit up. I waved as Kat and I made our way to the table. Will was already in the game room with a stack of quarters in his pocket. I sat on the side of the table so I could keep my eye on him.

"Looks like he'll be busy for a while," I said to Kat.

"So," she said. "What about Christmas?"

"What about it?" I said.

"Well, Will and I will be in D.C. with Jason. Your mother usually heads down to Palm Springs. So, where will you be?"

I smiled. "Don't worry about me."

"I do worry," she said.

"I'll be fine," I reassured her. "I'm spending Christmas Eve with my son and part of Christmas morning. That's all I need."

Kat shook her head. "In that big house all by yourself. What about New Year's Eve?"

"I'll figure it out, Kat. Promise. Don't worry about me."

"Hmm," she said.

We ordered our burgers. Kat got a glass of wine. I stuck with water. The dinner rush poured in. I heard Will let out a gleeful shout as he worked the knobs on the pinball machine. The thing was old and Magnum P.I. themed, the original version.

"You ought to get one of those things in the rec room," Kat said.

"Just what I need." I laughed. "You really want that noise all evening?"

"Good point."

A commotion drew my attention to the bar. A group of men started shouting at Sam, recognizing him. He rose and said something to the woman sitting with him. Her face fell.

"Trouble?" Kat asked.

"Wouldn't surprise me," I answered. The shouting drew Will's attention. He'd run out of quarters. He turned away from the pinball machine and made his way over to Kat and me. "Food will be here in a few minutes," I told him. I'd ordered him a lemonade with a curly straw. He climbed into his seat and took a sip.

"That's Detective Cruz," he said.

"It is," I answered.

"They're trying to say he didn't pursue enough leads with the Sutter family," Will said, louder than I cared. It drew a few looks our way.

"Shh." I put a finger to my lips. "Never mind what kind of gossip you hear, Will. Detective Cruz is very good at his job."

He was also off duty. I looked around the bar. Two other off-duty deputies sat at one of the high tops. They noticed the group of men harassing Sam and left their seats.

"Maybe we should get our sliders to go?" Kat asked.

"I'm not done playing!" Will protested.

"It's okay," I said. Thankfully, it looked like the men were backing down.

"I think that's Denny Harvey," Kat said as the server brought our tray of food. "He's a cousin or second cousin of Mickey's. Ed's nephew's kid, I think."

"They're everywhere," I said, taking a bite of my burger. "I never realized how deeply Harveys and Sutters were embedded in this town."

"I go to school with Sierra Harvey," Will added. "Mickey's her cousin too. She says she thinks he did it. She says her mom calls him a douchebag."

"Will!" Kat and I spoke together.

"Sorry," he said. "I'm just reporting the facts."

The group moved off. Sam caught my eye above the

crowd. He gave me a wink. I waved back. He turned to talk to his date.

"Is that his girlfriend?" Will asked.

"I wouldn't know," I said, dipping my fries in ketchup.

"Because he keeps looking at you," he said. "Ms. Digby, my speech therapist, says it's rude to pay attention to someone else when someone's talking to you. You're supposed to keep looking at the person who's talking to you. I bet that girl thinks he's being rude."

Kat giggled over her fries. I narrowed my eyes at her. Will wolfed down four sliders, then started attacking his French fries.

A little while later, Paula Dudley, the owner of the Blue Pony, came out from behind the bar. Backed by two bouncers, she politely asked the group of Harveys to leave.

I braced myself, waiting for one of them to protest. I read lips well enough to see one call Paula something nasty. But all four of them rose together and headed for the front of the bar.

"I have to go to the bathroom," Will proclaimed and popped out of his seat.

"Oh no, you don't. I'll go with you," I said. No way I was letting him out of my sight with Sutters and Harveys and tempers swirling around.

"Gross, Mom," he said.

"I mean, I'll wait outside for you."

I had a bad feeling. The restrooms were toward the front of the restaurant where I couldn't see Will coming and going.

"Be right back," I said to Kat.

We weaved our way through the tables, toward the game room and the front of the restaurant. They were small, one-stall restrooms, and the door was locked when we went there. I tried the woman's door. It was open.

"No way," Will said. "I'm not going in there."

I opened my mouth to argue but saw the better of it. The look on my son's face told me I'd be wasting my breath.

So we waited. The noise from the pinball machine drew Will's eyes.

"Nice moves!" Will exclaimed as he watched a teenage boy work the levers. Shaking my head, I couldn't believe Kat actually thought having one of those things off my living room was a good idea. Beside it, the Pac-Man machine lit up and thumped away as a new player took the controls.

The door opened and Will scooted into the men's room. The Pac-Man player ran into a spot of bad luck and the lilting, electronic sound of failure reached my ear. I could barely hear myself think.

I could barely hear myself think.

I turned toward the bar. From this short hallway, I could see half of it. Sam's back was to me. He leaned in to hear whatever his date was saying. He shook his head, unable. She put a hand on his shoulder to repeat herself.

The pinball machine lit up as the teenage player hit the jackpot.

It's all I could hear. I felt the blood rush from my head and settle somewhere south of my knees.

It's all I could hear.

And now, I could barely bring myself to breathe.

"What's wrong, Mom?" Will said. He had to shout it.

Sam caught my eye. His eyes narrowed in question. He would ask me if I was okay, just like Will had.

My answer to both of them would be no. I was very much not okay.

🐝 35 🐝

"Kat," I said, taking two twenty-dollar bills out of my purse. "Can you take Will home?"

After finishing his sliders, he'd gone back to play pinball. If we let him, he'd be occupied for hours.

"Of course," she said. "But how are you going to get home?"

"I'll worry about that later," I said. "There's something I need to do."

It wasn't quite judgment in Kat's eyes, but deep concern. I knew what she thought. It wasn't like me to bail on my son. I would make it up to him. If he knew my reason why, Will would tell me to go. I was as sure of that as anything else.

Kat knew me well enough not to press me further. I said goodbye and weaved my way back to the bar. Sam sat alone now, his companion having gone to the restroom herself or something.

"Sam," I said. "I need you."

His eyes widened and the hint of a smirk settled on his face. "Well, I ..."

"He's lying," I said. "Jody Doehler's been lying."

"What now?" Sam said, sliding off his bar stool.

"You questioned him. We both did. He said he was waiting in line at the bathrooms. That's when he heard Mickey threaten to kill Skylar Sutter. Twice he testified he heard Mickey tell her he'd put her in the ground. Only he couldn't have. You can't hear anything over there except video games and pinball machines."

"Mara, what are you talking about?"

"See ... or rather, hear for yourself."

I tugged on Sam's sleeve and had him walk with me to the restrooms. He nodded to the bartender, gesturing for his check.

I pulled harder.

"I'm coming," Sam said. "Mercy, woman. What's gotten into you?"

I got him to the short hallway leading to the restrooms. The electronic pulse of the Pac-Man machine ramped up beside us. Underneath that, someone had just started shooting ducks on the hunter's arcade game of it.

"Stay here," I said. I walked over to the bar and sat at the end where Jody said he saw Skylar and Mickey. I picked the stool closest to the bathroom hallway.

I turned to Sam, cupped my hand on one side of my mouth and shouted. "Twinkle, twinkle, little star, how I wonder what you are."

The guy sitting next to me turned and, reasonably, looked at me as if I'd sprouted horns.

"Up above the world so bright?" I said. He shook his head and turned back to his beer.

I walked back to Sam.

"Could you hear me?" I asked him. "What did I say?"

Sam's expression wasn't much different from the guy at the bar.

"You don't know, do you? Admit it."

Sam put his hands up in surrender. "No. I couldn't hear what you were saying."

"I was practically shouting," I said. In fact, I had to do almost that for Sam to hear me as we were standing right next to each other. He leaned in so he could hear me.

"Come here," I said. I tugged on his sleeve and he followed me out of the bar and into the parking lot.

My ears were still ringing from the noise.

"He's lying," I said again. "There is no way Jody Doehler could have heard what he said he did. Not here. Not in that bathroom line."

"Mara," Sam said. "It's busy in there tonight. How do you know whether anyone was playing in the game room?"

"It was a Sunday night," I said. "And when have you ever been to the Pony when it wasn't just as loud as that? Plus, that was the April Fool's bash. Dollar pitchers. It was probably twice as packed as tonight. And we just had to come outside to have a normal conversation. Jody was particular in what he said. Both when you interviewed him and when he testified. But it's a lie. He just flat out couldn't have heard Mickey threaten Skylar like that."

Sam gritted his teeth. "It doesn't mean ..."

"No," I said. "I know. It doesn't prove Mickey didn't kill Skylar. I believe he did. But I think we need to talk to Jody Doehler again. Now."

"This isn't up to you," he said. "Jody was cross-examined. Well, I might add. I was in that courtroom, Mara. Elise Weaver's already blown some holes in his credibility. Mickey's guilt doesn't hinge on Jody's story. Plus, it wasn't just Jody's story. Chad Carmichael and Sarah Bosch said they saw an altercation between them too. The same exact night, Mara."

"I don't know. I'm not saying it all makes sense. But I can't ignore this, Sam," I said. "I have a duty. So do you."

Exasperated, he shook his head. "What exactly are you proposing we do? You wanna call Elise Weaver and tell her how to win her case? She doesn't need your help. She's got Judge Denholm helping her out enough."

"Tell me you think I'm wrong," I said.

He took a step back and looked at the stars as if they could talk some sense into me.

"Say it," I said. "Go back in there and see what you can hear. Put yourself in Jody's position. Think about it. Chad and Sarah never said they saw Jody here. We all just assumed he was telling the truth. Something's wrong. I feel it. Sam, who came to you first with the story about the Blue Pony? Chad and Sarah or Jody?"

He reared back. "Chad called me. I'd have to look at my notes, but I think Jody called me the next day."

"Something's not right. Could he have known? Could Jody have known about Chad and Sarah's statement somehow? Then he just backed it up because he thought it would help? Sam, please. Go in there. Tell me what you hear."

I swear, steam started coming out of Sam's nose. He paced in front of me. I held my ground. Raising my finger, I pointed to the front doors.

"Fine," Sam finally said, storming off toward the entrance.

I waited. It was freezing. I'd left my coat on the rack near our table. A minute passed. Then another. It took almost fifteen before Sam came back out.

A car pulled up beside me. An Uber driver. Shivering, I went back into the bar. The door flew open and Sam's date came charging out, her expression reading red murder. She climbed into the back of the car.

Sam followed her a few seconds later.

"Oh," I said. "I'm sorry. I didn't mean ..."

Sam waved toward the driver. His date responded with a middle finger as the car turned and headed toward the street.

"Yikes,' I said. "I really am sorry. She seems ... um ... she seems nice."

Sam waved it off. "Don't get me started."

"Well?" I said.

"Well what?" Sam grumbled.

"Well, what do you think?"

He scowled. In the dim light with his dark hair and features, he looked downright devilish.

"Son of a ... I think you're right. I think Jody Doehler is full of it. He couldn't hear a thing in there if he was at the Blue Pony that night at all."

I had ... feelings. I couldn't really sort out whether it was relief or dread. Both, actually.

"So now what?" I asked.

"Now," he said, "I go have a chat with Jody Doehler."

"Good," I said. "I'm going with you."

"Mara ..."

"Non-negotiable. Plus, you're my ride now."

Sam made a noise. An actual growl. But he waited as I went inside to get my coat.

❧ 36 ❧

Jody Doehler lived with his grandmother on the outskirts of town, a ramshackle ranch with crooked shutters and more lawn art than grass.

"Why don't you stay in the car?" Sam pleaded.

'No way," I said. "You don't have a warrant or anything. It's better for both of us if I stay close."

"I don't need a warrant to talk to the kid," he said.

There were two vehicles in the driveway. A blue Dodge Caravan and an old F-250 with a flat tire. The truck was Jody's. I'd seen it parked at Georgette Sutter's the day I went out to her house.

I pulled my coat around me as Sam and I trudged up the uneven paving stones. He rapped on the screen door, causing two large dogs into a round of deep-throated barks. Decades of instinct kicked in and Sam moved his hand to his right hip. He was carrying. He was always carrying.

"Shut your yap!" a creaky female voice called out. She got a hold of the dogs and opened the storm door. Squinting up, she tried to recognize Sam.

"I'm Detective Sam Cruz," he said. "This is Mara Brent.

We were hoping to catch Jody Doehler at home. Your grandson?"

She had maybe twenty strands of wavy gray hair on her entire head. She had a cigarette dangling from her lip. She took it out and pointed it to her left.

"He ain't here much," she said. "Spends most of his time up at *her* place."

"Her?" I asked.

"My sister," she said. "Though she likes to say HALF."

"Mrs. Doehler," I said. "You mean Georgette Sutter? Your son is up at the Sutter residence?"

"Most of the time," she said. "Look at this place. Paint peeling. Crap all over the driveway. You know my washer hasn't been working for two weeks? Says he's waiting for a part. Pff. He's got me schlepping down to the laundromat while he's out there cleaning her windows, taking her shopping, wiping her ass, for all I know."

I winced.

"I really need to speak with Jody," Sam said. "Do you have any idea when he might be back? Isn't that his truck parked out front?"

"That piece of crap? That's what he left for me. My van needs a new alternator. Said he'd fix that too when he got around to it. I can't get up in that cab. I'm waiting on a hip replacement. Thinks he's doing me some kind of favor. He's such a fool."

"Why is that, Mrs. Doehler?" I asked.

"Thinks he's gonna get rich when my sister croaks. Now that *her* grandson kicked it. And that weird granddaughter of hers heading back to whatever fancy house she has. My sister ain't gonna leave Jody a cent. And he'll come crawling back here."

"Mrs. Doehler," Sam said. "Do you get the impression your grandson would do anything to make Georgette happy?"

"Like a puppy," she said. Livia Doehler put her hands up under her chin as if she were a begging dog. "You find him, you tell him he's got work to do here! What do you want to talk to him about, anyway?"

"Well," I said. "You're aware Jody is a material witness in the case against Mickey Harvey?"

"Got his name in the paper," she said. "Yeah. I'm aware. They said there was gonna be a reward for information leading to the arrest. Well, you arrested that kid. Thug, that one. You know I dated his grandpa a lotta years ago? Almost married him too. Should have. Boy, that would've sent Louie's family into a state. Anyway, the reward. Said ten thousand. I want you to know. Jody hasn't paid a dime of rent since he was eighteen. That was supposed to be the deal."

"What deal?" Sam and I said it together.

"I'm just saying. Your material witness. If he's eligible for that ten grand. I want a lien on it or something. Who do I talk to about that?"

"Mrs. Doehler," Sam said. "Do you think Jody would have made up a story in order to get reward money in the Sutter murders?"

"Wouldn't put it past him," she said.

"Mrs. Doehler," he said. "Would you have a problem if we looked around your house a little? Does Jody have a computer here?"

I could see Sam's wheels turning. Mine were too. Could Jody have actually fabricated his entire story to please Georgette Sutter or to get a reward?

"I don't care what you do," she said. "But you tell that good-for-nothing grandson of mine he owes me."

"Sam," I said, tugging on his arm.

"Wait one second, Mrs. Doehler," he said, giving her a charming smile.

"Sam," I whispered when we were out of earshot. "What are you thinking?"

"I'm thinking there's more to Jody's story than he's letting on."

"Me too," I said. "But I can't let you into that house without a warrant."

"She owns it," he said. "She's consented. I want to get a look at his computer. See what kind of searches he's been running. Also his phone, see where he's been."

"I don't want any loose ends," I said. "She may own the house, but Jody's got a right to privacy to his room. She just said she charges him rent. Any half-good defense lawyer would argue that makes him a tenant."

"Fine," he said. "I'll write one up."

"Good," I said. "I'll help you get it through. In the meantime, I want to talk to Grandma George one more time."

37

"It's not a good time," Nikki Sutter said the next morning. She stood in the doorway, blocking my entrance.

"Nikki," I said. "I'm not here to go over your testimony. Though I'll admit, I wish you'd told me beforehand what you revealed on the stand."

"I didn't know it would come up. How could I know she'd ask me about all of that? Besides, you didn't ask," she said, casting her eyes down. She looked gaunt. Her cheekbones cut sharp angles beneath her hollow eyes. The trial, perhaps staying here, was taking its toll. It was almost as if Waynetown itself began to eat away at her.

"No," I said. "I didn't ask. But Detective Cruz and I both were after information about who might have had an axe to grind with the people who died down the hill."

"I won't apologize," she said. "That was my truth to tell. I don't know how that woman knew what my Uncle Chris did. And what did it matter? Skylar's dead. Uncle Chris, Aunt Jenny, they were all dead. It doesn't matter. I just wanted to forget about all of it. This family has been through enough. My grandparents have been through enough. Our business is out there. On the news. The internet. In that podcast. They're taking my trauma ... *my* trauma and using it to sell ads."

It was hard not to get angry. I was frustrated, yes. At the same time, Nikki Sutter was a victim herself. I worried Elise had only scratched the surface of the abuse Chris Sutter may have subjected her to. I wished I'd known. I would have fought for her. I would have done everything within my power to make sure the man who hurt her faced justice.

"Olliver, my boyfriend. He's scared," she said. "A private investigator called his work. You know, to verify that he was actually at work the day before the murders. Is that woman going to try to make it sound like Olliver flew back here and murdered my uncle and my brother? He was halfway across the country ..."

Nikki took a breath, as if she were revving up to lose it. I put a hand on the door. "No," I said. "She can say all she wants. I don't think there's any real threat of Olliver getting dragged into it. But Nikki, I'm not here about any of that. I'd like to talk to your grandmother again."

"She wants to talk to you too," Nikki said. "She just finished taking Grandpa Lou's breakfast tray. He's been agitated. In and out. He thought I was her last night. I guess I kind of look like Grandma George when she was younger."

"I don't want to cause them stress," I said. "Oh, also, is your cousin Jody here? I have a few additional questions for him too."

A few minutes before I arrived, Sam texted to tell me he'd gotten Judge Ivey out of bed. He'd signed his warrant for Jody's laptop. He expected to serve it within the hour.

"I haven't seen him," Nikki said. "He might be on the grounds somewhere. You can ask Grandma."

"Ask me what?" Georgette said. She walked down the

hall. Nikki moved to the side. Georgette had a dish towel in her hands. She tossed it over one shoulder.

"Can I bother you for a few minutes?" I asked.

"You're never a bother." Georgette smiled. "Nikki, don't be rude. Let Mara in. Lou just finished his coffee. I've got half a pot on. You want?"

"I'm fine," I said. "And I won't take up your whole morning."

"Get in here," she said. "You're lettin' all the cold air in."

I came in. Georgette proceeded to grab the shoulders of my coat and help me get it off. She gave it to Nikki and made a shooing gesture to her. Nikki took my coat and headed for a hall closet. Georgette looped her arm through mine and led me into the front room. Lou Sutter sat in his recliner with a TV tray in front of him. He had an old episode of the *Price Is Right* with Bob Barker on.

"You can stream those now," Georgette said. "He'll spend the whole day watching the game show channel. It keeps him calm. *Family Feud* is his favorite. Though I always found Richard Dawson creepy."

"I'm glad," I said. "That it keeps him calm."

Georgette showed me to one couch. She took a seat on the other end of it.

"You sure I can't get you something? You look skinnier than the last time I saw you."

"No," I said. "Thank you. I'm fine."

"You worried?" she asked.

"About the trial?" I said.

"That lawyer Mickey's got. She sure stirred up a storm."

"She has," I said. "And she shouldn't have been permitted to. To be frank, Judge Denholm has allowed a lot of testimony in that I don't believe he should have."

I looked down the hall, but Nikki was nowhere to be seen.

"He shouldn't have allowed the jury to hear things about what may have gone on between your nephew and Nikki."

Georgette's eyes glistened. She stared off into space for a moment.

"I'm sorry," I said. "I cannot begin to fathom how difficult this year has been for you."

"She should have told us," Georgette said. "Or I should have seen it. That's something I'm going to have to figure out how to live with."

"Georgette," I said. "There's something I need to ask you about. I have some concerns about another witness. Can we talk about Jody Doehler?"

"Jody?" she said. "What's he done?"

"Nothing. Well, there are some ... discrepancies in his story that I'm trying to clear up."

"What kind of discrepancies?" she asked.

"Georgette, you're aware Jody provided critical testimony about Mickey and Skylar's relationship."

Georgette reached for her own cup of coffee and took a sip. "He said he heard that little bastard threaten to kill my niece. He wasn't the only one."

"Actually, he was," I said. "We have other witnesses who saw Mickey get physical with Skylar. But Jody's the one who said he expressly heard Mickey threaten to kill her. I'd like to talk to him more about that claim. I may have to call him back to the stand."

"Jody's a little soft in the head sometimes," she said. "He's a good boy when he does what he's told. That sister of mine could never keep him out of trouble. That fell to Louie and me. Isn't that right, honey?"

Lou Sutter had a finger pointed at the television. "I don't know how that wheel doesn't knock more of these idiots in the head. I saw it do that once. Funniest damn thing ..." He chuckled to himself.

"Have you seen Jody today?" I asked. "Nikki thought maybe he'd come down to do some work for you."

"He's down at C.J.'s house," she said. "I've been thinking of letting him live there. Patty's daughter doesn't want anything to do with it. She said she'd sell it to me. Nikki owns Kevin's house. I'd like it if she moved in. I want to keep an eye on her after all of this."

I had a feeling that was the last thing Nikki needed. Waynetown wasn't good for her. She'd moved on, put the trauma of her younger years with Chris Sutter behind her. Now, I hoped guilt wouldn't tie her here when all was said and done.

"Georgette," I said. "I have to ask you something. Do you mind if I'm blunt about it?"

"I wish you would be," she said.

"Jody," I said. "Is it possible, that is, can you think of a reason he might have lied about what he heard between Mickey and Skylar?"

"What do you mean, lied?"

"Well," I said. "I'm no longer convinced he actually overheard Mickey threaten to kill Skylar. Where he said it happened doesn't track. There's a bit of a hole in his story."

"You think he lied?"

"I think I have more questions than answers about his story now," I said.

"Does that woman know that?" Georgette said. "His lawyer?"

"I don't know what she knows," I said. "I'm just trying to make sure I prepare for every contingency. I believe Mickey's lawyer is going to rest her case soon. If there's any chance Jody was lying, I need to talk to him. I need to know why."

"You think she's gonna win, don't you?" Georgette said. She went still.

"Like I said, I'm just trying to cover all of my bases."

"Four thousand!" Lou shouted at the television. "She's out of her damn mind. That Lincoln alone is worth four thousand."

He batted his hand at the screen and turned his recliner toward the window. Bob Barker told a hapless contestant from Kenosha, Wisconsin, that she'd overbid the Showcase Showdown by over three grand.

"Grandma." Nikki came around the corner. "I'm heading into town to meet a friend. Can I bring anything back for you and Gramps? I can hit the grocery store."

"We're good, honey," Georgette said. "You have a good time."

"Call me if you think of anything," Nikki said. She gave me a wave, then left through the front door.

"So, Jody," I said. "Do you know where I might find him? I need to talk to him about his testimony."

"I don't understand," she said. "If he was lying, what does that have to do with you? Isn't that the other lady's problem?"

"I just want to talk to him," I said. "That's all. If he's called back to the stand, he needs to be prepared."

"Are you going to call him back?" she asked.

"I'm not sure."

"Hmm. Well, I just don't see the point in any of it. Mickey's going to jail. I was in that courtroom too. I saw that jury. They think he did it. Don't you worry, honey. You're doing a good job. I think God put you into our path for a reason. I think my Kevin is looking down, and he's smiling, knowing you're in his corner. And he's right there next to his daddy, my Thomas. You know, that's what gives me peace. Knowing Thomas and Kevin are together."

It was then I noticed the new portrait on the wall next to Thomas Sutter and baby Tina. Kevin Sutter's picture hung beside them. Georgette had lit three candles beneath them.

"I appreciate the vote of confidence," I said. "But I really do need to talk to Jody again. If you see him ..."

"Oh, I'm sure he'll make his way up here sometime today," she said. "You want me to call you when he does?"

I rose to leave. "That would be helpful, yes. Only, would you mind not telling him what we talked about?"

She shrugged. "If you don't want me to, honey, I won't."

She put a hand on my back. "Don't you worry. I told you. I had a feeling about you the day we met. It's all going to work out. My advice to you? Eat something. You're skin and bones."

I laughed. "I'll try."

"Wait here," she said. "I'll go fetch your coat."

She walked out of the living room, leaving me alone with Lou Sutter. He had a far-off expression in his eyes. I could hear Georgette humming as she walked down the hall.

An awkward moment passed. Lou's program had ended and the TV went dark.

"How are you doing today, Mr. Sutter?" I asked.

He didn't answer. He just kept staring out the large bay window, watching as Nikki's car rounded the drive and disappeared down the hill.

"Always telling everyone what to do," Lou said.

I looked behind me, then back toward the hallway. It was just the two of us.

"Rosemary always said she'd end up killing them all," Lou said. "She will too. That one's got a mind of her own. Tried to spread her wings. She's got 'em clipped now. Poor kid."

He seemed here and not here. Did he mean Nikki? I'd thought the same myself. She'd spread her wings and flown to

Seattle. Now, with the murders and the trial, she might never fly back there.

"Rosemary?" I asked. I envisioned the Sutter family tree I had taped to one wall of my office. Lou's older brother Ray had married a woman named Rosemary. But she'd died decades ago. Did he think Nikki was Rosemary?

"She'll say they deserved it," he said. "She's probably right. But maybe that's not for us to decide, isn't that right, kid?"

He looked straight at me now and gave me a quick wink.

"She?" I asked. "Mr. Sutter ..."

He reached into the side pocket of his recliner. He brought his hand out. For a split second, I thought he was holding a remote control. Then, the metal gleamed in the sunlight coming through the window.

It was a handgun. A small, semi-automatic. My memory flashed to the pictures of the nine-millimeter Luger Will once showed me as he hypothesized about the Sutter Seven murder weapon. No. It couldn't be.

"Mr. Sutter!" I shouted. I'd been here before. Early last year, I'd stood in my boss's office as he pulled out a similar gun and pointed it straight at me.

No. Not again.

"Mr. Sutter," I said. "Let me take that from you."

"Better not do that," he said. "You don't want to get your fingerprints all over it."

It was then I noticed he covered the handle of the gun with a small blue handkerchief. He turned it, pointing the barrel away from me, then lifted it. He stayed stock still as I took the gun out of his hands.

"Better hurry," he said. "Before she comes back."

"Where ... where did you get this?" I asked.

"She tried to bury it out behind the woodpile in the back

of the house," he said. "She doesn't think I go back there anymore. I go where I want."

"She," I said. My brain was still trying to catch up with what my eyes were seeing.

"Georgie! That boy will do anything for her," Lou said. "If Jody's lying, it's to save Georgie's skin. She told me he'd be too dumb to figure out what to do with that thing. But she went too far this time. If she'd left Kevin alone ... but she didn't. She's gone too far this time. You understand? I should have listened. We all should have listened. Rosemary was right. My wife will be the death of us all."

I heard Georgette Sutter's lilting voice as she sang an old standard. Her footsteps drew closer. I slipped the wrapped pistol in my purse and took out my phone.

Sam, thank God, answered right away.

"I need you," I said. "Get a crew out to Lou Sutter's. And hurry!"

Georgette rounded the corner and held out my coat for me.

❧ 38 ❧

Georgette Sutter asked for two things when Sam brought her into the interrogation room. A cup of tea, and for me to sit right next to her.

"No sugar, honey," she said to Deputy Remick. "I don't like any of that stuff."

I saw myself in the large, one-way mirror on the opposite wall. No make-up. My hair pulled into a ponytail. I wore a pair of leggings and an oversized cardigan. I hadn't gone to Georgette's expecting to be here today. I hadn't expected any of this.

"Mrs. Sutter," I said. "I want to reiterate; you have a right to have your own lawyer present. Do you understand that?"

"Of course I understand it," she said. "I signed your paperwork. Let's get on with this. I've got a pot roast in. Nikki's no good in the kitchen. Lou won't eat it if it's too dry."

Sam caught my eye. He knew what I was thinking, and a subtle sweeping gesture from him told me what was on his mind.

Not now. Let her keep thinking she'll be home in time for dinner.

"Mrs. Sutter," Sam said. He had two pads of paper in front of him. One for his own notes, one for Georgette if she was willing to put her statement in writing.

"I waive my right to an attorney," she said. "I want to talk. It's about time. Ask me your questions."

She caught her own look in the mirror and smoothed an errant hair behind her ear. She wore a pink-and-white tracksuit with a flower pattern on the collar. She straightened it and adjusted her glasses. It dawned on me she relished the attention.

"Mrs. Sutter," he said. "Your husband produced a gun and gave it to Ms. Brent today. We're going to test it. Am I going to find your fingerprints on it?"

"I suspect you will," she sighed. "It's mine. Nice one, isn't it? Smith and Wesson. M&P Shield. I've had it for years. Lou got that one for me for Christmas. I've got a permit for that. It's sad, but I had to be able to protect myself when I was in the bait shop by myself. It made Louie feel better. Got so used to carrying it around. I kinda miss it now."

"Mrs. Sutter," Sam said. "It will take a day or two for our ballistics testing to come back, but that same type of weapon was used in the shootings of your family members on May 18th."

She stared blankly at him.

"Mrs. Sutter," he said. "If you know something about what happened that day, it's better if you came out with it now. There won't be any denying the science if that gun comes back as a match for the murder weapon. We'll know. We have the bullets that came out of the gun that day. Each gun leaves unique markings when those bullets are fired. If ..."

"I know all of that," she said. "I watch *CSI*. I'm not an idiot."

Sam sat back. "So what do you want to tell me?"

She pursed her lips and shook her head. "That little, soft-headed idiot. Did you find him?"

"Jody?" I asked. "You mean Jody Doehler?"

"He had one job!" she shouted. "One. I told him to do what I said. But no, he couldn't keep his mouth shut. I knew it. *Knew* it. The second those kids came over I knew it would be trouble."

"What kids?" Sam asked.

"You mean Chad Carmichael and Sarah Bosch?" I asked. "They came to see you. After the murders."

She nodded. "They wanted my forgiveness. Can you believe that? Crying their eyes out about seeing Mickey get rough with Skylar that night and not saying anything to anybody else. Came over here acting like they were trying to see if *I* was all right. What they really wanted was for me to tell them it was okay they didn't do more to help her get away from that little monster."

"And Jody overheard." Sam filled in the blanks. "He heard them tell you about that night at the Blue Pony."

"I knew it," she said. "Tried to get him out of the room. Saw his wheels turning. Then he had to make up some dumb story about hearing Mickey Harvey threatening to kill poor Skylar too. You didn't need it. I knew it was going to cause me trouble. I've tried with that boy. You know, my sister wrote Jody off years ago. If she'd just shown him just the tiniest bit of affection. He's a special case. A good boy at heart. He just ... I don't know. I guess they call it ADD or whatever the P.C. police say. He just can't focus. You have to keep him busy. That's the key. Give him jobs to do. You let him stay idle, he gets into trouble. That's what I told Thomas about Kevin. Those two were a lot alike. I should have stepped in more than I did. I didn't want to get in between a father and his son. That was a mistake. I know it now."

"Mrs. Sutter," Sam said. "I spoke to you the day after the shootings out at the farm. Do you remember that?"

"Of course," she snapped. "I told you, I'm not an idiot."

"Okay," he said. "You told me you were at home the morning of the 18th. You told me you got up at seven and were cooking breakfast for Lou. Was that true?"

She folded her hands and rested them on the table. "You need to understand how much I did for Kevin. How much Lou did for Kevin. His own mother abandoned him. Ran off to Seattle with Nikki. He had nobody but us looking out for him. We handed him that business. Gave him a future. A purpose. He promised me he'd turn his life around."

"You mean his drug problem," I said.

"Well, of course, honey. What else would I mean? Karen, Thomas's wife. Nikki's mom. She was too permissive. Let those two kids get away with everything. Spare the rod, spoil the child. All that. Do you know how much money we spent putting that boy in fancy clinics trying to get him to kick those drugs? Thousands of dollars so he could take yoga classes and find inner peace. Fat lot of good it did. Oh, and he was a liar. Such a good one. Said he'd take care of me. We gave that business to him so he could carry it into the next generation. Not so he could sell it off to some pot dealer. That really broke my heart. He owed me. You know what we sold that place to him for? Fifty grand. It was a gift."

"Kevin never offered to give you a piece of the sale to Verde, did he?" I asked.

"He did not," she said. "Not that I would have touched it. That's dirty money. Sold his soul to the devil. You know how much I've had to hear from people in town about that? He didn't even ask. Didn't say, Grandma George, what do you think about this? I would have told him. Would have set him straight. I made that business what it was. When I married

Louie, they were only selling worms pretty much. It was my vision. I did all the legwork and the bookkeeping. Got the billboard on I-75. Put out flyers. It was my idea to expand the general store."

Lou Sutter's words came back to me. He said Rosemary Sutter always said she would be the death of them all. I wondered how well Lou's brothers and their wives took to Georgette telling them all what to do with their family business. The thing was, she was right. She had turned the bait shop and general store into a lucrative Maumee County staple.

"Lies," she said. "Lies after lies after lies, Kevin would tell. I gave him so many chances."

"It's part of the disease," I said.

"Oh, spare me," she said. "I don't want to hear that crap. That boy never had to face the consequences of his actions. Karen, his mama, always carried his water. I knew she wasn't the right girl for my Thomas."

"Mrs. Sutter," Sam said. "Tell me what happened the morning of the 18th of May. Did you go down to talk to Kevin?"

"Wanted to see if he'd lie to me again," she said. "I saw him with Mickey Harvey over at the car wash on Baldwin street. I'm not an idiot. I know what they were doing. I know they sell drugs over there. Piece of trash, that boy. Just like his old man. Just like that whole family."

"You're saying you knew Mickey was selling drugs to Kevin?" I asked.

"Damn right I did," she said. "So I had Jody drive me out there. I wasn't going to stand for any more lies. I'd had enough. Sure enough, I saw that little thug's car in Kevin's driveway. Right there. Under my nose. On Sutter property. I knew why he was there. I knew what Kevin was doing."

"What happened when you confronted Kevin?" I asked.

"Same as always happened," she said. "He lied. He said Grandma, it was just the one time. He swore to God. Can you believe that? It's bad enough he lied to *my* face."

"What did you do next?" Sam asked.

"Told him I wasn't going to stand for it. Told him how ashamed his father would be. I told him I wanted him off the property. Let his mother figure out what to do about him."

"What did he do?" I asked.

"That little ... he laughed at me. Called me names I won't repeat. He told me he did the family a favor by getting rid of the store. He had the nerve ..."

She hiccupped. Tears filled her eyes. Sam was quick with a box of tissues and slid them across the table.

"He ... he said my Thomas didn't like working at the store. That he only did it to please me. He said Thomas and Karen were planning on selling their shares and moving far away. It was a lie. I know it. My baby would have never done something like that. Kevin said Thomas hated me. Can you believe that? He said my baby boy hated his own mama."

"You got angry," Sam said.

She nodded. "It was so hurtful. So vile. He said my Lou was in on it. That they were all trying to figure out a way to tell me. Then Thomas had his accident. Now why would he say all those things?"

"What happened next, Mrs. Sutter?" Sam asked.

"I threw the book at him. The literal book. Thomas always kept a Bible on the table in the front hallway. You know that was his house before Kevin got it. Lou and I built it for our son. I threw it at Kevin. I'm not proud of that. Then Kevin ... he came at me. Told me it was his property, and I wasn't welcome on it. I could see it in his eyes. He was high. Strung out. I saw the track marks on his arms and I knew.

There was no helping him. He was going to kill himself, and then I'd have the shame of that on our family name. So ... I just ... I did him a favor. I put that hateful boy out of his misery."

"So we're clear," I said. "You're telling us you shot Kevin?"

"He was beyond saving," she said. "You don't know what he put Thomas and Karen through. Time and time again. There was no help for him. And he showed me the evil in his heart. I did what I had to do."

Sam pressed his hand to his brow. It almost seemed like he was trying to keep his head from popping off. I could relate.

"I didn't go over there with a plan to shoot that boy," she said. "I keep my gun in my purse. Always. Like I said. I could never be too careful when I was in that store by myself as the years went on. Louie actually showed me how to use it. And Kevin swore a false oath to God in my presence. He profited off those vile people. He was lost to us already. I told you I saw Mickey leaving Kevin's house. He didn't see me. Jody parked a little ways up the hill in the bushes. I knew there was only one reason Mickey would be there. He was selling more drugs to my grandson."

"Mickey's cell phone," Sam said. "We had him at Skylar's house. But you're saying he was really at Kevin's."

"I don't know about cell phones," she said. "Hate those things. But yes, Mickey was leaving Kevin's right before I went in. That's really what tore it for me. That's when I knew Kevin had truly sold his soul to the devil."

"So you killed him," I whispered. I kept the rest of my thoughts unspoken. She'd killed her own grandson.

"Well," she said. "I knew I had to get out of there. Jody was supposed to be waiting for me in the car. I started out the front door. I guess Jody heard the shot and came running. He was scared. So he came on up to make sure I

was okay. Such a good boy. That's the thing. He always
wants to make sure I'm okay. Hardly leaves my side.
Anyway, like I said I figured we'd better get on out of there.
We started to go back to the car. That's when that boy
started running toward us."

"Boy," Sam said. "Do you mean Ben Watson?"

"I guess so," she said. "Well, he maybe heard the shots too.
Or maybe Jenny told him to come see what was going on. He
froze. Kinda like a deer in headlights. It all happened so fast.
He turned around and started running back to Chris and
Jenny's. I panicked. I'll admit. But, well, I still had the gun,
and I panicked."

"You shot him in the back," I said. "You. You shot Ben
Watson in the back."

"Well, he was running away from me," she said. "Who
knows what he'd have told Chris and Jenny. I just needed a
minute to explain it all. That boy was going to ruin it before I
could."

"What happened next, Mrs. Sutter?" Sam asked.

"I gave the gun to Jody. I needed a minute to catch my
breath, you see. I told him, well, I told him to see who was
home over there. I told him to take care of it."

"At Chris and Jenny Sutter's?" he asked. "You're saying
you told your nephew to take care of it. To take care of the
others."

"Yes. It got kind of out of hand after that," she said. "I
should have gone with him. I was having some chest pains
then. I went back to the car. Or started to. Jody went into
Chris's house. Well, I guess Jenny was in the kitchen. Jody ... I
think he was trying to protect me. That's the thing. So, I heard
more shots. You know, I can't feel too sorry for that. I swear I
didn't know Chris was doing that stuff to Nikki or the other
girls before last Christmas. I kinda wish I had. He got what he

deserved. And Skylar? That girl was heading down the same path as Kevin. You mark my words."

"What did you do then?" Sam asked.

"I went to the back door. Well, at that point, I'd seen what Jody did. Jenny against the wall. Chris and Skylar in the hallway. Well, we were in it then. Jody asked me, what are we gonna do, Grandma George?"

"What did you tell him?" I asked.

"Well, I told him, in for a penny in for a pound, at that point. I saw a light on over at C.J.'s. I told Jody to go in the car and get a clip for the gun. He was empty by then. Couldn't be too careful. For all we knew Kevin had more drug dealers on the way. So, Jody did what I said. *That* time anyway. I told him to see what was going on over at C.J.'s. He did. He said I'll take care of everything, Grandma. Well, I'll be damned. He did."

"You're saying Jody Doehler shot Patty Sutter and Mark O'Brien on your orders?" I asked.

"Well, it's not like I told him go over there and shoot them. He just kind of took that initiative."

My head spun. Georgette spoke about the brutal killing of seven people, as if she'd just asked Jody to take out the trash for her. With cold horror, I realized that's exactly what she thought.

"I told him it was all gonna be okay," she said. "Nobody'd be the wiser. And we did the family a favor. Kevin was beyond hope. I told you that. Chris? Well, I don't need to repeat that bad business. You tell me. You know."

She pointed a finger at Sam. "Don't you sit there and try to tell me a bullet through the head isn't the best thing and only way to deal with a sicko like my nephew, Chris."

Sam slowly blinked but didn't answer.

"I'm sorry about the others," she said. "Especially Skylar.

But I'm telling you. That girl was headed down the wrong path too. Did you check her for drugs? If Mickey got my Kevin hooked again, it was only a matter of time before she was too. Oh, and you ask Nikki. You would not believe some horrible things that girl said to my granddaughter after Nikki was brave enough to tell the truth about Chris. The least of it was calling my baby girl a liar."

"Mrs. Sutter," Sam said. "I'm going to need you to write down what you said to us today."

"If you want me to," she said. "Just, go easy on Jody. He really did think he was making a problem go away for me. He's a good kid when he follows directions. See, that's the thing. He didn't do what I told him. I told him, just keep your mouth shut, Jody. Evil took hold of all of them at the bottom of that hill. Every single one. Kevin. Chris for doing what he did to my Nikki. Jenny and Skylar for calling her a liar. That lawyer friend of Patty's was only after her money. Trust me. I told Jody, just sit tight. Evil takes care of its own. Told him, just keep your mouth shut and keep walking the path of God and everything would turn out okay for us. He couldn't do it though. Had to blab that nonsense about hearing Mickey threaten Skylar. Kept telling me about it like I should be proud. I fixed it, Grandma George. I fixed it. He sure fixed it all right. I should have just shot him too. Oh, you're too smart for your own good, Mara Brent."

She took the pad of paper from Sam and started writing.

"We'll give you a few minutes," Sam said. He met my eyes. I rose and followed him out of the interrogation room.

Sheriff Clancy waited for us in the hallway. He'd been on the other side of the glass and heard every word.

"Jesus Christ," he whispered. "She's a psychopath!"

"I think so," I said. "She seems to honestly believe she was ridding the world of evil."

"I didn't see it," Sam said. He squeezed his eyes shut. Cocking his arm, he slammed his palm into the wall.

"I didn't see it!" he shouted. "I was so focused on Mickey friggin' Harvey ..."

"She knew what she was doing," I said. "She knew nobody in the world would suspect she was responsible for killing members of her own family. And she's right. If Jody Doehler had simply kept his mouth shut, she might have gotten away with it."

"It was you," he said. "My God. Mara ... if you hadn't put it together. If you hadn't made me listen to you at the Blue Pony."

"If I hadn't been so wrapped up in beating Elise Weaver," I finished for him. "I lost sight of it all too, Sam."

"Enough," Clancy said. "None of that means a thing now. Let's just get back to work."

"Jody Doehler," I said.

"Just got word," Clancy said. "State troopers picked him up in Toledo. They're bringing him in now. And we should have preliminary ballistics on Georgette's gun. How the hell did you find that thing?"

"I didn't," I said. "Lou gave it up. He told me he saw Georgette try to bury it behind their woodpile. He was lucid enough to remember to grab it. And I think he knows exactly what she's done."

"My God," Sam said. "I need a drink."

There was a commotion down the hall. Jody Doehler came through in cuffs. Two deputies had to drag him forward.

"Grandma!" he shouted. "Grandma!"

"Get him out of my sight," Clancy said. "Interview two is open."

I pressed my back against the wall. I think I needed it to hold me up.

"You okay?" Sam asked.

I nodded. "I am. Do you need me for that interview?"

Sam looked back at Jody. They got him back to his feet and pushed him inside the door.

"I've got it," he said. "But stay close."

"I will," I said. "I've got a phone call to make. I need to tell Elise Weaver we're dropping the charges against her client."

"I'm sorry, Grandma!" Jody Doehler's wail echoed down the hall.

"Oh Jody," Grandma George yelled back. "Will you for once in your life just shut up!"

❦ 39 ❧

Twelve hours later, I stood in front of Judge Denholm to go through the formality of dropping the case against Mickey Harvey. The entire Harvey family had lined the back wall of the courtroom. The Sutters had wisely stayed away. Outside, Sheriff Clancy had called in support from the Ohio State Troopers, just in case.

"Mr. Harvey?" Denholm said. "I hereby order the case against you to be dismissed in its entirety. These fine deputies here are going to see that you get processed out as quickly as possible. To the rest of you back there. We've had enough bloodshed spilled in this town. You've got a prosecutor here who was brave enough to do her job right in the end. I want you all to go on home. Welcome your son, your cousin, back with open arms. Plan a big party in his honor. I wouldn't mind an invitation. But this feud is over. You understand? I don't want to see any more of you back in my courtroom. The same goes for any Sutters who are out there. We clear?"

Except we would see a Sutter in here again unless Graham Sutter pled out on his vehicular homicide charges. That was tomorrow's project for me. Judge Denholm's words seemed too little, too late. He'd let this trial turn into a circus. It worked to inflame the tensions all through town. I just hoped today's message got through. As it was, I expected it would go viral. He got his show. I hated that I was just cynical enough to believe that was entirely his point.

"Anything more from you, Ms. Weaver?" Denholm asked.

"No, Your Honor," she said. "My work in Waynetown is done."

"Have a safe trip back home then," he said. "And we're dismissed."

He banged the gavel with a bit more gusto than usual. Ed Harvey practically vaulted over the railing to get to his boy. The deputies let him. Elise got out of their way. As the Harveys began their celebration in the hall, it gave Elise and me a rare, quiet moment together alone. Soon enough, she'd be out taking her place on the courthouse steps to give the media the show they came for.

"I have to admit," Elise said, smiling. "I would have liked the chance to finish the battle in here. I had a hell of a closing."

I put the last of my files into my briefcase. "Oh, I'm sure you did."

"I would have won, too," she said.

I paused. "You sure about that? Because from where I sat, all you had was a bunch of tabloid headlines and family secrets. Your client was still lying about where he was the morning of the 18th. His cell phone still put him at the scene of the crime."

"You and I both know it was a different crime, Mara," she said.

I did know. Now. Georgette's statement put him at Kevin's house, helping him score.

"It's too bad he hadn't just told the truth about that to Sam," I said. "It would have saved him a lot of aggravation."

"You sure about that? It seems to me your Detective Cruz had his mind made up from the outset. He came at this investigation with a closed mind. So did you," she said. "Though, I have to admit, it's killing me that you were the one to figure out Jody Doehler was lying. I should have caught that one."

I pulled my briefcase strap over my shoulder. "You're right. You should have. But of course, there was still the physical evidence, Elise. Your client had Skylar's blood all over his clothing. Clothing he tried to dispose of. You still sure you'd have swayed the jury?"

"A bloody nose," she said. "Nothing more. Mickey grabbed an old shirt and gave it to her to clean up with. He forgot about it."

"A bloody nose," I said. "One he probably gave her."

"You'd make a brilliant defense attorney," Elise said. "You'd be great at a lot of things. I could use you. And I could pay you. Probably three or four times what you make here."

"Money isn't everything, Professor Weaver," I said. "I like the job I have."

"Hmm," she said. "Well, all the same. I just regret the opportunity to wipe the floor with you. Next time."

This time, I laughed. "And I know you well enough to know you're only saying that because you aren't sure you could. Admit it. Denholm was a disaster. He let you get away with things you know he shouldn't. If it weren't for that ..."

I let my words trail off. If it weren't for that ... My own need to win might have had me put an innocent man on death row.

"If it weren't for that," Elise repeated. She had a twinkle in her eye.

We stood there, eye to eye. She had nothing left to teach me, but I had a lot left to learn.

Finally, Elise raised her hand to shake mine. "Next time, counselor," she said. "Next time."

"Can't wait."

With that, she took her leave. The press hadn't waited for the courthouse steps. They gathered in the hallway. Camera flashes went off as Weaver the Cleaver sliced up the day as her victory.

Later, Kenya would ask me if it bothered me. It didn't. Well, maybe a little. But the lesson I learned would stick with me. It was one her predecessor, Phil Halsey, had never learned. Winning didn't matter. Justice did. Today, I thanked God I'd been open-minded enough to let it in.

❧ 40 ❧

One Week Later ...

"The star is crooked," Will said. I took a step back and cocked my head.

We made a change. Every year since Will was old enough to help, we'd put the tree in the dining room. This year, we put it in the corner of the living room so we could see it where we spent the most time.

"I think he's right," Kat said. She sat on the floor cross-legged, unwrapping the next ornament.

"Oh," I said. "That one's my favorite. Will, do you remember making that for me when you were six?"

It was a painted horseshoe with Will's picture glued in the middle. He sat atop Mulberry, a school pony he rode at a camp.

Kat tested the hook and handed it to Will. He took it and found a middle branch to hang it on. The branch immediately sagged under the weight of, well ... a metal horseshoe.

"Now there's a design flaw," Kat giggled.

"Shh!" I said. Will delighted in unwrapping each new

ornament. Most he'd made for me. Within minutes, our Douglas fir was festooned with cardboard gingerbread men, noodle candy canes, and paper mache Santas.

My cell phone rang. I went to answer it, leaving Kat and Will on garland duty.

Sam Cruz's number popped up. I put him on speaker then walked into the study, closing the door.

"Working on Saturdays again?" I asked.

"Not for long," he said. Before I could ask what he meant, he launched into the reason for his call.

"I just wanted to give you a heads-up. All the labs came back on Georgette Sutter's gun. There's no doubt it's our murder weapon. It's all perfunctory now with her and Jody's confessions, but I just thought you should know."

"Thanks," I said. "You were on my list of people to call, anyway. Kenya just signed off on a plea deal for both Jody and Georgette. Second degree for her. First for Jody."

"Wow," he said. "Surprised he went for it."

"It'll keep the needle out of his arm," I said. "But he's never going to see the outside of a jail cell again. Neither will she."

"How'd she take it?" Sam asked.

"Indignant," I said. "Her lawyer will likely argue for leniency in sentencing due to her age. I doubt she'll get it."

"How'd the old man take it all?" Sam asked.

"Grandpa Lou? Well, Nikki Sutter is taking him back to Seattle with her. She's getting him into a great facility out there where she can visit him every day. She says he seems happy about it. Knowing what he knew about Georgette was eating at him."

"I don't know if I'll ever get over all of that," Sam said.

"Me either," I said. "But so far, it seems like the town is.

That's all that really matters. Graham Sutter pled out as well."

"There's a for sale sign up on the Sutter farm and all the houses," he said. "Gotta admit, it was weird to see."

"End of an era," I said.

He was silent for a moment. "Sam?" I said. "I want you to know. You did good work on this case. Nobody could have guessed that Georgette killed her own grandkid. The case against Mickey was solid. If you're getting blowback, I'll be the first to ..."

"I'm not getting blowback," Sam said. By the change in his tone, I guessed he was smiling. "I'm getting promoted. That's one reason I called."

"Promoted?" I asked.

"Clancy offered me lieutenant. I've accepted."

"That's fantastic news! Though, I'll admit, it'll be a real loss not having you handling my murder cases for me. How did Gus take the news?"

Detective Gus Ritter was still the oldest and saltiest detective in Maumee County. He'd mentored Sam.

"Haven't told him yet," he said. "I'm hoping he doesn't notice."

This got a laugh out of me. "Well, congratulations. It's well deserved."

"Anyway, they're throwing kind of a party for me next week. Not sure whether it's a don't-let-the-door-hit-you-on-the-way-out-of-the-bureau kind of deal or a welcome to command. But it's at the Pony, Friday after work. You should come. Uh, your whole office should come."

"Wouldn't miss it," I said. From the other room, Bing Crosby's "White Christmas" started playing.

"I'll let you get back to your weekend," he said. "See you Monday."

"See you Monday," I said. "Congrats again, Sam. It's great news."

"Thanks," he said, and we hung up.

I went back to join Kat and Will just in time to hang the last strand of garland. Kat gave me a quizzical look, asking me "who was that" with her eyes.

I shook my head, dodging the question. We each stepped back. I put an arm around Will as Kat got the lights. We admired the sparkling splendor of the tree.

"It's perfect," I said.

"The one at Dad's is bigger," he said. "But this one's my favorite. Maybe don't tell him."

Kat and I laughed together. "It'll be our secret," I said.

"You'll have a Christmas party?" Will asked.

"I will," I said. "Don't worry about me. I'll have you in the morning. Then we're all getting together downtown on the 26th. Kenya's idea."

"I like her," Will said.

"Me too."

"You know, Mom," Will said. "It would maybe be a good idea if you got a boyfriend too."

I froze. So did Kat. She shrugged her shoulders, showing she had no idea he was going to say that either.

"A boyfriend?" I said. "I don't think I'm ready for that yet."

"You are," he said. "And I like when you smile. Dad stopped making you smile. You should be with somebody who makes you smile."

Nobody in the world could fill my heart like Will could. So I smiled, big and full, as the Christmas lights twinkled. I saw Will's sweet face reflected in the ornaments. I held him tight. Together, we looked forward to the bright promise of the New Year ahead.

UP NEXT FOR MARA BRENT...

Mara must get inside the mind if a sadistic killer if she wants to serve justice. But this time, when evil touches her, it may not let her go. Don't miss Mark of Justice.

Click here or copy into your browser to find out more ==> https://www.robinjamesbooks.com/moj/

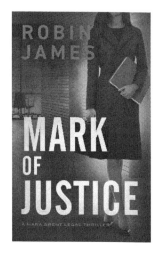

NEWSLETTER SIGN UP

Sign up to get notified about Robin James's latest book releases, discounts, and author news. You'll also get *Crown of Thorne* an exclusive FREE ebook bonus prologue to the Cass Leary Legal Thriller Series just for joining.

Click to Sign Up

https://www.robinjamesbooks.com/marabrentsignup/

ABOUT THE AUTHOR

Robin James is an attorney and former law professor. She's worked on a wide range of civil, criminal and family law cases in her twenty-year legal career. She also spent over a decade as supervising attorney for a Michigan legal clinic assisting thousands of people who could not otherwise afford access to justice.

Robin now lives on a lake in southern Michigan with her husband, two children, and one lazy dog. Her favorite, pure Michigan writing spot is stretched out on the back of a pontoon watching the faster boats go by.

Sign up for Robin James's Legal Thriller Newsletter to get all the latest updates on her new releases and get a free digital bonus prologue to Cass Leary Legal Thriller series. http://www.robinjamesbooks.com/newsletter/

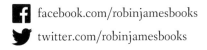

facebook.com/robinjamesbooks

twitter.com/robinjamesbooks

Made in United States
Orlando, FL
23 June 2023